THE
Whaler

THE
Whaler

· INES THORN ·

The Island of Sylt series

Translated by Kate Northrop

amazoncrossing

Text copyright © 2016 Ines Thorn

Translation copyright © 2017 Kate Northrop

Previously published as *Die Walfängerin* by Aufbau Verlag in Germany in 2016. Translated from German by Kate Northrop. First published in English by AmazonCrossing in 2017.

Published by AmazonCrossing, Seattle

www.apub.com

Amazon, the Amazon logo, and AmazonCrossing are trademarks of Amazon.com, Inc., or its affiliates.

ISBN-13: 9781611099249
ISBN-10: 1611099242

Cover design by PEPE *nymi*

Printed in the United States of America

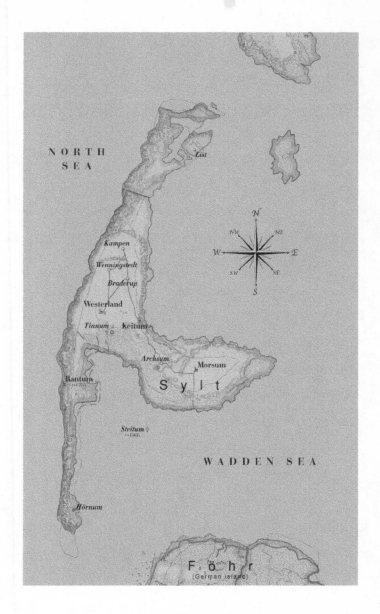

The Island of Sylt

PART 1

The North Frisian Island of Sylt, Germany, 1764

CHAPTER 1

On the island of Sylt, there was one god for the summer and another for the winter. The summer god was worshipped in church and referred to as the Almighty. The other, the winter god, was Captain Rune Boyse. On this day, he stood atop the dunes, feet planted wide in heavy leather boots, arms crossed over his chest. He was observing his flock, their backs hunched under their loads, as they rushed over the bright sandy beaches collecting flotsam left by the storm. Boyse was a large man with a thick black beard, brilliant piercing eyes, and hair almost as long as that of the crucified Jesus which hung in the little village church in Rantum. He wore charcoal-gray breeches of tanned deer hide and his sailor's jacket, but he didn't look at all like a sailor. He looked like the man who ruled the entire island.

Only the older folks still remembered how Rune Boyse had become the winter god of Sylt. He had gone to sea for the first time when he was young, barely eleven years old when he joined his father and brother-in-law on a whaling ship as a ship's boy. The ship had become stuck in the ice near Greenland, and almost the entire crew had starved to death. Only Rune Boyse and his brother-in-law managed to escape the icy grave. Rumor had it that the boy had saved his sister's husband's life, but it couldn't be proven, because the man had left for the mainland a year later, after his wife died. Rumor had it, too, that young Boyse had encouraged him to leave. No one on the island knew the details, no one except for one woman. The rest only knew that Boyse's brother-in-law hadn't left Sylt of his own free will. But whatever the rumors were, one thing was clear: Rune Boyse held the island tightly in his grip. He wasn't a governor, but his word had great weight among the people. Even the elders listened to what he had to say. Since he had survived out on the frozen sea, it was said that he was favored by the old gods, and was stronger and cleverer than any other man on the island. He knew what went on in every household, upheld law and order, and was respected by everyone for his sense of justice. He was especially admired among the women. Despite the admiration he received, he chose to remain alone, and no one knew the intimacies of his heart or mind. Not even now, as he reigned over the dunes, watching his flock like the Almighty Father in heaven.

During the night, once again a ship had foundered near the island. It had probably belonged to a Hamburg merchant and been on its way to Norway. The rough sea had captured part of the cargo, countless red winter apples from the old country around Hamburg, and cast them onto the beach. There they lay, red dots on the pale sand, just waiting to be collected. The sky was gray, steel gray like the sea tossing foamy whitecaps onto the beach, the flying spray settling on clothing, hair, and faces. A few seagulls cried as they soared above, through the air scented with salt and seaweed and a hint of the delicious aroma of apples.

The crowd was unusually silent. Everyone was bent over, eyes glued to the sand, desperately trying to grab apples before a neighbor got to them. From the dunes, it looked like a swarm of ants cautiously trying to stay out of each other's way but still covetous of every single apple. Old Meret—who could speak with the dead, so they said—dragged a half-full sack up the dunes, her face taut with the effort. Two old men carried a heavy crate between them, which they had to put down every few steps. A mother with a baby wrapped tight to her chest had folded her skirt up, revealing her pale legs, to make a basket for the apples. A stray dog shoved one of them back and forth with its nose, and two boys were filling their caps. A small child sat down in the wet sand and tried to bite into an apple, crying loudly when it couldn't. Entire families had banded together and were picking up whatever they could. Some of them could already imagine the perfume of baked apples.

Even toothless old Wilhelmine, who couldn't really walk anymore, had been set down on the beach by her daughter-in-law to try her luck. She was sitting there trying to fish out the fruits with a stick. Apples were rare on Sylt, especially in January. A gaunt woman shoved someone aside with her hip, and a little girl squealed as another child darted in front of her.

"There, look! There's another!" Thies Heinen, one of the few men participating in the hunt, pointed to an apple that was partly hidden by beachgrass. Maren straightened, pushed a strand of hair off her face, and smiled at Thies. As usual, when she looked at him, she felt her heart grow warmer. They had been together for more than a year, and it was common knowledge that they would marry one day. Thies Heinen, the most handsome young man on the island. True, he wasn't rich, but he was strong and dependable. His chest was broad like the chests of the men who loaded the ships in the harbor, and his blond hair always looked as though he'd just walked in out of a storm. His blue eyes gleamed.

"What are you thinking about?" he asked. "Should I be worried?"

Maren laughed with genuine pleasure. "Isn't this wonderful?" she said, waving a hand at her willow basket, already more than half-full. "Of course, it doesn't mean we won't have to go hungry again before spring, but it's certainly helpful. Oh, I can already taste the apple cake!"

Most of the residents of Sylt were terribly poor. Many of the men went out in their fishing boats to catch herring, but the herring population had been declining for years, and their nets often came back empty. Others went on whaling ships to Greenland, but even that was uncertain. The earnings were contingent upon how many whales they caught. It often seemed as though the whalers came home with less than when they'd left, because not every ship found whales to hunt. Only the captains and officers of the whaling ships had a guaranteed income, receiving payment even if their ships returned empty to the harbor. Many of them could even afford to build solid Frisian houses with reed roofs. Of course, not in the village of Rantum, which was built on the narrowest part of the island and was completely exposed to the whims of the weather, helpless before the forces of nature. Between the North Sea on the west side and the Wadden Sea on the east, the land could be crossed in about a thousand paces. By God, it wasn't much. And after every storm, there was a little bit less. There were hardly any meadows, no trees, and absolutely no arable land. Only the dunes, covered in beachgrass, creeping willow, crowberry, yellow beach roses, and sea holly. A sheep could barely find enough to eat there, and certainly no cow. Bog heather grew in the valleys between the dunes, and occasionally marsh gentian, which could be brewed into a healthful elixir. Sea buckthorn, which the people of Sylt made into punch, preserves, and juice, grew there too. Otherwise, the landscape was sparse, and not exactly blessed with color. Especially not in January, when the dune plants were all murky shades of gray and brown.

The houses, or rather huts, of Rantum clung to the Wadden Sea side of the dunes, to find at least a little protection from the strong winds. The clotheslines fluttered with shirts, breeches, and skirts, and also, always, fishing nets. Dried sheep dung for heating was piled against the sheltered side of the houses, and in the most protected corners were little plots of kale. The houses were small, just a kitchen with box beds and a living room. Wealthier households had a formal parlor on the wind-sheltered east side. Separated from the living areas by only a breezeway were a work area, a smoke room, and a small stall for the occasional sheep.

The people who lived in Rantum were mostly herring fishers. There was a smithy and a small general store where they could buy whale oil for lamps, soap, flour, and dried beans. In all, the village consisted of these, a little church, and around twenty houses, and not even one of them was half as fine as a real captain's home.

The captains built in Keitum. There, the island was wide enough to raise sheep on either side in the marshes. Nice fat salt-marsh sheep with soft wool, which was knit into warm things that would keep out the damp and rain because of the salt it had absorbed. Stockings for fishermen and whalers, thick sweaters for winter, lined coats, and blankets that would keep you warm even when the fire had gone out. And most important, there was arable land, largely protected from the sea. Land where they could grow barley, oats, rye, and broad beans. There they had real vegetable gardens, and they planted carrots, cabbages, and turnips, and some even kept a few chickens.

In Rantum, there were just a few narrow strips of land on the Wadden coast, capable of growing only some tough grasses. Even if some courageous soul plowed a field there, planted it, and cared for it, the next storm tide would rise to cover it, and the field would become hopelessly salted.

Only the Wadden Sea offered a small bounty. Young people went out to seek shellfish and seagull eggs, but even those didn't last all year: seagull eggs become inedible once they were brooded. Some people set snares for sandpipers, oystercatchers, and other seabirds, but birds were seldom caught, and hunger was a constant guest in the homes of Rantum. Hunger was not the only problem on Sylt. There was no firewood, for no trees grew on the island. There was only water, sand, heather, and of course the dunes. Those who could afford it had firewood brought from the mainland, but not many could. Most people began to collect sheep dung in early spring, to dry and burn throughout the winter. You could get used to the smell, but not to the neighbors who thought that because they owned the sheep, they owned the dung too. Fruit was extremely rare and extremely costly. There were no plum trees, quince trees, or apple trees on Sylt.

Thies, who was filling his sack slowly and deliberately, nodded.

"Today we have apples, and tomorrow, if we're lucky, we'll get parts of the ship. Good planks, pieces of the masts, decking. Then we'll have some wood for heating again."

Maren shuddered. She knew well enough that corpses came along with parts of the ship. And she also knew that the entire population of the village would be on the beach again. They would swarm over the dead, taking their boots, breeches, and skirts. They would empty pockets and hope to find a few coins sewn into the linings of coats. They would pull out earrings, search for sailors' sea chests, and break them open roughly. They would take Bibles, whale-oil lamps, and tools. And the beach overseer would turn a blind eye and would only come to bury the remains after the citizens of Rantum had left.

Maren hated the body stripping, but of course, she took part in it, like everyone else. How else could one survive on Sylt? She bent down for the apple that was hiding in the beachgrass. Suddenly she was shoved aside.

"Get your paws off it! That one's mine!"

Maren looked up. Grit Wilms stood in front of her, staring her down with narrowed eyes. Her hair had slid out from under her bonnet and was sticking to her cheeks, which were red with fervor. "I saw that apple first. It's mine."

Maren shrugged. "Thies pointed it out to me a while ago. It's mine. But if you're desperate for it, take it. There are others."

Grit Wilms was tall and thin with small, malicious eyes and hair the color of wet sand. She already had careworn lines around her mouth and nose. She gave a little snort. "Ha! Thies! Thies! All you talk about is Thies! If I wanted, he would be collecting the nicest apples for me, and you wouldn't even see his backside."

"Oh, really?" Maren smoothed her dress. She did that when she was angry. And she was always angry when she met Grit. Grit, who had been making her life difficult for years. Grit, who was never satisfied with anything or anyone, who ruined everyone's mood with her sourness. Grit, who criticized everything and insisted she was right until the bitter end. Grit, who acted like life was an endless succession of self-denial, sacrifice, and hardship. Maren was sick of her. And today of all days, she really didn't feel like dealing with Grit's bad mood.

"Then why didn't you keep him?" she asked more harshly than she had intended to. "Everyone knows how your mouth watered at the sight of him. And you haven't changed." She had to speak loudly, because the waves were pounding on the shore just a few yards behind her. Last night there had been a powerful storm. Not a hurricane, just a winter storm, but the sea was still wild. A fine mist of spray covered the entire beach and clung to their skin and hair. When Maren licked her lips, she could taste the salt. A few seagulls circled over the sand, eager for what the people would leave behind.

Grit picked up the apple, rubbed it clean on her pinafore, and bit into it triumphantly. "Everyone knows that you stole Thies from me." She shoved Maren's shoulder.

Maren took the blow in stride and looked around for Thies. He was too far away to hear, bent over in search of more apples. "I didn't take him away from you, and you know that, Grit. Even if he did dance with you once at the May Ball." Maren thought back to that party three years ago. She had just turned thirteen and had watched Thies and Grit dance that evening. She had also watched Thies drink far too much *Branntwein*, a strong local whiskey. That was the only reason he'd danced with Grit at all, and then he'd kissed her. At fifteen, Thies had still been almost a child at that time, a youth full of curiosity who wanted to try everything. Including love. Now he was a man.

"Didn't you? We were planning to marry. It started at the May Ball. 'Grit and Thies.' Everyone said it. 'Grit and Thies, Thies and Grit.' But you always want what other people have, and you couldn't stand it that he didn't choose you."

Maren wanted to give her a piece of her mind, but then she bit her tongue. There was no point in arguing with Grit. She'd never heard anyone say "Grit and Thies" before, and neither had her friends. But it didn't matter, because that's what Grit was saying now, and few people would risk contradicting her. A few months ago, Grit had decided that Maren had stolen Thies from her. Of course that was nonsense; Thies and Maren had been neighbors since they were small. When they were little, her mother had sometimes jokingly wondered if Thies and Maren would marry someday. But they weren't ready for that, not yet.

"Now you're married, and Thies isn't. Back then, you tricked a vow out of a fifteen-year-old boy in exchange for a cup of Branntwein. He didn't understand, and it was no more than a childish game." Maren was slowly starting to get angry. "Thies laughs about it now. And besides, you're cousins. Relatives shouldn't marry, or they'll have stupid children." She glanced at Grit's midriff, still as flat as the sea on a windless day after two years of marriage.

"Yes, I'm married. But to a man I don't love. One who's thirty years older and has a hunchback. I had to marry him because my father couldn't feed us. It was my duty as a daughter. You and Thies can laugh as much as you want. But she who laughs last, laughs longest."

Maren shrugged. "You didn't have to accept old Wilms. No one forced you to the altar."

Grit put her fists on her hips, and her head went forward like a chicken pecking for corn. Her chin trembled, and her voice became harsh with anger. "Of course I had to take Wilms. Thies wasn't able to provide for my family and me. He has nothing himself. Only his mother and his damn sister."

"His sick mother and his crippled sister, Antje, you mean? Two people that you didn't want to have to care for, didn't want to take responsibility for? You preferred Wilms, who doesn't ask for anything and gives you as much as he can. That's the truth." Maren knew very well that Grit wasn't lazy. On Sylt, it was expected that the young take care of their parents, and Grit certainly would have helped to care for not only her own parents but also Thies's mother and Antje. But she was so sick of all the accusations! It was really time for someone to make Grit shut up. For a moment, it seemed as though Maren's words had done the trick. Tears glittered in Grit's eyes, and she looked as though she'd been struck by all ten biblical plagues at once. The corners of her mouth turned down, and her thin chest quaked.

"If it weren't for you, I could marry Thies as soon as Wilms dies, and we could live off what I inherit from him." Her words weren't as harsh as usual, rather quiet and almost pleading. Although Grit's dress wasn't the latest mainland fashion, and Wilms never paid for even a single round of Branntwein at the tavern, rumor had it that he had a considerable amount of money tucked away under his pillow.

Maren laughed, unkindly and loudly. She threw her head back and spread out her arms. "Your husband is still alive, and Thies is still available. And that includes his mother and sister. We aren't engaged. Not officially, at least. But Wilms will have to hurry up and die, because *I'm* the one going to the *Biikebrennen* with Thies."

Maren took her basket and left Grit standing there. She walked back to Thies, who continued to help her collect apples. From a distance, she cast a glance that was a mixture of pity and triumph. "Did you hear what Grit said?" Maren wanted to know. "That the two of you have been together since the May Ball? And that she wants to marry you as soon as old Wilms dies?"

She laughed again, and hoped that Thies would join her, but he shook his head and watched Grit thoughtfully as she walked away. "Leave her be. She hasn't exactly had it easy. And there are good things about her too."

Maren would've liked to argue, but her gaze fell on Captain Boyse, who was still standing high on the dunes, smiling down at her. Suddenly she felt as though she'd been caught doing something wrong. *Hopefully, he didn't hear what Grit and I were saying,* she thought. The idea was absurd, given the powerful waves still pounding the shore. But Captain Boyse was the winter god of Sylt. He could hear anything that had been whispered on the island, if he wanted to. But it didn't work the other way around, and so Maren didn't hear when the captain said to himself, "Very good, my dear. Very promising."

CHAPTER 2

Captain Rune Boyse was looking out of his living room window at the gray clouds hanging over the island as they slowly began to break up. The wind blowing in from the southwest meant the day would be dry. The cloud cover might even clear completely, and the sun would transform the last remnants of snow into glittering jewels. Boyse wasn't usually so romantic, and he didn't usually like the snow. He was always surrounded by snow while hunting for whales near Greenland. But today was special. Despite being on land, Boyse wore his captain's uniform. Tonight was the Biikebrennen. Tonight the fire would burn, tonight the winter would turn toward spring, and tonight he would do what he'd been waiting to do for years. He ran a cloth over his brass buttons so they would shine and thought about his plans.

At sea, he'd forgotten how to believe in God. Otherwise, he might have prayed for guidance. Neither did he believe in Odin, the old god of sea and storm, as many on Sylt secretly did. And so he didn't believe in the power of the Biikebrennen, a fire which was lit every year to drive the winter away and honor Odin. But he did believe in the council, and the hearing that would take place tomorrow, before the whalers made their way to Hamburg or Amsterdam. Not many cases would be heard. A few persistent beach robbers, reported by the beach overseer, would have to pay for their crimes, and Old Meret had been accused of witchcraft again. They said she spoke to the dead and still worshipped the old gods. Rune Boyse knew this to be true, but Old Meret didn't have to worry. On Sylt, people stuck together, and as long as she didn't hurt anyone, no one would hurt her. There was something else that should be discussed. Rather, something that *had* to be dealt with. But only Rune Boyse and one other person on the island knew of it, and they didn't want to reveal their secret, at least not yet. The captain was a clever and patient man; he knew the time would come. But that time was not yet at hand.

He dipped the cloth in whale oil and began polishing his boots, whistling absentmindedly. When he finished, he looked around the room, proud of all he'd attained. The room was big, and heated by a fine delft tile stove. Around a large cherrywood table stood six high-backed chairs with leather seats. Boyse had an eye for beauty, and some of the beautiful things he'd brought back from his travels were displayed on shelves around the room: a meerschaum pipe with a porcelain bowl, dishes from China, a knife from the Mediterranean, bowls carved of olive wood, tankards and boxes of silver, gleaming candleholders, and a Bible bound in saffron-colored leather. Laid out on the terra-cotta floor tiles were Oriental rugs that Boyse had bought in Amsterdam, and the elaborately carved grandfather clock—as tall as a man and with gold-plated hands—stood by the wall and chimed every hour. Under the windows sat wide, beautifully painted chests covered with pelts and cushions. In the corner was an English secretary desk as tall as Captain Boyse himself, with a comfortable chair in front of it. It gleamed with fresh polish. In its numerous drawers were other little treasures and coins from many different countries. A row of ink bottles, including one made of sterling silver, sat on the table, and a wooden stand filled with carefully sharpened goose-feather quills stood next to them. Over the desk hung the nautical chart where Boyse marked all the routes he'd traveled. Lined curtains of thick green wool hung at either side of the windows to keep out the drafts in winter. Yes, Captain Boyse had a truly beautiful, comfortable home, rich with the scents of beeswax candles and lavender potpourri. A home that was meant for a family. Feeling satisfied with himself, he whistled a new song he'd learned about a sailor who was waiting for his true love.

The maid in the kitchen raised her eyebrows. The captain was whistling. He almost never did that. But when he did, one could expect surprises.

Maren was feeling as though ants had been crawling around in her stomach all day. The tingling was making her nervous. And clumsy. After her usual breakfast, gruel with watered-down beer, she dropped a bowl and broke it. Then she caught her pinafore on the door handle and tore it, and, to top it off, she pricked her finger with the needle while mending the hole.

"What's wrong with you, child?" Finja Luersen watched her daughter with quiet annoyance. "You're not usually so scatterbrained."

Maren laughed and then stuck her bleeding finger in her mouth. "The Biikebrennen is tonight," she said. "It's the most important festival on Sylt. The entire island is excited. How shall I stay calm?"

"Ah. So. You're nervous about the Biikebrennen." Finja cast a glance at her husband, but Klaas kept filling his pipe, pretending he hadn't heard anything. "Do you know something I don't?" she asked him.

Klaas drew on his pipe, exhaled a cloud of smoke, and smiled, making crinkly little lines form around his eyes. "I know just as much about the Biikebrennen as you do."

"You know what I mean."

Klaas glanced at his daughter, and Finja understood his meaning. "Maren, please go pick the last of the kale so we can have a full pot for tomorrow's meal."

Maren, finger still in her mouth, nodded, left the warm kitchen, and went out to the tiny garden. Every spring, Klaas brought an entire wagonload of soil from the next village to fill the plot so her mother could plant something. Kale, at least. The ground at the foot of the dunes was nothing but sand, and nothing could grow in it except a few scrubby bushes and scratchy heather.

The door had hardly closed behind Maren when Finja said, "So, what did you hear in the pub? Which matches will be made? Which girls will be engaged tomorrow?"

Maren heard her clearly, and she paused just beyond the door to listen, her burning curiosity outweighing her guilt.

There was a pause. Like most of the islanders, Klaas was a quiet man. "I heard the captain wants to marry," he finally said.

There were many captains on Sylt, at least eighty of the island's nearly three thousand citizens. But Maren knew immediately which captain he meant, because there was only one captain with that much power and influence over the islanders, almost as much as God had himself. No one really remembered why Boyse had so much power on Sylt, but everyone knew it was his job to make the decisions. But when Maren thought about it, she realized no one knew him well. He was a recluse. Although it was rumored that he had a lover in every harbor, here on the island he hadn't shown interest in anyone. He was handsome, but in a very different way than Thies was. Thies was sensitive, understanding, and sometimes even a little indecisive, but Boyse seemed to be wild, stubborn, and stern. It was easy to imagine what might happen if he were crossed: he'd square his already chiseled jaw, and his smoke-gray eyes would darken until they seemed almost black.

Maren had once heard Old Meret calling her mother's attention to the distinct Cupid's bow of his upper lip: "Our captain is a fine specimen of a man, still young and untamed. His wife won't be very happy during the day, but at night she will be rewarded."

The old woman had giggled, and a pink blush had stained Finja's cheeks. "Don't be silly," Finja had said. "As though a little dimple could have an effect like that." Old Meret had peered at her closely.

"There was once another man who had the sign of love on his face, and I think you remember him well."

Finja's cheeks had reddened even more. "That was a long time ago," she'd said quietly. "No one remembers anymore. No one wants to remember."

Maren didn't like Boyse, but she couldn't say why. Sometimes she felt as though he could look directly into her soul and know all her thoughts and feelings. Thoughts that she wouldn't dare face herself, even under cover of the quiet night. Feelings that made her blush with shame. Yes, Maren believed that Captain Boyse could see into people's minds. It scared her, especially because he didn't reveal his own thoughts. Nothing was hidden from him: no secret tryst, no quarrel between neighbors, no tiny act of thievery. And if someone was in trouble, Captain Boyse intervened without making any fuss about it. *Yes,* Maren thought, *he behaves as though the entire island belongs to him. The island and all its people.*

Still, she felt almost compelled to watch him at festivals or in the church. He was so dark, so mysterious, and the other whalers often spoke of his heroic deeds at sea out near Greenland. They said he caught more whales than any other captain. That he was the only one who dared explore waters that others avoided. That he didn't show concern for his men or himself while hunting. And that in harbors like Amsterdam or Hamburg, he could drink vast quantities of Branntwein without slurring or staggering, not even a little. There was a lot of talk about Boyse. When he became the subject of conversation, only the men who'd actually been to sea with him kept silent and smiled.

Thinking about Boyse made Maren uncomfortable, and she turned and rushed to the kale patch, her cheeks burning. She knew her parents' words had not been intended for her ears.

Finja and Klaas continued their conversation in private, unaware that they'd been overheard.

"Who does Rune Boyse intend to marry?" Finja asked.

Klaas shrugged. "Some say one thing, others say something else."

Finja, beginning to lose her patience, sat down beside her husband on the kitchen bench. "I want to know exactly who said what." She clearly didn't believe what her husband was telling her. Rune Boyse and marriage? It was unimaginable! Why would a man who could have any woman on Sylt and a woman in every harbor tie himself down? He was almost thirty, but marriage and children—hearth and home—didn't seem to suit him. He'd always been an adventurer. He was just as much at home on the sea as he was on Sylt. Or had he settled down? Was he ready to start a real home? Finja had seen many girls cry for him because he was uninterested in them. "I'm not made for marriage," he had told every one of them. And now he wanted to marry?

"I don't know much. But I heard that he's interested in someone from Rantum."

Finja raised her eyebrows. "Someone from our village? There aren't even very many marriageable girls here. Why not someone from Keitum, where the captains' daughters live?"

Klaas shrugged silently, and at that moment, Maren returned, her cheeks red from the wind, her arms filled with kale. Shouts followed her in from outside. Finja, happy for the distraction, hurried to the window. A group of boys were pulling a wooden wagon piled high with firewood up the highest dune. Two others approached the house. Finja turned. "Do you have anything for the bonfire?"

It wasn't just expected that everyone on Sylt would contribute something to the Biikebrennen; it was a religious obligation—even more sacred than the yearly Christmas donation for the sea captains' widows and orphans. Since wood was so scarce on the island, four whole weeks ago, everyone had begun collecting the driftwood that washed ashore. They searched their barns and stalls for spare boards, or, if they had no wood, they gave a few bundles of straw or rags. When the boys knocked, Klaas went with them to the west side of the house, which served as stall, storage room, barn, and smokehouse, and gave them a few old ship's planks.

"Do you have a jar of whale oil, so our Rantum fire will burn even higher and longer?" little Hauke asked. His father was one of the whaling ship officers who would be leaving for Hamburg in the next few days.

Klaas sucked on his pipe again. "What do you think, boy? I'm a herring fisherman. I have no whale oil. Ask those who work on the whaling ships." But he gave him a jar of rapeseed oil anyway. "Be careful. Don't spill it."

He watched the boys go, and then he climbed the dune behind his house and peered over at the larger dune where the fire was being laid. It was a complicated task, and all the young men participated, while the older men watched and gave advice. Klaas smiled as Old Meret climbed toward him carrying a bundle of dried seaweed.

"Do you remember when you were a little boy?" she asked, gazing over at the heap of wood. "Back then, you still believed in the old gods. And what do you believe in now, Klaas Luersen?"

Klaas didn't answer, but Old Meret didn't seem expect him to either. On the other dune, with a great deal of loud cheering, the big straw figure that symbolized winter was just then being stuck onto a pole in the middle of the pyre.

"Who remembers the old traditions now?" Old Meret said. "Which of the young people know that the fire is lit in honor of the great god Odin? The winter must be driven away, and the spring must be awakened. Then, foolish boys will jump over the sacred flames because they believe they will be rewarded with health or love." The old woman giggled a little. "Do you still remember, Klaas, how you used to jump? You jumped for Finja. Farther and higher than all the others. And you got her. But you've never thanked Odin for it."

"If he's as powerful as you say, he doesn't need my thanks."

Old Meret started at his words. She raised a finger. "Do not sin, Klaas Luersen. Those who do not give Odin his due will suffer misfortune."

After Klaas left the house, Finja hurried from the kitchen into the parlor. There, in the best room of the house, stood her old hope chest. Her father had made it for her, and he had built a hidden compartment in it. "Every girl must have a secret now and then," he'd said, tilting the chest and showing her the false bottom. Finja had no secrets from Klaas. No secrets but one: there was one thing that he didn't know, couldn't ever be allowed to know. She pulled up the bottom and removed a small velvet-covered wooden box. The seal and name of a good Sylt household gleamed on the lid. *Rán Hüüs* was the house of Rán, the Norse goddess of the sea. Inside the box was a signet ring with an image of Rán and a large, heavy gold pendant in the shape of the sea goddess. She examined the items carefully, weighed them in her hand, and then sighed. A dark sense of foreboding crept in, as it had for years. Whenever Finja thought it was finally gone, it reappeared again. She pressed the gold to her breast and heaved another sigh. Then she said a fervent silent prayer and hid the box again.

Maren had put on her best clothes, a traditional white knee-length skirt, red stockings, a red bodice, and, over it, a warm vest made from the pelt of a young seal. She had brushed her blond hair until it shone and had plaited it into a thick braid. She had even stained her lips and cheeks with a little red beet juice. Klaas grimaced when he saw her. "What's all this about, Maren? You're not going to a wedding."

Maren giggled. "Maybe I am."

Finja spoke. "What are you planning?" She tilted her head and peered at Maren suspiciously. "You're sixteen. Your time hasn't come." She'd spoken harshly, but Maren continued to smile.

"Other girls my age are already married. Grit, for example. She's been sharing old Wilms's bed for two years."

"But you don't need to be. You have time. Besides, you're two years younger than Grit." Finja rarely spoke so severely; usually she couldn't stand to deny Maren anything.

Even Klaas was surprised. "Leave her be, Finja. She may be young, but she's not stupid. Don't you remember the old saying? 'Happy is the wooing that is not long doing.'" His mouth stretched into a smile. "Just remember how young *you* were."

Finja stared at Maren as though she'd never seen her before and then shook her head. "Child, you have no idea what you're doing. I know that you think we're hopelessly old-fashioned. But let me tell you, take your time with men. Many a girl has unknowingly invited sorrow in far too quickly."

Maren swallowed. Her mother's words made her feel uncertain. No, it wasn't the words so much as the tone of her voice. Finja was a gentle woman. She didn't often try to control her husband and daughter. But now her manner was firm and strict.

"But I want to go to the fire with Thies," Maren explained.

"You're going with us," her mother declared. "You know the custom. You're only allowed to go to the Biikebrennen with a sweetheart once you're engaged. And as far as I know, you're not engaged. If you don't want to go with us, you can stay home. Now get dressed properly if you want to go. The others are all on their way already."

Maren looked at her father, crushed. She had imagined climbing the dunes hand in hand with Thies, for everyone to see. Grit above all. Now she'd be walking behind her parents like a child. But Finja and Klaas would soon see that she was grown up. Ready to live the life of a woman.

A little later, Maren trudged sullenly up the dunes with the Ottensens, the Lorenzens, the Thakens, the Hennings, the Bohns, and the other families of Rantum. There had been a fine drizzle falling over the island all day, and the sand was hard as stone. Now the rain had stopped, and twilight was washing the last bits of color from the winter landscape, making it grow ever darker until it became gray. It was a good day to sit at home by the hearth; but even though it was damp and cold, everyone climbed up the dunes. Klaas walked slowly and had to stop now and then because his rheumatism was particularly bad that day. The youngest Ottensen child coughed so hard that one could almost hear the rattling in her chest, and someone had tied a hot stone in a sling to old Mrs. Thaken so she wouldn't freeze. Still they were full of laughter and banter, singing and chattering in anticipation of the festival. The people of Sylt had spent the whole winter in their houses, sheltering from the heavy storms and bitter cold, and now it was time to call the spring.

Everyone wore their best clothes. Their shoes had been polished until they shone, and the women's wrists, hands, and necks glittered with every piece of jewelry they owned. All of them wore their freshly aired-out traditional formal wear, but no one wore it as haughtily as Grit. And she had every right to, for on her dress, a few real gold coins danced, catching the light of the torches. They walked up the narrow dune path like geese, craning their necks toward the festival, eager to capture and enjoy every tiny moment of it. Sand crunched quietly under Maren's feet. The children chattered excitedly and pulled their parents forward. Even the elderly who could barely walk anymore perched on the backs of their strong sons and were carried up the hill.

Just before Maren and her family reached the top, Thies met them. Maren reached for his hand, casting a triumphant glance at her mother, and they climbed to the top together, arriving almost last. The area at the top was filled with people. Two fishermen were spreading herring over an old grill, and spiced wine was being heated over a barrel of coals. The citizens of Rantum stood around in groups, and laughter sounded in the darkness again and again. Maren thought it was very much like the atmosphere in the church on Christmas. Nothing exciting had happened yet, but the air was practically flickering with possibilities. Holding Thies firmly by the hand, Maren looked over at Grit. Grit's dress might be decorated with gold, but her face didn't show the least glint of joy. Angrily, she stared daggers at Maren and Thies, threw back her head, stuck her nose in the air, and turned away.

When everyone had finally reached the top of the path, the villagers of Rantum arranged themselves around the huge unlit bonfire. A reverent, almost hallowed silence overtook the group. Only the children, with colorful lanterns in their hands, laughed and scampered around the few men holding flaming bundles of straw. As the beach overseer for Rantum, it was tradition for Rune Boyse to take the first step toward the fire, but this time, Old Meret stepped forward out of the circle. She leaned close to the woodpile, her small figure glowing in the light of the torches. She looked as though she had been dipped in gold. Maren poked Thies in the side. "She looks like an angel, doesn't she?"

Thies shook his head. "Some people say she's a witch, and now I'm not so sure that isn't true. What's she doing there?"

Then Old Meret raised her arms and tilted her face up toward the dark night sky, which was lit only by a pale sliver of the moon. "Odin, lord of storm and sea, guardian of seamen and fishermen, guider of wheel and sword, is our great protector. To earn his goodwill, today we sacrifice animals and goods to the hungry flames," she called in a deep, powerful voice that sent shivers down some people's backs.

Maren turned to Thies again, who was staring as though spellbound at the strange, almost ghostly apparition of Old Meret. "What's she talking about? We don't sacrifice animals. That would be cruel." At that moment, a flock of wild geese flew over the hill, honking loudly. Everyone looked up. When they saw the birds, they froze and went silent. Old Meret pointed to the geese, as though she had summoned them. There must have been about a dozen, and they circled over the group and cried out, as though they had something to tell the crowd.

Only Grit, who was standing behind Maren, seemed relatively unimpressed. "What a lot of drama," she said. "Now all we need is for one of them to land on Old Meret's shoulder." But her scoffing was immediately interrupted. Old Meret raised a finger in warning to her, and it seemed to Maren as though the old woman was looking directly at her.

"Do you see them?" the old woman cried. "Do you see the wild geese? You all know the story of the wild geese. In the old days, part of our island sank into the tide. Before the disaster, which I myself did not see, our island was shaped like an oval, like a seagull's egg. After the storm, it looked like a torn piece of seaweed. The entire village of Steitum disappeared. Now, the ghosts of the lost souls of Steitum take the form of wild geese and mourn their loss every year at the Biikebrennen. Those who see them are doomed to disaster."

Everyone stared up at the geese, who were still calling. Men put their arms protectively around their wives and children, and some of the little ones began to wail. Captain Rune Boyse was about to put an end to the eerie, haunted atmosphere, but then the geese flocked together and flew away. The villagers exhaled in relief, and Old Meret continued, her arms still stretched to the heavens and her shape silhouetted by torchlight. "Our shouts ring at the feet of the gods. *Wetke tiare!* Take our sacrifice, great Odin! Ho! How the winter will soon burn on the pole! Spring, open your blossom eyes. Awaken and watch the fiery wheel roll to the sea!"

At that moment, a young man who would be going whaling for the first time that year pushed a wheel wrapped in burning straw across the dune and let it roll down into the water. Now the villagers were free of all debts to their neighbors, free from the sin of the harm they had done to one another. It was a new beginning.

A collective sigh could be heard, and afterward there was a thoughtful silence. Old Meret used the moment of quiet to deliver the final threatening words of her speech. "You have forgotten! Forgotten the gods, forgotten the father, forgotten the meaning of the sacred Biikebrennen! We old ones must call them!" Then, exhausted, she let her arms drop to her sides.

Captain Boyse stepped up next to her holding a long, flaming pitch torch in his hand. *"Tjen di Biike ön!"* he shouted. Light the Biikebrennen! Then he threw his torch into an opening at the bottom of the huge pyre, and the others with torches or bundles of burning straw followed suit. The pyre crackled, smoke billowed up, and then flames shot into the night sky, thanks to the donations of oil and fat. Sparks flew upward and sprayed the sky with golden stars, which fell glowing to the earth. Cries of jubilation broke out. The girls clapped, and the boys threw their hats in the air. And in the blink of an eye, the fire from the village of Hörnum could be seen in the distance, glowing in the dark night. Then the fire of Keitum, and afterward, Westerland. The smallest children were lifted onto shoulders, and they pointed southward, to where the Biikebrennen on the neighboring island of Amrum could be seen. Faces glowed with happiness. The villagers took one another by the hand, not caring whether they stood beside friends or enemies, and made a circle, walking slowly and ceremonially. Then the musicians began to play an old song, and the plaintive melody could be heard far across the island.

When the song was over, Old Meret raised her arms once more and turned her eyes to the sky. "Odin, great lord! Protect us and our island," she cried in her dark, conjuring voice.

Then she lowered her arms, suddenly looking unspeakably exhausted. She staggered out of the circle, supported by a neighbor who quickly supplied her with a tankard of hot wine. At the same moment, it seemed like the fire lost some of its power. The golden sparks ceased rising, and even the crackling of the wood became quieter. An oppressive silence hung over the crowd, but only briefly. Then murmuring, whispering, hissing, and grumbling began.

"The Biikebrennen should be a happy festival," someone said. "Send that old witch home. We don't want her dark prophecies here."

"Yes, send her away so she doesn't ruin the festival. We want to celebrate and enjoy ourselves," someone else added.

Then several voices rose in chorus. "Send her home. Send her home. Send her home!"

CHAPTER 3

Old Meret left after practically being driven away. In a few moments, the merriment of the festival took hold again. Young boys cavorted and shouted as loudly as they could, and girls took each other by the hand and danced around the fire, leaping like young deer. The older men had gathered together and filled their pipes, and soon a thin white cloud floated next to the mighty pillar of smoke from the Biikebrennen. The married women had also gathered and were chatting and singing songs, but the mood was still slightly dampened in spite of all the noise. The cheerfulness was contrived, and it became more hysterical and wild by the moment. The songs sounded shrill, and the laughter sounded hollow. Hanging over the festival was a dark foreboding, which couldn't be driven away by laughter or song. Maren had taken Thies's hand and pulled him into the circle of youths. One of the boys, who was passing around an old sailor's flask of rum, kicked a foot in the direction that Old Meret had disappeared in.

"I wish the old witch would finally die. She only brings trouble to the island. Just last week my mother dragged me to church. I had to light a candle because I met the old woman at night and forgot to greet her."

The other boys jeered. Even Thies made a face. Only Maren shook her head. "I don't think she's dangerous. Maybe she has some strange ideas, but she certainly isn't a witch, at least not an evil one that we have to be afraid of. She's never hurt anyone. But I *am* sure she has the second sight." She paused to think. "I'm happy, at least, that I only have one set of eyes." And then Maren laughed brightly. Only Grit shook her head as though Maren had just said something monumentally stupid.

"We'll be leaving in a few days," one of the boys said. "Let's celebrate properly one last time!" Then he started singing a bawdy song, and the others joined him, laughing.

Captain Boyse stood with the minister, observing the antics of the young people. He was particularly interested in one of them. He smiled when she smiled, and scowled when she took someone by the hand.

"You will be leaving for your long voyage in a few days," the minister said, shuffling his feet in the sand. "I can't say that I'm particularly pleased about it. When you're on the island, I can depend on people to go to church and behave themselves. But as soon as you're gone, things become unpredictable."

"What do you mean, Father?"

"Well, sailors' wives are expected to be faithful, but it seems to me that doesn't always apply to all of them."

Boyse's forehead creased. "Girls who have lost their virtue and unfaithful wives have to wear a red band on their foreheads. I didn't see a single woman or girl wearing one today."

"No, and it's no wonder. It just means that since you've been back on the island, you've been keeping order. And when I baptize the spring babies whose 'fathers' were at sea nine months before the birth, of course I record the names of those sailors as fathers in the parish register."

Boyse nodded. "As we agreed. And in exchange, Father, you receive a barrel of good rum from me every November. So I'll hear no complaints. The most important thing is that there is peace on Sylt. And so there is."

Boyse left the minister standing where he was, straightened his tunic, and ran a hand over his hair and beard once more. Then he straightened his shoulders and made his way over to Finja and Klaas Luersen, who were standing with neighbors and singing songs.

"I'd like a word with you, Luersen."

Klaas separated himself leisurely from the group and followed the captain for a few paces. They walked away a little, where no one would hear them. Klaas didn't follow as reverently as another man might have done. He had respect for Boyse but didn't fear him.

"I'll come straight to the point. I'd like to marry your daughter."

Klaas drew on his pipe. "Ah. And why our Maren, of all the girls? You could easily find richer, more beautiful girls." Klaas loved his daughter dotingly, but he knew she wasn't a good match for the captain. She was too outspoken, and too poor. She was pretty. Yes, she was very pretty, with her gray eyes and long blond hair. But she was also headstrong. She wouldn't make a good wife for someone who was used to giving orders.

"I have chosen Maren. She belongs to me and my family."

Klaas was astonished by the certainty of Captain Boyse's words. Any other man would have praised Maren's virtues, her skills, and her beauty. But Boyse didn't waste any breath on those things.

"Does she know?" Klaas asked. He never could have imagined that the girl who had been the talk of the Rantum pub could be his daughter.

"She doesn't know. At the moment, she's dancing with Thies Heinen around the fire. And I don't like it, if I may tell you."

"You may, but it won't change anything. Maren is sixteen years old, Captain. Should she sit at home twiddling her thumbs? She's young, and she wants amusement like all the other young folk. She still has time before she has to marry. But when the time comes, Maren herself will decide."

"I'd thought to announce the engagement this evening. We can marry next winter. You and Finja can think about whether you'd like to leave your cottage here and come live with us in Keitum. I have plenty of room. You know I have one of the best Frisian houses there. You would want for nothing. There's even plenty of firewood and Branntwein."

Klaas regarded the captain for a moment before he spoke. "A tempting offer, to be sure. Although surprising. But we won't do anything that Maren doesn't agree to. You may ask her yourself whether she wishes to be your wife, though I think she's too young for marriage. Everything else will happen as it must." Then Klaas tapped his pipe out on the heel of his boot and turned to go. He sighed softly, because he knew that marrying Boyse would be the best way for Maren to have a comfortable life. But she was headstrong and was used to making her own decisions. *Maybe the people who think we've spoiled her are right,* Klaas thought. *The ones who think she always gets her way and doesn't understand her duty to her family.* He knew they were right. Finja had been over thirty when she finally became with child. Finja and Klaas had always known that Maren would be the only one. And so they adored her and spoiled her, and almost always let her have her way. They were happy when Maren was happy. And now Klaas wondered for the first time whether they had prepared their child properly for life. It was clear to him that neither Finja nor himself would be able to decide whom Maren would marry. She would have her own way again, but this time, Klaas feared, she would make the wrong decision. However, he could do nothing about Maren's stubbornness and nothing about the selfishness that sometimes possessed her. He turned back to glance at Boyse and prayed silently that he'd have patience with Maren. Patience and a thick skin.

Boyse straightened his tunic again, although it was already hanging smoothly. Again, he smoothed his already-neat hair. Then he strode toward the group of young people.

"It's time to leap the fire!" one of them shouted. "Thies! Go! Jump for Maren!"

"Stop!" Boyse commanded. "First, I wish to speak with Maren alone."

Her face was glowing with joy and excitement as she swept a loose strand of hair from her forehead. Her eyes flashed; her breath came fast. "Now? Can't it wait until tomorrow?" But then Maren saw the captain's face darken, and she went to him. Boyse took Maren's hand and spoke quietly, so the others couldn't hear.

"Maren Luersen, daughter of Klaas and Finja, will you marry me in a year?"

"What?" Maren's eyes went wide in surprise. She had been ready for anything, but not this.

"Will you marry me?" Boyse sounded slightly aggrieved. Any other woman on the island would have fallen to her knees with joy and thanked her creator. But Maren stood proudly in front of him, not even lowering her eyes.

"Why me?"

"Because I have chosen you. Would you deign to be my wife? I can wait one more year if it must be." Now he sounded even more impatient.

Maren felt laughter rising up inside of her, tickling her throat, filling her mouth, but shortly before it broke out, she managed to swallow it again. Then she looked Boyse directly in the eye. "I thank you kindly for your proposal, but I'm already in love. In love with Thies Heinen. This evening, we promised to marry each other. He will make me happy."

For a moment, everyone stood as though frozen. Those who had been listening in secret immediately wished that they were very far away, and more than a few thought of the wild geese who were supposed to bring doom and disaster. No one dared to deny Rune Boyse anything. It was unthinkable that a woman he had chosen would refuse him. But Maren did. She even held his gaze without flinching, while Thies stared at the ground and suddenly no longer looked like someone who'd just spoken of true love.

"Do your parents know about this?" the captain asked.

Maren smiled and shrugged. "They knew that I wanted to go to the Biikebrennen tonight with Thies. This time they wouldn't let me, because we're not engaged yet. They'll have to allow it next year."

"And you believe they will still be in agreement?" Boyse asked.

Maren smiled again. "Why wouldn't they be? Thies is a good, hard-working man. We love each other. For me, that's the only reason to marry." She spoke the last words almost triumphantly. "He will make me happy," she repeated. She believed it too. So far, her life had been all about waiting. She would finally find happiness when she was married, when she no longer had to obey her mother and father. Her entire childhood and youth, she had been waiting for her real life to finally begin. Maren could see how the others in Rantum lived, how many marriages weren't blessed with love and happiness, but she was sure that it would be different for Thies and her. Thies. That was happiness. Even if she didn't know exactly what happiness looked like or how it should feel.

Boyse's face became cold and hard as stone. Only his eyes gleamed with hurt, and his mouth was pressed into a thin line. He bowed his head a little. "I will respect your decision, Maren," he said. "But I advise you to think it over once more very carefully before you make your final choice. You are still young, and much can change. I will ask you again in the winter."

Maren's answer was on the tip of her tongue, but her friend Maike tugged on her arm. "He's right. You should think about it."

Maren shook her head. "Reflection and love are not good bedmates. My feelings have decided. That's the way it will stay."

Captain Boyse bowed his head slightly, and then turned quickly and walked stiffly away.

Finja and Klaas had been watching from a distance. Now Finja went to her daughter.

"He proposed to you, didn't he?"

Maren nodded, still feeling amused. "Yes. Can you imagine?"

"It's not a laughing matter, child. He meant it seriously. You need a man who can manage you. Boyse would be a good match for you." Finja spoke the words, but anyone who knew her could tell that she hadn't spoken from her heart. There was fear flickering in her eyes.

"That's nonsense!" Maren threw her head back. "I can manage myself. Boyse is old. Life with him would be deadly dull."

Finja looked at her daughter thoughtfully. "You're still very young, Maren. Young and impetuous. I wish you'd grow up a little. Don't do anything that can't be undone. Wait a year, do you understand me?" Again, her voice was hard and unyielding.

Maren bit her lower lip obstinately. "I don't know what you mean," she lied. "Thies and I just made our promises to each other and swore by the sign of the fire. Why should we wait another year when we're certain? I don't know why you're saying this."

"Oh, yes, you do. But I'll be glad to tell you again. I know that you believe Thies is the man of your heart. I like Thies too. He's an honest, hardworking young man. But don't get engaged to him. Neither officially nor secretly. It can only be to your sorrow. If he really loves you, he won't mind waiting for you for another year."

"It's too late." The echo of triumph still hadn't completely disappeared from Maren's voice. "I've made up my mind."

"But it hasn't been announced. You can still change your mind."

Maren pursed her lips. She grabbed Thies by the hand and shook her head. Thies, who'd been silent up until that moment, obviously wanted to say something, but Maren gave him a warning glance, and he closed his mouth again. He didn't look happy. He looked like he didn't feel comfortable in his own skin.

"Maybe we should wait," he said. "We have time."

But Maren shook her head. "I want my life to begin!"

CHAPTER 4

Even though the winter was harsh and cold, it was much too short, as usual. At least for the women and children. The twenty-second of February, which came after the Biikebrennen, was *Petritag,* or Saint Peter's Day. It was a sad day for most of the island dwellers; it was the day the sailors took leave of those they loved. They brought their sea chests to the big gaff-rigged Dutch sailing *smaks* in the harbor, where they waited for an offshore breeze. The Dutch smaks were coastal transport ships which would bring crew members to their assigned ships in Amsterdam. As they went out to sea, the women and children waved good-bye with white handkerchiefs. The men would return in the autumn. Thies was leaving too, and Maren stood with the other women high on the dunes and waved farewell to her sweetheart. Finja had been able to stop Maren from making her engagement public: it had been easy to convince Thies to wait another year. But for Maren, the promise at the Biikebrennen had been as much of a commitment as a public engagement party to which everyone on the island had been invited. She was Thies's fiancée, and she would behave that way, no matter what the rest of the islanders might think or have to say about it.

Thies didn't want to sign on to Captain Boyse's brig, because Boyse had a reputation not only for being strict but for returning weeks later than all the other captains, albeit with his ship packed with barrels of whale oil and blubber. Thies had promised Maren he would look for a job on a merchant's ship, but who knew whether he'd be able to find one?

The ships disappeared over the horizon after passing Hörnum. The women sighed again, dried the last tears from their cheeks, and tucked their handkerchiefs back into their bodices. But the children had already almost forgotten about their fathers and brothers and were playing happily on the beach.

And so spring came to the women of the island, and then summer followed with bright, clear days of dazzling light, which became weaker in August and were already a milky autumnal haze by September. When the migratory birds made their way south over the island, the women and children waited on the dunes again and kept a lookout for the returning men.

Maren had spent the entire time thinking of Thies, envisioning his adventures and imagining his return. She had recalled the magical moment of their engagement again and again. She could still remember the evening as though she were experiencing it anew.

She had stood a little to the side while Old Meret had made her proclamations. Thies had put his big warm hands on either side of her face, stroked her lips with his thumb, and then kissed her so tenderly that her heart had grown warm.

"I like you very much, you know," he told her. And when she was silent, losing herself in the dark fire of his eyes, he asked, "And you? What do you think about me?"

Then the words slipped out just like that, without her having to think. It made them even more honest. She told him how she felt, without even knowing exactly what it meant. "I love you," she whispered. And then Thies kissed her. Not just on the lips, like he had before, but a real kiss, with an open mouth, so she could taste him and feel his breath. He pushed apart her lips with his tongue, and Maren, at first a little shocked, allowed it. She had to stand on her tiptoes to reach his mouth, and the entire time she imagined that everyone in Rantum could see her. They would finally understand that she and Thies belonged together. She wished he would never stop kissing her. His mouth tasted good, and the kiss left a languorous, warm feeling in her stomach. Then he let her go, and Maren's gaze fell on Captain Boyse. She saw him crease his brow, and all at once, she was flooded with a sense of shame. At the same time, perhaps for the same reason, she didn't want to let Thies go. She stretched again, her lips seeking Thies's.

"You're as impetuous as a young horse," he said softly, his voice rough with emotion. Maren was confused and ashamed in a way she didn't understand.

"But we're engaged now, aren't we?" she asked quietly. "I would never do such a thing with any other man. Now you're going to marry me."

Thies laughed again. "Anything you desire, my darling."

He'd taken her hand in his and had kissed her ring finger exactly on the place her wedding band would be. And Maren had felt grown up and courageous and magnificent. For half of the evening. Until Boyse had asked for her hand in marriage.

The autumn storms came, and with the storms came the time of return. First, the men who'd been on the merchant ships arrived, and then the whalers. But not all of them. Peter's oldest son had lost his life at sea, and Thaken, the helmsman from Rantum, didn't return either. Grit's husband, Wilms, had also found his grave at the bottom of the sea. By November, almost all the men had returned home. Only those who had sailed on Captain Boyse's whaling ship to Greenland were still gone.

Thies returned in October. Maren greeted him with a cry of joy and fell into his arms, touching his face as though she were touching happiness itself. Her joy wasn't even dampened by the funerals that she'd had to attend.

"Where have you been?" Maren asked. "Tell me about your adventures." Her hands constantly caressed his arms, his face, and his wild hair. She had missed him, had missed their conversations, his warm hand in hers, and the special voice he used only when he spoke to her.

Thies was quieter than usual, but he still allowed himself to enjoy Maren's attentions. "I wasn't able to get work on a merchant's ship, so I went with whalers. We went north to Spitsbergen, but we only caught two whales. It didn't make me rich. I only hope that the pay will get my mother, my sister, and me through the winter." Maren knew exactly what he hadn't said. *I can barely take care of my mother and sister. How can I even think about starting my own family?* At once, she was filled with fear. Gray, tough, sticky fear. But when Thies kissed her, stroking away the worry lines on her forehead with his fingers, the fear simply dissolved like mist in the sunlight.

"We'll find a way. There's always a way," she said, nestling against him. "I can make fishing nets the way my mother taught me."

Thies hugged her close and sighed into her hair.

"What's wrong?" Maren asked.

"Nothing. Nothing that can be changed." He looked at her and pushed a strand of hair away from her small face with its big sea-gray eyes.

"It's good that you can make nets. But they won't fetch very much. There aren't many herring fishermen left on Sylt. Your father is one of the last in Rantum. The shoals of herring moved away long ago."

"Don't worry so much!" Maren said dismissively. "It will be all right."

Thies became even more serious. His eyes darkened. "It's not as easy as you think. I've been thinking about it all summer. This winter, I could attend Boyse's seamanship school. I'm already a good sailor. At least, the mate I last sailed with told me so. He even gave me a recommendation and a book to study, to prepare myself." He showed Maren the book, *The Art of Navigation*, by someone called Nahmen Arfsten, about the basics of seamanship.

"Seamanship school," she repeated. Many captains and ship's officers spent their winters teaching the young men of the island the art of seamanship. They learned to read charts and even to draw them, to discern the direction of the wind, and to handle all the tools of the trade. The young men learned what it really meant to guide a ship through a storm between sandbars, icebergs, and rocks. They learned everything about the trimming of sails and even how to keep a crew's spirits up when they were at sea for months. Shortly before Saint Peter's Day, several of the students who had learned enough went to the mainland to Tønder, the nearest city that offered the officer's examination. Maren knew that each year there were very few who passed the exam, but Thies, she was sure, could be one of them. So far, he'd worked as an ordinary seaman and had earned the correspondingly low pay. As an officer, he would earn far more. But that wasn't all.

"But then you'd have less time for me," she said quietly. *Then you will be with Boyse all the time,* she thought. And she didn't like that thought at all, although she didn't actually know what bothered her so much about it. Boyse was the best teacher on Sylt. Young men practically lined up to study with him, even though he was strict and unforgiving. Since he'd proposed to her, Maren had avoided Boyse whenever possible. If she met him in Rantum, she kept her head bowed, but she couldn't stop her heart from beating a little faster. He had confused her, and he confused her more every time she encountered him. Before he'd proposed, her world had been clear and orderly. She had been happy about marrying Thies and about their future together. It was as though the captain's proposal had taken away a little bit of her love for Thies. She hated him for it, and she hated, too, that Thies depended on his school.

"Yes, that's true. But you can use the time to embroider your trousseau," Thies answered.

She took his hand and leaned her cheek on it, relieved and happy at his words. "Do you love me?" she asked.

Thies nodded.

"Do you love me so much that you believe the two of us can take on the world together?"

Thies swallowed and avoided her gaze, but then he nodded again. "Yes. I believe in you and me. I believe in the power of our love. We'll be able to do anything we set our minds to."

CHAPTER 5

When she heard the knock, Maren knew who was at the door. She looked pleadingly at her mother, who was sitting on the edge of her chair looking pale and thoughtful.

Finja hadn't broached the subject of marriage since the Biikebrennen. Only recently, once all the seamen had returned to the island, had she brought it up again. "So, have you thought about it?" she had asked Maren.

"There's nothing to think about. I love Thies, and that's all that matters," Maren had replied.

"And when you have no firewood and can't afford to buy milk for the children? Does love still matter when you're hungry and cold?"

Maren bit her lip. "Love can overcome anything."

"No, my dear, it can't. But you won't believe that until you've experienced it for yourself. There are things more important than love. Respect, friendship, and strength, for example. Thies is a good man, but he's not strong."

Maren thought of Thies's broad shoulders, his powerful back, and his strong hands. "Of course he's strong."

Finja shook her head. "I'm not talking about physical strength. I'm taking about strength of spirit. Will Thies stand by you in good times and bad? Will he be a dependable friend when the passionate flames of love have burnt low? Poverty can make people self-centered."

Maren's forehead creased with confusion. What kind of questions were these? And how was she supposed to know the answers? She only knew that before Thies's father had died, his parents had fought with each other every day. The father had constantly berated the mother because he'd given up another good potential partner for her, and the mother had accused the father of not being able to provide for his family. They'd spent many dreadful years together until the father had finally died. To this day, long after the father's death, the mother resented him because he'd left her with nothing. But Thies was different. Maren knew that. Thies would take care of her. In good times and bad. She spread her arms wide. "We love each other. Why shouldn't that be enough?"

Finja tilted her head doubtfully. "Maybe it is, maybe it isn't. Love doesn't necessarily last forever. A few years ago, Grit and Thies were inseparable. And then, as she was already embroidering her trousseau, he turned his attentions to you."

"He was still a child when he promised to marry Grit. He grew up."

Finja shook her head again, as though she wasn't particularly convinced. "You still have a little time. Look deeply into your heart."

Now, when the knock sounded a second time, Klaas got up and opened the door. There stood Captain Rune Boyse. "You know why I've come?" he asked tersely.

Klaas nodded. "Welcome to our home."

He walked ahead into the good sitting room. Maren and her mother were already waiting there. While Maren sank into the big comfortable armchair, Finja sat on the edge of her chair, sliding back and forth nervously. Just yesterday, when she'd heard Rune Boyse had returned to the island, she'd questioned her daughter again.

"Have you thought about marrying Boyse?"

Maren had raised her eyebrows. "You can ask me as often as you wish. My decision stands."

"I think you've made the wrong decision." Finja had looked concerned. "If you think carefully, you'll understand. Thies already has difficulty providing for his family. You know that yourself. Boyse can give you everything you need. Not only now, but also in the future. You could have children without worrying that they'd go hungry. They would sleep in warm beds, and when they got sick, a doctor would be called. It's not only about love; it's about much more. It's about your entire life."

Maren nodded wearily. "You've told me all this. But I won't change my mind. Thies and I will marry. What is life worth without love? In winter, he'll attend the seamanship school and then go to Tønder for his examination. Next year, he'll go to sea as an officer and will earn enough to support us."

Finja sighed. "I would forbid you to see Thies, but I know you. If I did that, you'd elope with him. I can only pray that you won't regret your decision."

Now, Boyse stood on the threshold and examined the room carefully. There were only a few delft tiles—a sign of wealth and status on the island—decorating the walls. There was a shelf full of clay crockery, simple vessels, though decorated with a beautiful pattern. The high-legged sofa, upholstered in a soft green material, was threadbare. There was no clock and, under the window, only a single chest that was covered by an old sheepskin. The rough floorboards were bare, and there were no curtains at the windows to keep warmth in the room.

Klaas slipped past the captain and poured two glasses of his best rum. "Come and sit down, Boyse." He asked Boyse about his time at sea and about whaling. But then Boyse, like Finja, began to slide nervously toward the edge of his chair.

"Enough pleasantries," he finally declared. "You know why I've come." He took the glass in hand, took a deep swallow, and then looked Maren directly in the eye. "Have you considered my proposal?"

Maren nodded and gazed down at her hands, which were folded in her lap. She didn't dare look him in the eye.

"And?"

Maren took a deep breath and looked at him. "I can't be your wife."

"Why not?" A small smile was playing over the captain's lips.

"It has nothing to do with you. It's . . . I just . . . can't. Because . . . I love someone else. But I already told you at the Biikebrennen." When Maren had finally gotten the words out, she sighed with relief.

"Still Thies Heinen?"

Maren nodded. "We're in love."

Boyse grimaced. "Love? You still believe in it?"

Maren's forehead creased. It annoyed her that Boyse spoke as though she were a stupid child who still believed in Father Christmas. "Yes, I do!" Maren's words felt hollow and a little too sullen.

"That's your last word?"

"Yes, Captain."

He turned to Finja, who looked pale and tense. "You weren't able to do anything about this?" he asked her.

Finja sighed. "I wish I could."

"Well, one day you may have to. And I just hope for all of us that it won't be too late." The captain's words were enigmatic and baffling, and Finja's hands began to shake. But she remained silent and lowered her eyes.

Boyse sighed and stood up. He smoothed his tunic. "Now everything necessary has been said." He turned to Klaas. "Thank you for the rum."

Then he turned around a little stiffly and left the parlor, leaving so quickly that Klaas managed to stand only after the door had already closed behind him.

Maren looked despondently at her mother. "Now it's been said and repeated and written in stone. He won't come again," she said quietly.

"Yes. You've decided. I can only pray that you've made the right decision." Finja sighed and then reached for the rum and drank the generously filled glass in one draft, although she didn't normally like spirits.

Maren saw fear in her mother's eyes and worry in her father's, and she herself wasn't completely at ease either. She had made the right decision; that was clear to her. But would Boyse accept her rejection? He was a proud man, and he was used to people obeying his orders. Now Maren had defied him. She asked herself if it would have unpleasant consequences. There were plenty of girls on Sylt who wished nothing more than to be Captain Boyse's wife. But so far, he'd ignored all the interest directed at him. Now he was thirty years old, and several of the islanders had already begun to wonder why he was taking so long to get married. Had he been waiting for Maren? No, she couldn't imagine that. She knew she was special, but also that Boyse had much better prospects. She was proud too and wasn't about to let herself be talked into something she didn't want.

She stood up and smiled in spite of the mood. "Thies isn't rich, but he'll be a much better son-in-law than Boyse would be," she declared. "He will provide for you just as well."

"Oh, really?" Finja looked up. "Will he?"

At that moment, Maren realized that she had truly disappointed her parents. She realized that Finja and Klaas had hoped for an easier life after her wedding. Klaas had difficulty getting out of bed in the morning, and no one knew how long he'd be able to keep going out to fish. There were days his rheumatism was so bad that he could barely bend a finger and every movement hurt him. It would have been a relief for him to know that Maren and Finja would be well provided for when he couldn't catch herring anymore. Finja was growing older too. Her eyes were becoming worse day by day. How many times had she cut herself recently when she gutted the fish Klaas had brought home? She couldn't knit in the winter any longer either because she couldn't see the loops. That meant she wasn't able to contribute to their earnings. Maren understood all of this, and also that she had to provide for her parents. They had worked as hard as plow horses all their lives. Now that they were growing older, it was her duty as a daughter to take care of them. But how? Her love for Thies wouldn't keep Klaas and Finja warm in winter or put food in their mouths. And Thies had been right: her fishing nets wouldn't earn much. But even though she felt guilty about her parents, and although it hurt her to see their disappointed and fearful faces, she still knew she'd made the right decision.

"I really do love him," she said softly, with her eyes lowered. "I'm sure he's the man I should marry. And I'll do everything I can to make life easier for you both."

Then Finja stood up and stroked her shoulder gently. "I know, Maren. I know." As she spoke, she sounded unspeakably sad, and a shudder ran down Maren's back.

Christmas was approaching, and with it came the snow. It wasn't particularly cold, but it had been snowing ceaselessly for days, and the drifts of snow made the roads unpassable. The dune paths were coated in a thin layer of ice and were so slippery that even people who were steady on their feet needed a walking stick to use them. The landscape looked like something out of a fairy tale. The heather was dusted with white, and the scrubby brown bushes and grasses were coated with a shining layer of silver. The sea looked like a vast mirror that stretched from horizon to horizon. Smoke rose from all the chimneys of Rantum, and delicious smells wafted from the smokehouses. The women baked Christmas confections, and in front of the barns, plucked geese were hanging, although they were very lean.

Maren had a special gift for Thies. She was knitting a pair of stockings for him, but they weren't just any stockings. They were stockings made of women's hair. Her *own* hair. Since Maren was a small child,

Finja had regularly cut off a few locks of her daughter's long hair and saved it, as was the tradition on Sylt. And now Maren had cut her hair very short and had spun fifteen years' worth of growth into a fine, soft yarn. She smiled at every loop, because she was proud of her gift. Stockings and gloves made of women's hair were very special on the island. They not only kept the wearer warmer than sheep's wool but were also better protection against moisture. But the girls and women prized their long hair, so it was considered evidence of great love to sacrifice her hair to knit something for a man.

Finja had been against it. "Do you really want to do that? Even before you're married? What if something happens? Who will take you to wife with short hair?"

Maren only smiled. "What could possibly happen? I've made up my mind."

"You're not only willful, you're stubborn as well," Finja said accusingly. But Maren just reached for the scissors and cut off her blond braid. But if she were honest with herself, she had to admit that perhaps she hadn't made the sacrifice for love alone. There was a feeling inside her that she couldn't quite put her finger on. Because she had refused Boyse, her parents couldn't approach their old age without worrying about survival. Maren was still plagued with guilt about that. That was why she had to prove that her love for Thies was the greatest that the island had ever seen. The sacrifice of her hair was the proof of it.

Then it was the morning of Christmas Eve, and Maren made her way over the dunes to bring Thies her gift. She also had small presents for his mother and sister in her pockets: a pot of heather honey for his mother and a prettily crocheted collar of fine yarn for his sister to attach to her dress.

Maren smiled all the way to the Heinen family home, full of anticipation and full of pride in herself. She knocked, and the door opened. "Oh, it's you," the mother said in greeting. "We weren't expecting you."

Maren's brow creased in confusion at the obvious coldness. "Have I come at a bad time?" she asked, slightly amazed.

"No, no. It's just that we've already had a visitor today." Finally, the mother stepped aside so Maren could enter the house.

"Who is it now?" she heard Antje call from the kitchen.

"Maren," Thies's mother called back.

"Oh, her," his sister replied, sounding a little disappointed.

Thies rushed joyfully from the work area and took her into his arms. "Merry Christmas! I was just about to come visit you and your parents."

"Am I one step ahead of you again?" Maren was glowing now. She reached into her basket and pulled out her gift. Thies unwrapped the package and looked thunderstruck. When Maren finally pulled the hood off her head and he saw that she'd sacrificed her hair, he gasped, found no words, and silently held her close and planted countless kisses on her short locks.

Then, his sister, Antje, entered the small living room. "What happened to you?" she asked, aghast when she saw Maren. "What happened to your hair? Did the lice eat it off your head?"

Thies held the stockings up for her to see. "She made these out of it for me," he explained with pride.

"Hmm," Antje said. "I liked it better on her head. Now she looks like a cabin boy." The mother laughed too, and Maren ran a hand over her head in embarrassment.

Then Antje took a pretty scarf which had been woven from brightly colored wool from her shoulders and held it up for Maren to see. "Look! This is what I got for Christmas." She was almost bursting with pride. "Feel it. It's as soft as a lamb's coat."

"Antje, stop. No one wants to know that." Thies made a move to grab the scarf away from his sister, but Antje quickly hid it behind her back.

"Oh yes? I think Maren would be very interested to know who gave me the scarf, and where Mother got the two delft tiles in the living room. You want to know, don't you, Maren?" Antje asked.

Maren nodded. She was already feeling a little betrayed, but she didn't know exactly why.

"Grit."

"Grit?"

"Yes. Grit Wilms, the widow. You're surprised, aren't you? You know, she can afford to buy nice things and doesn't have to cut her hair and walk around looking like a cabin boy."

All at once, the crocheted collar seemed cheap to Maren, and the heather honey seemed pathetic. She considered leaving them in her pocket; better not to give anything at all than such paltry things. But her pride won out. "Everyone gives what they can," she said with a defiant undertone, and handed them the honey and the collar. Then she straightened her shoulders proudly and gave Antje and her mother a challenging look.

Antje blushed but thanked Maren kindly, and the mother was suddenly very busy preparing a comfortable place by the fire for Maren to sit.

When Maren was alone with Thies at last, she said, "Is what they said true? Did Grit really come here to exchange gifts?"

Thies nodded and looked down at the floor, looking ashamed.

"What did she give you?" Maren asked.

"Nothing. Just a little thing. It's not important."

"Then it shouldn't be a problem for you to tell me."

Thies fidgeted in his chair and shook his head.

"Tell me!" Maren demanded.

Thies sighed. "She gave me a pair of women's hair stockings. But she didn't make them out of her own hair. She ordered them from the mainland."

"Oh!" Maren had made the stockings with such pride. Now her gift seemed worthless. She ran a hand over her short hair again and suddenly felt stupid, pushy, and ugly.

"Oh!" she repeated. "I didn't know that." Then she jumped up, feeling humiliated and sick. She pulled up her hood, wanting to leave the Heinens' house as quickly as possible, but Thies held on to her tightly.

"I'm so happy about the stockings you made for me, and I don't care about the ones from Grit," he said quietly. "I'm extremely happy about yours, actually. It's the most wonderful gift I've ever received. I will treasure them for the rest of my life. Thank you so much."

But Maren was still unhappy. "But you still have Grit's stockings. They're surely softer. She probably ordered the finest hair on the mainland." She ran a hand over her head under the hood. "My hair is quite ornery," she said with a sigh.

"To me, your hair is the softest in existence." He gave her such a gentle, tender kiss that a shiver ran down her back. She leaned against Thies's chest and sighed, feeling at least partly mollified. "It's just that your mother and Antje didn't seem to be very happy about my gifts."

"Hmm," Thies said.

She freed herself from his embrace and looked into his eyes. "We promised at the Biikebrennen that we'd always tell each other the truth. So please don't just say 'hmm.' I'd like to know why they suddenly seem to be so unfriendly toward me."

"What do you want to hear, Maren? Sometimes the truth can hurt."

"I don't care. I'd rather hear the truth directly from you instead of letting my imagination run wild and come up with things that are much worse in the end."

"They're not happy about our engagement."

Maren's brow creased. "So suddenly? I thought they liked me."

"They do. But ever since Grit has made it known that she's expecting a proposal from me, my mother and Antje can only think of the money that she'd bring into the marriage."

Maren grew angry. "Then Antje should marry a rich man. She should take Boyse, if she's dreaming of being rich."

"Don't be cruel, Maren," Thies said pleadingly, and Maren was immediately ashamed. He was right. It had been cruel to speak of Antje marrying, because she never would. She'd had polio as a child, and since then she could barely walk. What's more, she wasn't especially pretty, and she was poor. On an island where the women outnumbered the men, there would be no husband for her.

"Please forgive me," Maren whispered. "I didn't mean it like that."

"Now it's time for me to give *you* a gift." He smiled at her, and Maren saw the same look of joy and pride in his eyes that she'd come to him with.

"What is it?" she asked, feigning curiosity to make him happy. She didn't want to get a present now. Not after she'd heard about Grit's gifts.

He gave her a package that had been carefully wrapped in well-used tissue paper. "Open it."

Maren opened the paper and found a beautiful cap made of sealskin. "Oh!" she said. "How beautiful!" She rubbed the soft fur against her face and smiled at Thies happily. But then her face darkened. "Oh, Thies, it must have been terribly expensive! Where did you get it? It's so beautiful!"

Thies waved away her concern. "I just had to buy it, because the color of the fur reminds me of the gray in your eyes. Another whaling ship brought it from Greenland. Put it on!"

Maren did as he asked. She pushed back her hood and put the cap on her head. She could see from the look in his eyes how well it suited her, and suddenly she was happy, after all. She took both of his hands and held them against her chest. "We belong together, don't we?"

"Yes," Thies said. "Thies and Maren, Maren and Thies. Now and forever."

CHAPTER 6

The sky had been covered with thick gray clouds all day. A few heavy drops of rain fell every now and then on the last unmelted patches of snow. The wind was cold, but that was nothing unusual. Klaas sat in front of the house smoking his pipe and looked up worriedly.

"What's wrong?" Maren asked.

"We're in for a squall. A big one."

Maren looked up too. "The sky is almost always gray in winter. And the wind blows every day. How can you tell?"

Klaas blew a smoke ring, and he watched it rise. "I can feel it in my bones, child."

Maren's mouth twitched doubtfully, but she didn't say anything.

"Come. Let's tie down anything that could blow away. Then you can help me get my fishing boat up past the high-tide line. And tell your mother she should take the washing in and close the shutters tightly."

Maren looked up again. It looked like a normal January sky. Nothing indicated that a storm was brewing, but Maren didn't argue with her father.

By that afternoon, the wind had picked up, sweeping the fine sand from the dunes through the air, forcing it through every little crack around the windows. It caught in hair, stuck to skin, and burned in eyes. The sea reared up and cast six-foot breakers onto the beach, hissing and spitting like an angry cat.

Maren had forgotten to take in a couple of fishing nets. She went out but was unable to hold the door against the gale; it was seized by a gust and crashed shut behind her. She took a step forward, leaning against the wind. She had to gasp for air through the sand blowing into her mouth and nose. She saw her mother at the window and wanted to call to her, but the wind ripped the words from her mouth. The nets had taken on lives of their own. One hung on the fence with bits of heather stuck in it, sticky with sand and salty ocean spray. Maren tugged on it while the wind pulled at her skirts, lifted them up, and threw her pinafore over her face. When she had finally freed the net, she braced herself against the wind. The door of the barn flew from her grip and crashed against the wall. Maren hurried in, threw down the nets, and rushed back into the house.

It was dark indoors. Finja had closed all the shutters over the windows. Only an oil lamp with five wicks, two of which were lit, threw twitching shadows over the room. Maren's mother sat at the kitchen table with her hands folded, and Klaas sat across from her. Maren shook the sand from her hair and clothes, rinsed her mouth with water, and rubbed her eyes.

Her mother sighed. "It's going to be bad today."

No one replied, but Maren's fear was growing. The wind had become a storm, its howling competing with the sound of the crashing sea, tugging at the shutters, shrieking and shaking in the chimney. The fire flared once more and died. Hot ashes blew into the kitchen. Maren cried out and pulled on her mother's arm, though Finja sat motionless as she was struck with the flying embers.

"Come away!" she shouted, and Klaas, too, leapt out of his chair by the fireplace.

"I met Old Meret yesterday," Finja said softly.

"You shouldn't listen to her," Klaas replied.

"But her prophecies come true. You know that too."

"Yes. Sometimes she's right. And sometimes she's wrong. We still can't change anything."

Maren had never seen her mother so fearful. Finja's face had gone completely gray, and her eyes flickered darkly. They sat silently around the kitchen table, with their shoulders hunched, and listened to the wailing storm throw sand against the door and windows. The wailing grew louder; the storm had become a hurricane, blustering with uninhibited rage over the island. Maren's mother pressed her fists against her mouth and prayed silently. Her father paced nervously around the kitchen. Then the rain came, drenching the house with immeasurable force. It went on that way for hours.

Eventually, Maren, Finja, and Klaas settled into their sleeping alcoves, and although they were tired, no one could sleep. They lay tensely in the darkness and listened to the storm.

Toward the morning, as the storm began to let up, Maren managed to sleep a little. And when she awoke, her mother and father were sitting at the kitchen table again. Overnight the shutters had been torn from the windows, and what Maren saw outside shook her to the core. Not a single slat was left on the fence, the poles upon which the fishing nets usually hung were knocked over and splintered, and entire bushes had been torn out, leaving the land looking like a plucked goose on Saint Martin's Day. Inside, it wasn't much better. The reed roof had great holes torn in it, letting in the cold and rain. The kitchen was full of puddles, and the storm had chilled and soaked the house so thoroughly that it was impossible to get a fire started. It was still raining, the wind still howled in strong gusts, and the sea still sounded loud and threatening. But they seemed to have survived the worst of it.

"It's over," Maren's mother said quietly. "Everything is over. Whatever shall we do now? Old Meret was right again."

Klaas stood behind Finja and placed a comforting hand on her shoulder. "It will be all right. We've always managed to recover."

Finja shook her head. "Not this time. I can feel it. Old Meret prophesized it."

"How much has been damaged?" Maren wanted to know what was making her mother so dispirited.

"The storm took the barn roof off almost completely," Klaas said. "And the house's roof is badly damaged. The chimney came down, and the sand is up to the windows. I'm afraid my boat has been smashed to smithereens too."

Finja turned to Maren. "Go out and look around. It's not just that the house is damaged. It's destroyed. It's half-covered by a dune."

Maren started in surprise and looked to her father, who nodded. Then she put her shoulder to the door and tried to open it. She had to push with all her strength against the boards, but the door barely opened a crack.

"The sand is too high," her father explained. "Wait, I'll help you."

Together, they managed to open the door wide enough for Maren to slip outside. As she looked around, her eyes went wide with shock. Her father had been right. The back of the house was completely buried under sand, and in front, the sand was piled up to the windows. Roofing reeds lay shredded and broken on the ground. It looked as though there had been a war. Maren peered over at the neighbors' house. Mrs. Asmus stood in the ruins of her house, crying, as her husband, Fiete, walked over to Klaas.

"I've been down to the beach. Your boat is destroyed, and mine too. None of them survived in one piece." His face was pale, and he had wide, dark circles under his eyes. "What will we do now?"

Klaas raised his shoulders in a helpless gesture. "First, we have to see what can be saved."

"There isn't much. And without fishing, we won't be able to provide for our families."

Klaas nodded, thinking about his neighbor's words. "What you say is true."

"Have you got a plan?"

Klaas shook his head. He still seemed calm and collected, but Maren could tell he was despairing. She put a hand on his arm. "It will be all right," she said. "We've always managed somehow." But in her heart, she was afraid. She climbed the dune to look over at Thies's house and was met by another picture of disaster. She swallowed, again feeling that she owed something to her parents. If only she'd agreed to marry Boyse . . . She drove that thought away. Then she made her way to what was left of the barn, found a spade, and began to shovel sand away from the door and windows all by herself.

Klaas and Finja came to help her, but for all their effort, hardly any progress was visible by evening. The sand still stood high all around the house, and there were still holes in the roof, though they'd been covered with strips of heath sod. They layered on heavy clothes and were wrapping themselves in blankets in order to bear the cold of the night when Finja began to cry. She didn't say a word, and made no accusations, but she didn't need to. Maren understood her anyway.

When Maren woke up the next morning, her joints stiff with cold, she knew what she had to do. She washed, dressed, and hopped up and down to warm herself, but nothing helped. So she wrapped a thick scarf around her neck, put the sealskin cap on her head, and set off on the long road to Keitum. Pushing through her unease, she walked the seven miles from her parents' home to the widest part of the island. She knew that her plan would have consequences, but she had to try anyway. She owed at least that to her parents.

Three hours later, she stood breathless in front of Captain Boyse's beautiful big Frisian house, which seemed untouched by the storm. It stood white and shining behind the little front garden. The garden gate was made of a whale's jawbone, taller than a man. The shutters were painted sky blue, the roof was densely covered in new reeds, and the door was made of robust planks.

Both nervous and resolute, Maren raised the brass door knocker, which was fashioned in the shape of a whale.

Captain Boyse opened the door. "I've been expecting you," he said, and invited her to come inside. She followed him into the parlor and was nearly overwhelmed by the sheer luxury of it. The walls were covered in beautiful blue-and-white delft tiles. Under the windows stood painted chests with costly metal clasps, the table was surrounded by leather-upholstered chairs, and on the cupboard shelves, precious porcelain dishes were stacked. There was even a wonderfully carved and decorated grand-father clock, as tall as the captain himself. The lights weren't the usual dim tin lanterns, but polished silver stands set with expensive beeswax candles. The floor was covered in thick rugs that would be able to withstand the cold of the grimmest winter. There were porcelain pipes for tobacco on a small table that stood next to a rocking chair. Everywhere, exquisite souvenirs from every imaginable country could be seen.

Maren was impressed by the luxury and wealth, but Boyse seemed to move among his possessions as though they had no value but were just things he needed to fill his house.

"Have a seat," Boyse said. "Actually, I'd like to tell you to feel right at home, but I know that's not what you want."

Maren swallowed. His comment made it even more difficult to tell him about her difficulties.

"So, what can I do for you? Has the storm whirled your wits around so much that you've changed your mind and have decided to marry me after all?"

Maren swallowed again. She lowered her eyes to the colorful carpet and twisted her fingers together in her lap. *I'm here because I owe it to my parents,* she reminded herself. Then she gathered her courage. "The storm, it—"

"Yes, the storm," Boyse said, interrupting her rudely. "You would never have come to me freely. First, a storm had to sweep over the island."

"Yes. That's the truth." Maren responded with courage born of desperation and looked the captain directly in the eye. "It would be pointless to deny it. I haven't come to be your wife. I don't think you were expecting me to either. I've come to ask for your help."

"So. You want help. Go on."

"The storm hit us hard. The roof is half-gone, the chimney is damaged, and my father's fishing boat is destroyed."

"Any reasonable person would replace the roof, repair the chimney, and have a new fishing boat built," the captain responded, and Maren knew that he was saying it to humiliate her.

"Any person who had enough money would do that. But we have no money."

"Well, that's a pity. If you'd accepted my offer, you and your family would be comfortable and safe. Your father wouldn't have to fish anymore, and your mother would have no worries."

Maren sighed. "I know it's my fault, and I can't change it. But I came to you today anyway. I beg you, give my father a loan so we can go on living as we have."

"Why should I do that? You humiliated me in front of everyone, and you sent me away like a dog. You deserve to pay for that. Sometimes life gives us our just deserts."

Maren looked into the captain's face. Boyse's forehead was creased. His gray eyes glowed hard and cold, and his mouth had compressed into a narrow line. He was still offended by her refusal.

"I beg you with all my heart to forgive me, and to help us." She noticed that her voice shook a little.

"With all your heart?" Boyse repeated. "Are you sure that you have one?" He stood up and paced back and forth behind Maren's chair. Maren remained silent and looked guiltily at the table. She would have liked to get up and walk away, but she couldn't. Boyse was the only hope left to her family. Rantum had been hit hard. No one in her village had two coins to rub together.

"Shall I beg you on my knees?" Maren asked.

Boyse raised his eyebrows and regarded her as though he could already picture it happening. "You're going to have to do something," he said. "It's not going to be so easy to convince me. I already know from your beautiful eyes what I can expect. But no, I don't want to see you on your knees. I want a kiss from you."

Maren stood up angrily and faced the captain. Her eyes filled with tears that flowed down her pale, tense face. She had never felt so enraged in her entire life. She was filled with pure hatred for Boyse. She felt the redness of shame staining her cheeks, flushing her throat as she gasped for air.

"Look at me!" Boyse ordered, but Maren didn't raise her head. Then the captain put a hand under her chin and lifted it so she would have to look him in the eyes. Her eyes glittered with hate, anger, and desperation. She raised her hands pleadingly, unable to say a word, and held them there. She detested herself for what she was doing, and at the same time, she knew that it was necessary. If you were hungry, you couldn't be proud. If it was raining through your roof, you weren't in any position to make demands.

"I beg you! I can't kiss you," she said again.

"I also begged you for something, yet you denied me. Kiss me, or you can leave immediately."

So Maren closed her eyes and waited for his mouth to press roughly against hers. But she only felt his thumb, tracing the outline of her lips very gently. Then he lowered his mouth so lightly and tenderly to hers that a shiver ran down her spine. Boyse put a gentle hand on the back of Maren's neck, pushed her lips apart with his tongue, and played so tenderly with hers that her knees went weak. The kiss stirred and softened her until her entire body tingled, as though she had swallowed ants. A ball of fire exploded inside of her and blazed through her entire body. For the first time in her life, she felt heat in her lap, and the blood pulsing hotly through her veins.

But just as suddenly as he had begun, the captain stopped. She opened her eyes with difficulty, trying to find her way back to reality. She looked at him in confusion. Boyse's face was as cool and collected as if he had just signed a contract for a load of firewood.

As Maren smoothed her dress with shaking hands, the captain opened a hidden drawer under the tabletop and removed a purse of coins. "Here," he said. "That should be enough. Make sure that you pay it all back, to the penny. If you can't pay with coin, you'll have to find another way."

Maren nodded and was about to turn and leave, but Boyse held her back by the arm. All at once, his face had become gentler than it had been a few moments ago. "I have a Christmas present for you," he said, taking a wrapped package from a chest and giving it to her. Maren, still red with shame and humiliation, felt her eyes fill with tears again. It was bad enough that she'd had to kiss him. But it would be even worse, and more humiliating than ever, to have to accept a gift from him.

"I . . . I don't need a present from you," she stammered.

Boyse gazed at the package and then shrugged. "If you don't want it, I'll give it to another woman." He took a deep breath, watching Maren, who was still unable to even take a step. "And now go. I have things to do."

This last humiliation shook her out of her frozen state. With a sob, she rushed out of his house and wept half the way back to Rantum. She had been branded, heart and soul, and had no idea how to change it.

CHAPTER 7

Maren placed the purse on the table. "Now we can repair everything. Now, Father, you can buy a new fishing boat." She spoke softly, her soul still trembling and her cheeks burning.

Klaas's brow creased, and he cast a glance at Finja, who had a wary look on her face. "What did you have to do for it?" Klaas asked severely.

Maren shook her head. "Nothing I'd have to confess if we were Catholic."

"Will you marry him now?" Finja asked, relieved and fearful at the same time. "Did he force you to marry him?"

Maren shook her head. "I'm not going to be his wife. Not now or ever. I won't let myself be forced. I'm engaged to Thies, and it will remain so. Soon we will marry, and I'll be his wife."

Finja gestured at the purse. "Then how are we going to pay this back?"

Maren stiffened. She hadn't expected gratitude, but maybe a little appreciation. After all, she'd had to kiss Boyse to secure the loan. She'd had to swallow her pride. Didn't that matter?

"I'll work," she replied, feeling offended and defiant. "I'll ask the village bird trappers if I can pluck the wild ducks they've caught. And I can sew. Maybe I'll learn to stuff feather beds." She felt tears beginning to fill her eyes. She wanted to bite back her words, but it was too late.

"You don't have to worry. I'll pay back everything you've ever done for me with double the interest. I won't owe you a thing." Then she left the house and climbed the dunes, to cry there in peace.

Klaas sighed deeply as the door closed behind Maren. "We shouldn't have been so hard on her," he said.

Finja shook her head. "No, it was the right thing to do. She's our only child. She has responsibilities toward her parents. Remember, Klaas. We married because our parents arranged it. It was our good luck that over the years we grew to love one another. But it could have been different. Just look at Grit."

She sighed and wiped the tears off her cheek with the back of her hand. "There's no right to happiness. There's no right to love either. There's not even a right to survival. But one has a duty to at least try."

She stood, her shoulders drooping with sorrow. Then she took the broom and began to clean up the storm damage.

Maren sat on top of a dune among uprooted bushes and tangled beach-grass, gazing at the sea. It was low tide, and farther out she could see the remains of a shipwreck. The wood that stuck out above the water was covered with mussels and barnacles. When the tide came in, the wreck would disappear, but nothing would change for Maren.

I'm at Captain Boyse's mercy, she thought. *And if I can't repay my debt, God knows what he'll do.* Then she thought about Thies. He would help them as much as he could, but how could that possibly be enough? She stood up and gazed over at the Heinen family home. She could see Antje, who was collecting shattered wood in the yard, dragging her lame leg behind her, as though it, too, were made of wood. *Everything is ruined,* she thought. And before her tears could start again, she got up and walked down the dune toward Thies's home.

"So?" Antje didn't stop her work when she spied Maren. "Have you come to help, like a future sister-in-law should?"

Maren shook her head. "I just wanted to see how you are and have a word with Thies. I can't stay. We have too much to do ourselves."

"Thies isn't here," Antje answered harshly, straightening up and fixing Maren with a slightly angry stare.

"Where is he?"

"He's at Grit's house. Repairing something there. In exchange, she's giving him enough wood to repair our house." Antje spoke tiredly, without any malice in her voice.

"At Grit's house?" Jealousy reared inside her.

"Yes. In times like these, you can't be too choosy about who helps you. Besides, she's his cousin. And I hear you were visiting Captain Boyse, yourself. Apparently, he gave you money."

"Who told you that?"

Antje shrugged. "We live on an island. How long do you think something like that can stay secret? I heard it from Grit, and she heard it from the captain's maid. She was eavesdropping on you from the kitchen."

Antje's eyes swept over her future sister-in-law from head to toe. "I knew that you'd do almost anything. But I never thought you'd sell a kiss like a harbor whore. No, I never could've imagined that."

"I didn't sell a kiss. I'm going to pay back every penny of that money to Boyse. It was a loan."

"I honestly don't know what's worse." Antje took the broom in her hand and eyed Maren again. "You should be glad that Thies is so good-natured," she said. "But even his patience has limits. He'd wanted to go to your house to see if he could help. But then he decided he'd rather go to Grit. I think he made the right decision."

Maren nodded sadly and turned to go. She could understand Thies's choice, but shouldn't he have been loyal to her anyway? He knew that she'd turned down Boyse twice. For him. Wasn't that proof enough of her love? Couldn't he *imagine* that Boyse had forced her to kiss him? "Tell him he should come, when you see him," Maren said. "It doesn't matter how late it is when he gets back."

"I don't know if he'll have time," Antje replied.

That evening, Finja, Klaas, and Maren sat in the parlor, the only room still covered by an undamaged roof. Furniture from the other rooms had been brought in, pillows and blankets had been laid out on the floor to dry, and damp wood had been spread out around the fireplace. It smelled a bit musty. A single oil lamp cast a meager glow over the room. It was cold enough that Klaas, Finja, and Maren were wearing thick coats, and Finja had even wrapped her legs in an old blanket. Though Finja still looked pale, she seemed to be more invigorated than she had been that morning. There was light in her eyes again, and her shoulders didn't droop as much.

Klaas had a piece of paper in front of him and a goose-feather quill in his hand, and was making a list of what needed to be done. "The fishing boat is the most important thing," he said thoughtfully. "That's the only way we'll be able to earn a little money. Mr. Nickelsen from Hörnum is going over to the mainland tomorrow. I hired him to bring back wood for me. But it will still be a while before I can go fishing again. The next priority should be repairing the roof. You can both cut reeds tomorrow. We'll dry them here in the parlor. I rebuilt the chimney today. It doesn't draw as well as it used to, but it works for now."

Finja spoke. "We still have enough oil for the lamps, a dozen eggs, and half a smoked side of mutton. Tomorrow I can go to Old Meret's house to bake bread. We'll have enough to eat for the next few days."

Maren sat listening, though not really hearing what they were saying. She was focused on the sounds outside. Thies still hadn't come. It wasn't very surprising, because his house had been badly damaged too.

Everyone in Rantum had worked until it was fully dark to clean up after the storm. But couldn't he have come afterward? Just for a few minutes? To say a few words? He must know that she needed his comfort. His comfort, and more importantly, his forgiveness. She wondered if Antje had even told him that she'd been there that morning. Had he taken it badly that she'd asked Boyse for help? Above all, what did he think about the fact that she'd had to kiss Boyse? Thies was a proud man, and Maren's heart was heavy with guilt. But the kiss had not been voluntary. It had been forced. It wasn't her fault. Though, when she thought about the tingling inside of her that the kiss had provoked, she truly felt as though she had betrayed Thies.

"Maren? Do you have any questions, or anything to add?" Klaas glanced at her, and Finja examined her daughter closely.

"I'm going to go to the bird trappers' place tomorrow, right after I cut the reeds. Maybe I can find work there. I could also—"

She broke off then, because she heard footsteps outside. "That must be Thies," she cried, jumping out of her chair and hurrying to the door. She grabbed her cloak and raced out into Thies's arms. "Finally," she whispered into his warm chest. "Finally, you're here."

But Thies pulled himself roughly from her embrace. "Is it true?" he asked. He didn't sound angry or enraged, just sad.

"Please forgive me," Maren whispered, her head bowed. "I didn't want to. He refused to give me the money otherwise, and we needed it to survive. Please forgive me."

Then Thies sighed, and finally took her in his arms and whispered, "I wish you'd come to me."

"But you don't even have enough for yourself," Maren said feebly.

Thies stiffened. "That doesn't mean my fiancée should let herself be kissed by another man." Again, he sounded more sad than angry.

Maren stepped back so she could look him in the eye. "And you went to Grit, didn't you?"

Thies made a face. "Yes, I did," he replied, without further explanation. He still sounded a little hurt.

"And what was I supposed to do?" Maren asked. "We have nothing."

"Still!" Now his voice was hard. "Did you have to go to Boyse, of all people? Wasn't there anyone else you could have asked for money? You know how I feel about him. If he weren't a captain, I would have struck him when he proposed to you. I only restrained myself because I wanted to attend his seamanship school."

Maren shook her head. All at once, she was as sad and discouraged as she had been that morning. "No one in Rantum has money, only debts, Thies. You know that as well as I do. What was I supposed to do?" She sighed deeply and then added, "You went to Grit for help. So what are you accusing me of?"

"I didn't take money from her. I worked for her and got the wood as payment. That's different."

"Well, Boyse didn't have any work for me," Maren replied sharply, and stepped away from him again. "Do you think it was easy for me to ask him for a loan?"

"Your father should have done it. He's the head of your family."

Maren swallowed. "My father didn't know I was going to Boyse. If he had, he probably would have forbidden me. We don't even have a roof over our heads anymore. His boat was destroyed, and he can't even go fishing. I went in secret. No one knew."

Maren could tell by the look in Thies's eyes that he didn't accept her excuses. She raised her arms helplessly. "Wouldn't you do everything in your power to help your family?"

"*I* would," Thies answered. "But I'm the head of my family."

They stood facing each other, their arms hanging by their sides, their heads bowed. Close together, yet worlds apart.

"Can you forgive me, Thies?" Maren asked after a little while.

Thies swallowed and finally nodded. "These are hard times. We all have to do what we must." Then he took her in his arms again, caressed her back with his big warm hands, and pressed his cheek to her hair. They stood that way for a long time, until Thies gently pushed her away from him again. "I have to tell you something," he said, and Maren could tell by the sound of his voice that it wasn't good news.

"What is it?" She felt a cold shudder go down her back. Her heart pounded with fear.

"The storm changed something else," Thies began, and Maren's heart shrank.

"What do you mean?" she asked in shock.

Thies avoided her eyes, gazing over at the high dunes. "We have to postpone our wedding." He sighed, as though relieved that everything was finally out in the open.

"But why?" Maren put a hand on either side of Thies's face so he had to look at her. "Why?" she repeated softly. The world had just become a shade darker, and the crashing of the waves droned in her ears. Was this Thies's way of punishing her because she'd gone to Boyse? No, Thies wouldn't be so cruel to her. "Why?"

"There's no money for a celebration. I need everything I have to repair the house."

Maren nodded. She knew that he was right. "What if we don't have a party? What if we just have a nice meal with your family and mine?"

Thies shook his head. "No, Maren. It's no good. We can't marry this spring. It will have to be in October, when I come home. I want a big party with all our friends and relatives, the traditional way. No one must be able to say that Thies Heinen didn't give his bride a proper wedding. No one must say that she would have been better off with the captain."

She lowered her eyes and helplessly shuffled her feet in the sand, knowing that there was no cure for Thies's pride. "But you still love me?" she asked in a small, faint voice.

"Yes. I love you. That hasn't changed. That won't *ever* change. We will be married, but not in spring. In October."

CHAPTER 8

It took the villagers of Rantum months to repair the storm damage, even in the most provisional manner. Wood had to be brought in from the mainland, roofs had to be fixed, nets needed mending, and fishing boats needed rebuilding. Everyone helped one another, and the village rang with the sound of pounding hammers. Fortunately, the weather was kind to the islanders. It wasn't very cold, the storms blew wide of the island, and even the rain spared Sylt. Goods were traded back and forth: a side of bacon for wooden posts, three smoked eels for a fat bundle of dried reeds to repair a roof, a good pair of leather boots for as much pitch as was needed to make a fishing boat waterproof, and fine delft tiles for a bucket of lime and some clay. The children went to the mudflats to look for mussels, and the herring fishermen went out in their boats, dragging their nets along the ocean floor to catch other shellfish.

Maren made several fishing nets, but she didn't get much money for them. She placed every single coin she earned in a small wooden box, planning to bring it to Captain Boyse as soon as it was full. Maren would have liked to stay out of his way, but Sylt was simply too small to hide from such a powerful man. On Sundays in church, he pretended he hadn't noticed Maren, but when she went to the market in Westerland to buy thread and needles, Boyse somehow always appeared just as she was counting out her small coins. He never spoke to her, never smiled at her. He acted as though she didn't exist. And though she was still angry at him for the humiliation she had suffered, his contempt for her hurt. Then one day in Westerland, she turned a corner and walked directly into Captain Boyse himself.

"Oh, excuse me, p-please," Maren stammered, and quickly bent down to collect her purchases, which she had dropped in surprise. Boyse bent down too. As they both searched the ground for the needles, their eyes met. Only briefly, because then Maren let out a cry. She had found a needle the hard way, and the tip of her finger was bleeding.

"Let me see!" Rune Boyse ordered, taking her hand. He peered at the finger, then . . . then he stuck it in his mouth and tried to stop the bleeding by sucking on it. A wave of heat washed over her from the roots of her hair to the tips of her toes. Suddenly the situation seemed extremely intimate; she had almost never felt so close to anyone before. Heated blood pulsed through her body, and what Rune Boyse was doing suddenly seemed to be completely improper. She felt as though she were totally naked.

Maren squirmed with shame, but soon Rune Boyse let go, pulled a clean handkerchief out of his pocket, and tied it neatly around her finger. Then he stood up and walked away without speaking another word to her. The next Sunday in church when she sought his gaze, he avoided her eyes.

"Is there something going on with you and the captain again?" Thies asked her.

"What makes you think that?"

"You're staring at him as though you're waiting for something."

Thies's words made her blush because they were so close to the truth, but she shook her head vigorously. "No, I am not. I couldn't care less about Rune Boyse. The only thing binding me to him is my debt." But the truth was Maren felt deeply unsettled in the captain's presence. She was absolutely certain that he still wanted to humiliate her, and that he hated her because she'd rejected him. But somehow, his hatred didn't really feel like hatred. When she thought of his kiss, she blushed from the memory of it. She still chastised herself for allowing him to do it. She hadn't known then that a kiss could be as humiliating as a slap. And then there was her bleeding finger. She truly believed that it was some strange kind of cruelty that had made him do it, and yet, the moment had been precious to her. Precious for its intimacy.

February came much too soon, and the Biikebrennen and the men's departure with it. The women remained behind on their own with little to eat, with temporarily repaired houses, and with their fear of the next storm and for the lives of their men on the open sea.

Now that all the nets had been repaired, Maren worked for the bird trappers who kept their captured wild ducks in a barn between Rantum and Westerland.

The first time she had been there, old Mr. Lorenzen had explained to her in detail how he trapped the birds. There was a little freshwater pond near the Wadden Sea. Lorenzen lured the birds there with morsels of bait and caught them in his traps.

"They do it differently in Holland," he explained. "They drive the ducks through a maze of reeds covered with nets until they come to a dead end. Maybe we should try that method here sometime. But for now, we catch enough ducks in our traps." Then Lorenzen stuffed ten freshly killed ducks into Maren's basket. "Bring back the meat and feathers. If you want to keep a little of the meat for yourself, that's just fine. But work carefully."

Maren went home, sat in front of the house with a duck between her knees, and ripped out all the feathers. After a while her arms began to hurt, her hands were smeared with blood, her fingernails were cracked, and her back began to feel as though it were about to break.

She would have liked to hurl the ducks away and throw herself weeping into Finja's arms.

But Maren continued to pluck the birds with her teeth gritted, and put all the money she earned from Mr. Lorenzen in the little wooden box to pay Boyse back in autumn. Her mother often sat next to her, knitting wool from salt-marsh sheep, wool which was especially weather resistant, into stockings and vests that she sold at the market in Westerland. At the end of the day, Finja's eyes burned and her head ached, and she lay on her bed in the alcove with cool cloths on her forehead and moaned quietly.

They made very little money that way, but it was the only way for them to earn anything. Klaas went out to sea every day, but the shoals of herring had moved away. What Klaas caught was barely enough for his own family and a few neighbors. He couldn't bring in real money with it.

"What will happen if we can't pay back the loan?" Finja asked one day.

Maren shrugged. She'd been thinking about that too, but she hadn't come up with a solution. "We *will* pay him back," Maren finally answered. "We work hard. We can't do more. The main thing is that Father has his boat again and the house is repaired. We even have a little wood left over."

Finja laid her knitting in her lap and stretched her hands, which were covered in knots of gout. She rubbed her swollen joints. "I don't know how long I'll be able to keep knitting," she said. "I'm going to collect fuel for the fireplace. At least I can still manage that."

Maren knew that her mother also had serious back pain. She got up too, put the freshly plucked duck back in the pannier, and got a willow basket. Then she followed her mother to where the sheep grazed. Twilight had come, and the light had become weaker, so it was difficult to collect the sheep dung. They'd dry it to burn later in the winter. Maren found it disgusting to pick up manure, but it was a feeling she couldn't afford. She helped her mother until both baskets were well filled. They cleaned their hands by rubbing them with sand and snuck guiltily back to their house. It wasn't forbidden to collect dung, but the sheep's owners felt they had a right to it. The Luersens owned only two ewes, which hadn't lambed that year. They didn't produce enough dung to heat the fireplace even once, so Finja and Maren had no choice but to collect the dung of other sheep. Maren also went to the beach every morning to collect any driftwood that had been washed up by the tide during the night. She was not the only one. That meant the goal was to rise earlier than everyone else, in order to be the first one on the beach. As soon as the darkness had faded enough that the first delicate silhouettes of the day could be seen, Maren got up. She wrapped a shawl around her shoulders, climbed over the dunes, and walked down the empty beach to collect flotsam. Some days, she made a good haul: one or two pieces of wood, and even a splintered sea chest once. Other days, she came home with nothing but a bundle of seaweed to dry. She didn't wish disaster on anyone, and yet, she hoped every day that a ship would sink right in front of the island. There was even a prayer for it, which was whispered every morning by the beachcombers:

We beg thee, O Lord, not that ships sink in the howling of the storm down to the floor of the sea, but if you see fit to let them founder, then, O Lord, please guide them to our beach, so the poor people of the coast may be sustained.

When Maren finished collecting driftwood or dung, when there were no ducks left to pluck, and all the housework had been done, she sat and embroidered white linens with monograms for her trousseau. With every stitch, she thought of Thies. She missed him, but she would never admit it. Women on Sylt were accustomed to being alone for months on end. None of them complained about it. Why would they? It wouldn't help anyway.

When a shipment from the mainland arrived in Westerland, everyone who had ordered something met the ship in the harbor. One day, Maren went to collect a few things she had ordered for her wedding. Grit was there too, and she eyed Maren and smiled. But the smile was in no way kind. It was gloating. The wares were unloaded and distributed, and the women waited until their names were called.

"What did you order?" Grit asked.

Maren answered reluctantly. "Embroidery thread and a little lace for my wedding dress."

Grit laughed derisively, throwing her head back. "Do you actually believe that you'll use that lace?" she said tauntingly.

"Of course," Maren said, raising her chin. "I'll marry Thies in autumn. And there's nothing you can do about it."

"We'll see about that," Grit replied. Then her name was called, and Maren had to watch as Grit received a small ball of the very best Belgian lace. "Here, would you like to feel it?" Grit asked as Maren stood there with her simple, now almost coarse-seeming lace in her hands. "Mine is soft. So soft that a husband could really nestle up against it." Grit smiled again.

Maren stiffened. "Maybe *you* need lace for that," she said. "But I have a body that a husband would prefer to nestle against." But actually, she felt deeply ashamed. At first, her lace had seemed beautiful to her. But now that she'd seen Grit's, she felt tatty and unrefined holding her simple trim.

Grit's face twisted into an ugly grin. "We all know that you have a body men like to nestle up against. I've even heard that you can earn money with it." Grit laughed scornfully, and Maren's face burned. She couldn't just let the insult stand. She would have liked to tell her rival what had really happened, but she already knew that nothing would change Grit's opinion. So she didn't bother. But then something occurred to her. "Why do you need lace from Brussels anyway? Are you planning to marry again?"

"Of course," Grit answered sharply. "Whatever you do, I can do better. And as you know, I'm a widow. Soon my year of mourning will be over, and I'm not planning on staying alone for the rest of my life."

"Who are you going to marry?" Maren said, probingly.

"You'll find out soon enough. But you can be certain that you'll be more than surprised by my choice." With those words, Grit spun on her heel.

Old Meret had been standing nearby and had heard every word. Now she came to Maren. "I don't know what she's planning, but I fear it isn't good. Just yesterday, I saw a flock of wild geese flying over her house. Take care, Maren!"

"What could possibly happen? We've just survived a terrible storm. I think we're safe from bad luck for a while. Lightning never strikes in the same place twice."

"Lightning might not, but human nature is unpredictable. Take care anyway, my dearest!" Old Meret drew a cross on Maren's forehead with her knobby finger.

The summer passed and autumn came, and with it, the first ships returned. Maren had worked as much as she possibly could. She had plucked ducks until her fingers bled, and she had risen earlier than anyone else to collect sheep dung and driftwood as fuel for the winter fires. She had continued to knit in the evenings after Finja's eyes were tired, and on the few evenings when there was nothing left to do, she had worked on her trousseau. She had embroidered her monogram on sheets and table linens, on undergarments and nightdresses. Every evening she had fallen exhausted into bed, barely able to say her nightly prayers. And yet, the moments between prayer and sleep were the most precious of her day, because they were the moments she allowed herself to think of Thies. Thies, for whom she was doing all of this. Thies and their future together. She had put coin after coin in the wooden box, had denied herself every extravagance, had not even purchased the smallest sweet. She needed every penny to pay back Boyse. She wanted to have as little debt as possible when she finally stood at the altar with Thies. But the box filled more slowly than she'd expected.

She had gone from house to house, asking the villagers if they needed new feather beds that she could sew for them and stuff with fresh feathers. But no one had money for such a luxury. She even asked Grit, who had regarded her condescendingly. "A feather bed, from you? No, thanks. Anyway, you'd probably add horseshoe nails to mine. I'll order my feather bed from the mainland. Then at least I know it will be soft and warm."

So Maren had made a new feather bed for herself and Thies. She wanted to throw her old straw pallet into the fire immediately after the wedding and then curl up on the bed under the soft blankets she'd made, with Thies by her side. She could hardly wait! If he would only come home soon!

And then, at the end of October, he finally arrived. He'd been on a successful whaling voyage and had earned enough money that a wedding party could be planned. As a gift for Maren, he had brought a pair of white satin slippers.

"Oh, thank you!" Maren happily pressed the shoes to her breast.

Thies watched her with a smile on his face. "I have no idea on what kind of occasion you could wear them for here on the island, but in Hamburg they told me that a life without satin slippers was no life at all for a woman. If you ask me, I *do* know when you should wear them for the first time."

Maren smiled at him. "I'll wear them for our wedding. And I will be the most beautiful bride that Sylt has ever seen." Only briefly, she remembered the piece of simple lace which was the only decoration she had for her wedding dress, but then pushed the thought away. She would be beautiful. She would see her beauty reflected in Thies's eyes. Thies's eyes were the only mirror that counted.

Thies pulled her into an embrace. "I'm sure of it. But even without the shoes, dressed in sacks and rags, you would still be the most beautiful."

The wedding was planned for Saint Martin's Day. The minister hung the announcement on the church door, and Maren sewed the lace onto her mother's old wedding dress, which she had been planning to wear. Finja smoked eels, herring, and ham in the smoke chamber, pick-led hardboiled seagull eggs in saltwater, and crafted beautiful garlands out of paper and heather. There was a full week left before the wedding when Klaas examined the provisions.

"There's too little fish," he said. "We're islanders. Herring should be the main dish at the wedding banquet, and above all at the wedding breakfast the next day. What would a wedding be without herring salad with onions and beets?"

"Don't worry. We have enough of everything. No one will leave the table hungry," Finja said, trying to appease her husband. But Klaas was determined.

"I'll go out one more time to catch a few herring. Just to be sure. If there are any left over, we can pickle them."

Finja smiled, but Maren shook her head. When Klaas got up the next day before the morning dew fell and went to his fishing boat, Finja said, "We islanders aren't people who make promises and don't deliver. Let your father go. It's his way of showing his love for you."

Maren nodded. "I know," she said. "And I'm grateful to him. But . . ." She sighed and then didn't continue.

"But what?" Finja asked.

"But I have such a strange feeling. Like someone just walked over my grave."

Finja waved her worry aside. "That's just nerves. You know that you're about to experience the happiest days of your life, and that your entire life will change. What woman isn't nervous or scared before her wedding?" She looked at her daughter thoughtfully. "Do you regret getting engaged to Thies?"

"No!" Maren shook her head vigorously. "Thies is everything I ever wanted. And you? Can you be happy for me, or are you still wishing that I'd agreed to marry the captain?"

Finja's head came up. "Nothing is ever the way it seems at first glance," she said. But when Maren asked what she meant, she remained silent.

CHAPTER 9

It was unusually warm for the month of November. The sun had been shining on Sylt the entire day with a clear glistening light that cast sharp shadows and brought everything into focus. The wind blew very gently, so the dunes were able to warm up in the sun during the day. Now they were radiating their heat back into the evening air. Thies and Maren sat high on the crest of a dune, holding each other's hands and gazing at the sea, which lay like a shimmering piece of gray silk in front of them. Seagulls cried over their heads, and otherwise it was quiet. Only the heather crackled softly every now and then, and the beachgrass whispered stories from the old days.

"Are you nervous?" Maren asked quietly as she leaned against Thies's wide chest.

"Yes," he answered, just as quietly. "After all, you don't get married every day. And you?"

"My heart pounds just thinking about it," Maren answered. "But at the same time, I'm happy and eager." She straightened up and looked into Thies's eyes. "Do you also feel that life is truly beginning only now?" She didn't wait for an answer. "As children, we have to obey our parents. They decide for us what's right and what's wrong. But from the day after tomorrow, we can decide for ourselves. Isn't that wonderful?"

"Yes, it is." Thies caressed her hair as though he were placating a child. "But you can't expect to have too much freedom. We have duties. Our wedding won't change that. We have to take care of our families as long as they live."

"Yes, of course. But I still believe that we'll be very, very happy. This morning, I paid back part of Boyse's loan. It wasn't as much as we'd agreed upon, but still a tenth of the total. Now he can't complain. He knows that he'll get his money back eventually. Oh, I'm so happy about our lives!" A smile played on her face, but disappeared as she thought about her visit to the captain. She had planned to give the money to the maid and leave Boyse's property as fast as possible, but Boyse himself had answered the door. She had counted the money out of the box into his hand. He had watched her silently, and had gone back inside just as silently. He hadn't exchanged a single word with Maren, but he had still made her feel like a common beggar.

Thies's eyes showed shadows of doubt. "Don't you ever think our life might not turn out to be as wonderful as you're imagining? Aren't you afraid of being disappointed?"

Maren's eyes opened wide with shock. "Disappointed in you? Never. Why would you say such a thing?"

"Because sometimes things happen that you don't expect." The words hung in the air like a threat.

All at once, Maren noticed that the seagulls had stopped crying. The island was completely still. As still as a grave. A shudder went down Maren's back. "Yes," she said softly. "Sometimes things happen that you don't expect."

She thought of Boyse's kiss, which had been so different from Thies's kisses. It had set something in motion inside of her that she now longed for. When Thies kissed her, she felt safe, but the captain's kiss had actually stirred her and had made her feel things that she hadn't been able to imagine before. Although she hated Boyse, she couldn't stop thinking about his kiss.

Then she stood up, shivering. Far out to sea, dark clouds were gathering into towers. Beneath them, a last pale ray of golden light gleamed through as the sun set. Maren turned her eyes away. The image of the black clouds and the pale light suddenly seemed terrifying to her, almost poisonous. And there was the silence, the all-encompassing silence.

"Let's go," she said. "I have a lot to do before the day after tomorrow."

"Wait just one moment, my darling." Thies took her in his arms, kissed her gently on her quaking lips, and pulled her body tightly against his own as though they were one. He ran his lips over her eyelids, across her cheeks, and down her neck.

"No," Maren whispered. "Wait just two more days."

The next morning, the sea was rough. Little whitecaps danced on the waves and sent up a spray that settled like a damp veil over skin and hair. But the sea didn't seem threatening. Rather, the whitecaps seemed to be playing with each other like boisterous children. Clouds chased each other through the sky, and the clear sun sent brilliant white rays of light over the island every now and then.

Maren had gotten up early. She sat at the kitchen table with her parents, eating her gruel with watered beer and thinking that this was the second-to-last breakfast that she'd ever eat with her parents this way. Tomorrow was the wedding. Today, Finja and a few of the village women would decorate the church. A huge side of mutton would be roasted, cakes would be baked, and fish would be marinated. Antje and her mother were probably setting up the wedding chamber in their house, which would also be Maren's home soon. Maren had already packed her few items of clothing in a chest. She'd finished embroidering her trousseau, and it had been packed along with the rest of her belongings. Tonight, Klaas would bring her things to the Heinen house, so she would be able to find everything the morning after the wedding. But before that, she would walk down the long aisle of the church on her father's arm, wearing the dress her mother had worn. That summer, Maren had made a wedding wreath. It was woven from grasses and flowers and had been carefully dried so she could wear it tomorrow. She wondered if her mother would cry.

Maren looked up.

"Come, now, stop dreaming," Finja scolded. "There's still a lot to do."

Klaas got up. "I'm going fishing. I know it's a little late, the sun has already risen, but I should go one more time. We could use a few more fish, and I'm only in the way here in the house." He smiled drily, then bent over Maren and kissed the top of her head. "I wish you all the happiness in the world, and all the love under the sun," he whispered.

Then he disappeared.

Maren shook her head in surprise. "What was all that about?" she asked. "He doesn't usually talk so much."

Finja laughed quietly. "Just don't go thinking it makes him happy to trust another man with his one and only daughter. The house will be empty without you."

"I won't be gone from the world, just on the other side of the dunes. You'll surely see me more often than you wish to." She laughed. "Who knows? Maybe in a year you'll already be a grandmother."

Finja smiled, knocked on the wooden table for luck, and looked out the window. Outside, a raven was fighting with a magpie. When Finja saw it, she sighed.

"What's wrong?" Maren asked.

"Nothing. I don't know. I'd prefer if you didn't ask. You don't have to let an old woman make you feel anxious too."

"You mean Old Meret? Did she say something?"

Finja swallowed. "It's nothing. Surely nothing. Even Old Meret isn't right all the time."

Maren felt a shudder go down her back again. It gave her a feeling of unease, which she'd felt far too often in the last few days.

"What did she say?"

"Nothing bad, actually. Just that she didn't see you as a bride."

Maren laughed with relief. "That doesn't matter. Tomorrow in church she can convince herself with her own eyes."

By afternoon, Klaas hadn't returned, and the women were beginning to worry. Finja climbed the dunes, shielded her eyes from the glare with her hand, and looked out to sea. But from the island to the horizon, there was no sign of the fishing boat. Maren couldn't see anything either.

"Maybe he went up toward List, at the other end of the island. By the oyster beds. He probably didn't catch anything and decided to get oysters for the feast."

Finja nodded, but Maren could tell from her expression that she didn't believe it.

An hour later, she sent Maren to find Thies.

"You have to go out to search! Please! My father hasn't come back yet."

Thies nodded. "Tell all the other men," he commanded. Then he hurried to the beach, shoved his dory into the water, and pushed off from the shore.

Maren knocked on the doors of every house in Rantum. All she had to say was "My father hasn't returned," and the men immediately put on their oilskins and were soon on the sea.

Finja still stood on the dune, wringing her hands and praying softly.

"You'll see. He'll be back soon," Maren said, trying to comfort her mother. "He and all the others. The sea is no wilder than usual. He's been out in stormy weather before."

Finja nodded, then gazed up at the sky. The clouds had gathered more thickly and were showing violet around the edges.

"A squall is coming," Finja said quietly.

Maren looked up too. "That's not certain. The wind may be coming from the northwest, but many fronts just pass us by."

"Maybe. But my bones don't lie." Finja placed a hand on the small of her back. "I should have stopped him."

They stood on the dune for a long time, looking out to sea, but nothing happened. Sometimes Maren's mother briefly held her hand, as though to convince herself that at least her daughter was still there.

When twilight fell, the first fishing boat returned. Finja and Maren ran down the dune, almost tumbling in their haste, ignoring the sand which grated in their shoes and the prickly heather which caught in their clothes.

The fisherman was their neighbor Schwenn Jensen. He pulled his boat onto the land. When he saw Finja, he shook his head wordlessly.

"Did you see anything?"

Schwenn shook his head again.

"What about the others? They're still out looking for him, aren't they?"

Schwenn pointed at the black wall of clouds. "They'll have to turn back soon. God grant they have him with them."

"Did you go as far as List?" Finja wouldn't give up.

"From Hörnum to List. Two of us even went down the Wadden coast."

Then Finja sank onto the sand, covered her face with her hands, and began to weep. But Maren didn't want to believe what she already knew. She stood completely still, her eyes searching the waves intently.

She stood that way for a long time. Once Finja wailed loudly, and Maren shouted at her. "Stop howling! He hasn't drowned. I know it."

Finally, several boats appeared on the horizon. They recognized Thies's dory, which was towing another boat behind it. They were coming from List, directly from the oyster banks.

When Thies reached the beach, he didn't speak a word, just took Maren silently into his arms. The other men were quiet too as they pulled their boats up onto the beach. As they passed Finja, who was still sitting in the sand, they removed their caps and bowed their heads.

After a moment during which the horror had not yet spread from her head to her heart, Maren spoke, her eyes resting hopefully on Thies.

"That isn't necessarily his boat. Maybe it capsized, and he was able to swim ashore."

Thies shook his head. "It's his boat. You know that as well as I. And he couldn't swim. None of us can." It was true. Very few of the people of Sylt could swim. They were afraid of the cold North Sea, because immersion in its icy waters often resulted in death.

Thies put his arms around Maren and let her cry, holding her until she was calm again.

CHAPTER 10

The next morning, neighbors found the body of Klaas Luersen on the beach. When they came bearing the body of her dead father, Maren was standing in the parlor, running her hand over the fabric of her wedding dress. Finja had wept the entire night through. Now she sat at the table, her face pale and her eyes red.

"Old Meret was right," she said softly. "She didn't see you wearing your wedding dress."

Maren nodded. She was more than sad; she was also angry at her father. It was meaningless anger, because of course she knew very well that her father hadn't wanted to drown. But she felt betrayed anyway, because her happiness had been delayed for another year. A year of mourning.

Then the men knocked on the door, brought Klaas in, and laid him on the table. They said little, just patted Finja on the shoulder and nodded to Maren. "We'll bring a coffin soon," Schwenn Jensen told them. Then he, too, patted Finja on the shoulder and left.

Finja lit a candle, put it at Klaas's head, and sat down in a chair next to her dead husband. She gazed at him intently, as though his body could reveal why he had drowned now, of all times. Every now and then, she lifted her hand, stroked Klaas's pale, cold face, and sighed.

"It would have been a beautiful wedding feast," she said softly. "And now the wedding feast will be a funeral feast."

Suddenly Maren couldn't control herself anymore. A sob ripped through her chest, vibrated in her throat, and came out of her mouth as a terrible howl. She threw herself over her father's body, shook him by the shoulders, and even slapped him lightly in the face.

"Wake up!" she screamed. "Wake up, do you hear me?"

She pounded his chest until her mother finally pulled her away from him and held her in her arms as tightly as she could.

It took a long time for Maren to quiet down, and tears streamed down her cheeks until the neighbors brought the coffin, and Maren had to leave the room.

Thies's mother and Antje came over, warmed some water, and washed the corpse. Then they wrapped it in a shroud and laid it in the coffin. Thies held Maren tightly. The men had waited in front of the door. Now they lifted the coffin onto their shoulders and carried it silently to the church, which was still decorated for the wedding. The sexton rang the death knell as the men placed the coffin in front of the altar. With her entire body shaking, Maren ripped the dried bundles of heather from every pew, while the minister exchanged the numbers of wedding hymns on the slate for the numbers of funeral hymns. All night, Finja and Maren watched over Klaas in the church in silence, because they had discovered that their pain could not be shared even with each other. Every now and then, Finja had stroked the cold, sallow face of her husband and sighed.

When the first rays of dawn had touched the horizon, Finja spoke. "How shall we go on? Whatever can we do?"

As she spoke she didn't lift her eyes from her husband's face, and Maren knew that the question had not been intended for her. She didn't have an answer either. There was only one possibility. She would have to marry Boyse so he'd release her from her debt and they could survive. But Maren couldn't do it. Just the thought of it shook her to the core. She knew many people would think she was selfish, but she just couldn't. Hadn't her father and mother taught her to follow her heart?

When the sun rose, the whole village gathered at the church doors. The minister came and read the mass, and the congregation sang hymns. Some cried loudly, and some wiped tears from their eyes. They were grieving not only for Klaas Luersen but also for themselves. At the next church service, it might be one of them in a coffin. The islanders knew very well about the fragility of life, even though they generally preferred to repress that knowledge. On days like this, though, that fear broke through.

Finja sat next to Maren in the first pew. She had cried out all her pain; now she sat as though frozen, balling a handkerchief in her fist. Maren, too, was deaf to the words of the minister and the singing of the others. Her heart was heavy, and she couldn't breathe properly. What would become of them? She, too, asked this question. Once she turned to Thies, who was sitting in the row behind her. Thies nodded at her encouragingly, but it was no comfort to Maren. Later, when the coffin had been lowered into the earth and tears had washed away all the joy from her heart, a raven, black and heavy, settled onto Maren's shoulder. The raven of grief. It wouldn't be scared away easily.

The villagers came and shook her hand and spoke a few words that didn't reach her. Only when Captain Boyse appeared in front of her did she briefly awaken from her numbness.

"I'm so sorry, Maren," he said. "Now everything has changed."

She looked up. "The loan . . . Now we won't be able to pay it back."

"I know that. And you know the solution."

Maren's eyes went wide with shock. "How dare you! You would propose to me again over my father's open grave?"

Boyse shrugged. "You can call it what you will. I call it offering help in a time of need." He put his cap back on. "But perhaps this isn't the best time. I'll come to see you soon."

He stepped aside to make space for Grit. She didn't embrace Maren, only briefly shook her hand. "I told you so, didn't I?" she said, but Maren wasn't really listening to her.

"I would understand if you accept Boyse," Thies said that evening, when he was sitting with Maren in the Luersens' kitchen. Finja had already gone to bed in the alcove. "I'm not even sure it wasn't a kind gesture of the captain to ask you again to be his wife."

Maren bit her lower lip. "It was pure impertinence. That's how I see it. You can't buy love. Certainly not for money."

Thies frowned. "Maybe not *your* love. And maybe not now. But once you've experienced real poverty, when you're so hungry you can think of nothing else, when you're freezing cold and sick, then you, too, will think differently. I've been asking myself if I shouldn't give you up because I can't offer you a carefree life."

Maren leapt up and slapped her hand on the table so hard that the cups sprang into the air. "It's not right. I can feel it. It wasn't right for Boyse to ask me like that. It felt like extortion. But he's not going to get me that way. I will never be his wife. It doesn't matter if you want me now or not. I'll prove to you all that I can manage on my own."

Boyse came. He chose an evening five days before Christmas, and Klaas had been dead for more than a month. The grief was still present, but not as black and all-consuming as it had been in the beginning. Maren had supported her mother and had seldom left her alone, limiting her meetings with Thies. Or was it Thies who didn't come by every day anymore? Maren didn't know. She loved Thies as much as before, but she felt a bit betrayed by him. He'd offered to give her up! It was almost impossible to imagine: to give up the love of one's life! To her, it would be as if someone asked her not to breathe anymore. Maren hadn't told Thies how deeply he'd hurt her, because she knew he didn't understand how she felt. Occasionally, her mother had asked what would happen next, but Maren hadn't known what to say.

Once, Grit had come to buy a freshly plucked duck. "So?" she asked. "Are things looking up for the two of you?" Finja sighed and explained that she didn't know what the future held, but she didn't have much hope. And then Grit told her what the captain had said to Maren by Klaas's grave. She'd been listening to their conversation. "Wouldn't that be the best solution for everyone?" she asked manipulatively. "Wouldn't it be Maren's duty?"

Finja looked over at Maren, who was just starting to pluck another duck, and shook her head. "Of course it would be the best solution," she said. "But I can't force her to do it."

Grit had regarded Maren thoughtfully, wrinkling her nose. "It's bad enough that you have to ask her to do it. Anyone else would recognize her duty and fulfill it without complaint."

Finja nodded, as though she were in complete agreement with Grit. Later, she said to Maren, "I've never asked anything of you, and I won't start now. But if a solution throws itself at your feet, you shouldn't trample all over it."

Maren held her tongue, because there was nothing to say. Only two days later, at breakfast, she casually said, "I will take care of you, you know. Don't worry."

"How do you plan to do that?" Finja asked.

"I don't know, but I'll do it. I swear by God and my departed father."

And now Boyse had come. Her mother had invited him into the parlor, and he had a bowl of spiced Christmas cookies and a glass of grog in front of him. "Christmas is approaching," he said. "The time for forgiving and forgetting."

Finja nodded, and Maren waited for him to continue speaking. She ran a hand over her hair, which had grown to reach her shoulders again. Just yesterday evening, her mother had brushed it until it felt as soft as eiderdown.

"Forgiving and forgetting," Maren repeated, when the silence became too oppressive for her.

"Yes," Boyse said. He turned to her. "I've forgiven you for rejecting me. The forgetting might take a little longer, because after all, you made me look like a fool in front of the entire island. But a man can bear that."

"I'm sorry," Maren said. "Have I not apologized for that already?

"No, you have not. You allowed me to kiss you, but you only did that because you wanted money from me." The captain spoke the words kindly, but Maren could still feel slight contempt behind them. She folded her hands in her lap and waited again.

"Well, in any case I'm very glad that you've come, Captain Boyse," Finja said. "It's good to know that in times of hardship one isn't alone in the world."

Then all three of them were silent. The unspoken words flew around the room like a swarm of mosquitos, even dimming the oil lamp.

Finally, Boyse cleared his throat. "Maren, you know why I've come. Today I'm asking you for the third and last time if you will marry me."

Maren remained silent.

Finja sighed softly and even kicked Maren lightly under the table. But Maren still didn't speak.

"If you need time to think, I can't really say I understand, but I've waited so long that I can wait until tomorrow for your answer."

Finja spoke instead. "She needs to sleep on it first, Captain. So much has happened recently. She's still a little confused. She'll give you her answer tomorrow."

But then Maren stood up. "No!" she cried with determination. "No, I will not marry you. I am engaged to Thies, and I'm going to marry him. We love each other. Nothing has changed that."

"Is that your last word?" Captain Boyse, too, had gotten up.

"Yes, it is." Maren looked intently into his eyes, even though she would have preferred to run from the room.

"Well. Since there's nothing I can expect from you, then there will be nothing you can expect from me." He stopped and stretched his shoulders. "You owe me money. A lot of money. I want it back by Saint Peter's Day. Every bit of it."

"But we can't pay!" Finja cried desperately. She rushed to her daughter, grabbed her by the shoulders, and shook her, as though she could shake the stubbornness out of her. But Maren just let herself be shaken as though she were an apple tree, and watched her mother silently and sadly.

"Captain," Finja said, turning back to Boyse. "You're such a good man, you couldn't possibly be so cruel to us!"

Boyse sighed. "I'm not the one being cruel. I need my money. I will have it on my desk by Saint Peter's Day, or I will bring the case before the council."

Finja burst into tears. Boyse went to the door, and there he paused. "I wish you a joyful Christmas anyway."

The door closed behind him.

PART 2

1765

CHAPTER 11

Marrying a decent man was the most important thing for a girl on Sylt. The man determined the status and future of his bride through marriage. No, even before marriage. The prestige of a girl increased with the status of her admirers. It was less about the number of proposals and more about the quality of her suitors. Thies Heinen was one of the best suitors that a girl on Sylt could wish for, even though he was poor. He was honest and hardworking, responsible and courteous, and he was handsome. But Captain Boyse was the suitor that people whispered about behind their hands. He was rich, enigmatic, dark, and unfathomable. Boyse was a mystery, and so he was more interesting than Thies with his exemplary life.

Ever since Maren had been confirmed, her mother and other women had discussed who Maren would one day join at the altar. There was nothing more important for a girl; it had always been that way. The man made the woman. Maren sighed. She, too, would love to have been married to Thies already, instead of standing at the ship's rail, catching a last glimpse of Sylt.

There he stood, waving with a white handkerchief. Thies! Her Thies, surrounded by sailors' wives. She waved back tentatively, not sure he could actually see her among all the other people and animals on the big sailing smak. She recognized him easily. He was more than a head taller than the women and towered over them. His blond hair was tousled by the wind. She drank in the sight of him to carry with her on her long journey. Something that she could look forward to: that he would be standing there just the same way in the autumn, waiting for her. Then they would marry, and her dream would finally come true. A few had already turned to go, but Thies still stood on the dune, and Maren couldn't tear her eyes from him.

Tears ran down her face, but she quickly wiped them away so no one would see. She wasn't an island girl anymore. She was a ship's boy who would help the cook on a whaling ship.

After her father's death, before Christmas, Maren had gone once more from house to house to offer her services. She'd asked the bird trapper Mr. Lorenzen if she could pluck twice as many ducks in the future, but he had shaken his head. "I already trap all the ducks we need. It wouldn't make sense to trap more." So she'd taken her usual ten ducks and left. In the afternoon, she'd knocked on all the doors of Rantum to offer feathers and feather beds, and had also offered her knitting skills. But it was winter. The women had already spun and knit all the wool they would need; with so little time left before spring, nobody needed anything else made of wool. Only one person gave her an order for a feather bed: Grit.

"Well, I don't want to be mean. Make me a feather bed. Nice and soft and warm. But hurry up about it. I'd like to be able to use it before summer comes." Then she eyed Maren critically. "Pride goes before a fall," she said, and slammed the door behind her.

Nothing could have humiliated Maren more than getting this job from Grit. The next day she went to Boyse and brought him the silver coin that Thies had given to her after his last journey at sea. It was another entire tenth of the debt. The whole way there, she asked herself if Boyse would insist on kissing her again. Her skin began to tingle at the thought of it. All at once, she became red with shame when she finally admitted to herself that she had actually enjoyed the kiss. More than enjoyed it. It had awakened a part of her that she hadn't even known existed.

She knocked on his door, trembling, feeling annoyed at herself, and filled with expectation. But Boyse made no attempt to come any closer to her than was necessary. When she handed him the money, he regarded her indifferently, as though she were an insect on the kitchen floor.

"What am I supposed to do with this small change? I want all of it. Immediately. And I want it from you alone. Take the money that your beau gave to you, and don't sully my house with it."

Maren swallowed, but the lump in her throat wouldn't disappear. "I don't have any more. You'll have to wait until Thies can go to sea as an officer."

"But I won't wait," Boyse said. "Obstinacy is only for those who can afford it. You can't."

Then Maren became angry. "I didn't create the storm that robbed us of everything we had. And I didn't drown my father at sea either. If you were a man with a heart, you would help me."

Boyse laughed. "A man with a heart," he repeated. "I asked you once if you had a heart. I forgot what your answer was. It doesn't interest me anymore anyway. But *I* do have a heart. You can work on my whaling ship. I'm looking for a helper for the cook. If you survive the trip, your debts will be forgiven. But you will receive no other pay."

Maren's mouth fell open. "You expect me to work on a whaling ship?"

"If you can't pay your debts, then I will help you, child. After all, I'm a man with a heart." He spread his arms graciously. "I have no need of any other services you could offer me." He pointed at the firmly filled feather bed that lay in the alcove, and at two coats made of fine wool, which were spread out over a sea chest to dry. Then he stared so emphatically at her mouth that she blushed. Did that mean he regretted the kiss? Or that it had only been a bawdy joke, or a gesture to humiliate her? Maren was suddenly angry. How good that she'd never even considered accepting his proposal, even for a moment! Marriage with him would have been hell on earth. He would have ordered her around like one of his sailors. And now he was offering her this! It was monstrous.

Maren wanted to give him a prideful answer and ask about other alternatives, but his taunting, slightly condescending gaze induced her to say the words that she'd regret so often later. She straightened her shoulders. "Fine, Captain. I'll do it. I'll work on your whaling ship."

Boyse offered her his hand and she shook it, and with that, her fate was sealed. After that, she waited the entire day for some kind of message from Captain Boyse. A message that said he had just been making fun of her, and that of course he didn't want her to work on his ship. But nothing came. Just quiet old Piet, who had gone whaling with the captain for years, brought her a list that he'd made of things a ship's boy would need to bring on a whaling voyage.

The same evening, Thies came. They went walking on the beach together, even though it was raining a little.

"What's wrong? Why are you so quiet?" Thies asked. Maren considered informing him about Boyse's offer. Would it even make sense? She wondered if it had actually been genuine, or if it was just another trick to humiliate her. But somehow, she couldn't bring herself to tell him.

Instead, she said, "I heard someone talking about a female ship's boy. She signed onto a whaling ship so she could marry the man she loved." Then she looked at Thies to read his reaction in his face, but he only laughed.

"Was her sweetheart with her on the ship?"

Maren shook her head. "No. I think he actually didn't know where she'd gone."

"Did he actually take her back afterward?" Thies could only shake his head at such lack of judgment.

"I don't know. Why? What's so bad about going whaling?"

Thies took her face between his hands and kissed her on the lips. "You're sweet, do you know that?" he said. "You're not only sweet, you taste sweet too." Then he kissed her, but this time Maren didn't see any shooting stars. She freed herself from his embrace.

"Now tell me, what's so bad about the story?"

"A woman alone with so many men! She'd have to defend her virtue tooth and nail. I would never take her back after that."

Maren went pale and silent. After a long pause, she spoke again. "What if she had someone looking after her?"

"Why are you worrying so much about a girl that you don't even know?" Thies said. He took her in his arms again and kissed the worry lines off her forehead.

The day of the Biikebrennen arrived again, and this time Maren walked with Thies hand in hand to the top of the festival dune, while Finja wore a traditional Frisian mourning dress for the first time. Although Maren walked with Thies, she wasn't completely at ease. She still hadn't told him she'd be leaving on the sailing smak to Amsterdam the next day, and she had no idea how to do it. Even when she'd told Finja that she'd be working for Boyse as a ship's boy, she'd had to struggle to find the right words.

"There's no other choice, Mama. You know that."

But she'd been surprised when Finja had only nodded and said, "Maybe it's not so bad that you'll get to see something of the world other than just this island. Captain Boyse will keep an eye on you, of that I'm sure."

Maren had believed that once they were at sea, she'd be able to stay out of the captain's way as much as possible. But now she was standing at the rail of the *Mermaid* directly in front of him, and although the ship was filled with fifty sheep and seventy sailors, she felt the captain's gaze on her back, so she waved enthusiastically one last time. Thies slowly disappeared, becoming smaller and smaller, until at last she couldn't see him anymore. A sob escaped her chest, and she had to hold the rail tightly so she wouldn't fall down. She thought about the previous night.

After the Biikebrennen, she and Thies had stayed together. Maren couldn't bring herself to say good-bye to him. He still didn't know she was sailing for Amsterdam the next day, and he'd been surprised when she couldn't keep her hands off of him. He had taken her in his arms and returned her passionate kisses. When his hand had slipped under her bodice, she hadn't stopped him. Instead, she'd pressed herself against him and moaned softly. Moaned, like a proper woman. Then Thies hadn't been able to hold himself back anymore. He had pulled her into the smokehouse, where it was nice and warm. Maren was sure that Finja was asleep.

She allowed Thies to pull her dress down over her shoulders so he could kiss her neck and breasts. When he gently pushed her thighs apart, she paused for a moment.

"We aren't allowed to do that," she whispered. "We aren't married yet."

"We might as well be," Thies replied, his voice rough with passion. Then Maren thought about how many people lost their lives at sea. *Shall I die never having known love?* she thought. Then she wrapped her bare thighs around Thies's hips and became a woman.

Now she stood at the rail, unable to look away from the island. She wiped her tears away with a fist and asked one of the sailors, a boy from Sylt, how long the crossing to Amsterdam would take.

"You've never been on a Dutch sailing smak before, have you?" the boy asked. He continued without waiting for an answer. "This is a coastal ship, which was made to transport goods between the islands. You won't find any luxury here, but that means it's cheap. I only had to pay one Dutch guilder." He waited for Maren to confirm the cost, but she just nodded, because Captain Boyse had paid her way and added it to her debt.

"If we're lucky, it'll take us a week to reach Amsterdam," the sailor continued. But when he realized she wasn't going to have a conversation with him, he turned to another sailor, who was passing around a flask of rum.

Maren spent the entire day on deck, standing at the rail and gazing at the sea. Every now and then, she spoke with someone she knew from Sylt and, over and over again, had to answer the same question.

"What's a girl doing on a ship?"

And each time she replied, "I may not be a man, but I can work as hard as any of you." She felt the captain's gaze on her all day long and realized that he actually was keeping an eye on her, although she didn't know whether that should comfort or scare her.

Then the first night fell. Below deck, the sailors lay in four rows across the entire width of the ship, head to foot. It was cold and the wind whistled through the cracks. Before she'd left Sylt, she'd had to find warm clothes for the trip to Greenland. She had her father's women's-hair stockings. Her mother had knitted them for him years ago from her own hair. Maren had also inherited his oilskins. There was a tightly woven linen coat which had been brushed again and again with linseed oil until it practically repelled the wind and the water. The coat was far too big for her, but she didn't care about that. She took up the sleeves and gathered the waist a little, and made it work somehow. She also had her father's tall boots with her, but the shafts reached far past her knees, so she walked stiffly like a stork in them. Her mother had lined a wool cap with thick fabric, and along with it, Maren wore a wide scarf made of sheep's wool and warm gloves. Her sea chest, also inherited from her father, contained a Bible, a few undergarments, a thick sweater, a rough skirt, a wool blanket, and a warm fur sealskin vest.

Maren covered herself with the oilskin coat that had once belonged to her father, but she still couldn't keep her teeth from chattering with the cold. The boots were next to her head. She didn't have her sea legs yet and had been suffering from seasickness all day. But the others had explained to her that at night she couldn't get up to heave over the rail without waking many others. That's why boots stood near her head, and near the heads of many other novices. Her neighbor was just now throwing up, and Maren had to turn away because the smell made the nausea worse. It was stuffy below deck, the air so heavy from the sweat of many bodies that Maren could hardly breathe. In the evening, the sailors had closed all the hatches and had stuffed all the cracks with flax tow, so neither the February cold nor seawater could force its way inside. Many of the older men sat and blew thick smoke rings from their pipes. The smells of tired bodies, pipe smoke, and vomit mixed together until Maren felt she couldn't breathe anymore. She lay there curled into a ball, her hands pressed on her stomach, feeling as though she were about to die. She felt so wretched that if she died that night, it would seem like a relief. Not even thoughts of Thies could comfort her.

But then the night was finally over, and the hatches were opened. Maren got up and rushed onto the deck, breathing in the fresh air greedily and immediately feeling much better. Then she emptied the contents of her boots into the sea, rinsed them, and put them on. With her father's boots and oilskin coat, she thought at least she'd survive until they got to Amsterdam.

The next evening, a light storm blew in, and this time it wasn't only the landlubbers reaching for their boots. The old salts filled their pipes again, polluting the air with the smoke and telling stories that Maren would have preferred not to hear. They spoke of the shoals in the North Sea, on which many a ship had run aground. One old sailor from Sylt told a story he had heard from his father.

"Seventeen forty-four was a black year for seafaring. As black as a raven's wing. Rán, the sea goddess, was in such a rage that some believed she wanted to take revenge on the humans."

When Maren heard the sea goddess's name, she remembered the Biikebrennen from the previous year and thought about all the things that had transpired since then. When she looked back, how frivolous she seemed to have been! How much she had changed in only twelve months. Then, there had been no storm damage they couldn't repair. Then, her father had been alive. But now everything was different, and for the first time, Maren wasn't sure she'd survive as a ship's boy.

CHAPTER 12

It took them exactly eight and a half days to reach Amsterdam. The travelers streamed from the deck, and those who didn't already have jobs waiting for them at the docks left very quickly. Even aboard the Dutch smak, Maren had seen some of them approaching the captain and asking him to hire them for his whaling ship. But Boyse had assembled his main crew a long time since. Most of his sailors and officers were from Sylt, because Boyse preferred to know the men he worked with well, and he also kept an eye on them during the winter. Aside from that, he preferred to have a central team with special skills. For example, there were the forty-six harpooners, twenty of whom came from Sylt. Maren knew almost all the islanders by sight. It was only a few who came from List at the northern end of the island that she didn't recognize. One harpooner was even from Rantum. It was old Piet, and it was rumored to be his thirtieth year at sea. He was a taciturn man who rarely spoke, but she learned quickly that he could hear very well. When Maren groaned as she tried to lift her heavy sea chest, which was filled with underthings, sweaters, stockings, and jackets, Piet hurried over to her and took it.

Once ashore, Maren looked around, feeling overwhelmed. It was the first time she'd ever been off the island. She'd heard that the harbor of Amsterdam was big, but she was stunned by its size, the noise, and the masses of humanity. There were many large ships docked, and she recognized three whaling ships and a merchant's ship. The latter was enormous, dwarfing the other ships. Though once a merchant ship, it was now being loaded with all the necessities for a lucrative whaling expedition and being transformed into its new identity, a whaler under Captain Boyse's command. A pier stretched between the harbor wall and the ship, and workers were milling around on it. Several of them were carrying heavy sacks over their shoulders, and others were rolling barrels down the pier. Two men were hoisting a gigantic box onto the deck with a block and tackle, and under the furled sail, the captain stood with his feet planted wide and his hands on his hips, angrily shouting orders. Near Maren, a few sailors were sitting on upturned barrels and playing cards. The most amazing thing about them, though, was that one of them had black skin! Maren had never seen anything like him before. The old salts from Sylt had occasionally spoken of black men and women, but Maren had thought they were just telling big fish stories. She was helpless to do anything but stare at the man. When he noticed and winked at her, she smiled and quickly looked in the other direction.

There were many other kinds of men and women that she'd never imagined before. Men with dark, burning eyes and strange red head coverings walked around with curved sabers in their belts. She saw a man with a long beard who wore a floor-length black robe, a pot-like hat on his head, and a large brass cross on a chain. A woman in luxurious clothing and a fine fur cape got out of a fancy coach that had stopped in front of a shipping company building.

Maren was still standing next to her sea chest with her eyes wide when she was interrupted by a boy with a pushcart.

"Miss, are you looking for a place to stay?" he asked. "There's a little boardinghouse, very close by. No bedbugs, I promise."

Maren was confused. "A place to stay?"

The boy nodded. "Or are you traveling on today?"

"No," Maren admitted, and realized she was completely disoriented. She looked for old Piet, but he had disappeared long ago. The others from Sylt were gone too. She was alone and had no idea what to do or where to go. She was just about to nod and load her sea chest on the boy's wagon when she felt a heavy hand on her shoulder.

"Away with you!" said a commanding voice, and the boy scampered off immediately.

Maren turned and looked directly into Captain Boyse's face. His expression was neutral, but Maren thought she could detect a taunting gleam in his eyes.

"Barely arrived in Amsterdam and trying to get lost already," he said with annoyance. "Follow me." With that, he turned and walked briskly away.

Maren tried to pick up her chest so she could follow him quickly, but it was too heavy and bulky for her to carry. She pulled at it desperately, annoyed with herself and angry at the captain. Why hadn't he just told her where to go when they were still on the ship? He'd surely left her here to make her feel lost and alone in a strange city.

Boyse was getting farther and farther away. "Captain! Please wait for me!" she finally called. Only then did he turn around and come back to her. He took a stout length of rope from his pocket, looped it around the heavy sea chest, and hung it on Maren's back.

"You have a lot to learn," he grumbled as he walked off again, without turning once to look back at her.

Maren groaned and followed him. Soon she was sweating in spite of the cold, clear day. After she'd walked a few yards, she felt as though the rope would cut her shoulders off, but she gritted her teeth. After a few more steps, her knees were shaking, and she could barely put one foot in front of the other. Then she began to stumble under the weight. She would have liked to call out to the captain again, but she bit her lip and bravely trudged onward, step by painful step.

When Captain Boyse finally stopped in front of a low house, Maren was already beginning to see dark stars in front of her eyes. She didn't wait for him to help her lower the chest to the ground. Instead, she simply let the rope slide from her shoulders. The chest crashed to the ground, and a piece of the lid splintered off.

"Do whatever you want with your own things. But mind yourself if I catch you being so lackadaisical with things on the ship. I prefer to discipline disobedient ship's boys in the morning. With a belt, directly on a bare bottom."

"What?" Maren cried. In her mind's eye, she could already see herself with raised skirts in the middle of the deck on the whaling ship, while the captain belted her naked backside for all to see. But Boyse had already raised the iron door knocker, and a woman opened the door.

"My salty dog!" she cried joyfully, and threw her arms around Boyse. "I had to get through the winter without you, and now you're probably just going to be here for a few days."

Maren reddened with anger. *He has a lover here,* she thought, *and he proposed to me.* Maren observed the woman carefully. She still had her arms around the captain and was obviously whispering amusing things into his ear. She threw her head back and laughed. She was no longer young, over thirty. Her hair was long and red, and she wore it loose, without a cap. Maren sniffed. Maybe a woman could leave her hair uncovered in her own home, but certainly not on a public street! And then it occurred to her that she was standing in front of the woman's house. Well, she still thought her dress was too low-cut, her bodice was laced too loosely, and her skirt, which only reached her ankles, was indecently short. What's more, the woman had darkened her eyebrows with kohl and stained her lips and cheeks with rouge.

"Oh, how I missed you!" she cried again, kissing Boyse wantonly right on the lips. "But come in now, come in." The woman turned to Maren and smiled at her kindly. "He gets the craziest notions," she said. "Now he has a cabin girl instead of a cabin boy."

Maren would have liked to complain loudly that the woman's charming "salty dog" had forced her to take the job after she'd turned down his marriage proposal. She wanted to tell her how he'd courted her, but the woman just continued to smile at her in a friendly way. "Come on, I'll help you with the sea chest," she said companionably, and to Maren's amazement. Maren bit off the terse answer that had been forming in her head. The woman led her into a room that housed a rough wooden table and a few benches. The floor was made of compacted clay instead of boards. The walls had been painted with white lime, which had become yellow from pipe smoke. The air smelled of stale beer and rancid fat.

"It would be best to find yourself a good place to sleep now, before the others arrive," the woman said. "My rooms are all occupied. You'll have to sleep here in the taproom with the rest of the swabbies."

Maren swallowed. "On the floor?" she asked.

The woman shrugged. "If you can manage to reserve a bench for yourself, of course you can sleep there too. In any case, I definitely recommend a position near the fire because the wind whistles through the cracks like ten drunken sailors."

Maren nodded, spread the oilskin coat on the bench closest to the fire, and sat down on it carefully. Then she looked up at the captain. "What happens next?" she asked.

"What are you expecting? A dancing bear? Or circus performers to keep you from getting bored? No. You wait here until the crew is assembled. Then we all go on board."

Maren nodded. The captain spoke to her as though she were the lowliest of women, but then she realized it was probably just the tone of voice he used for all ship's boys. And they really were the lowliest of a whaling ship's crew. She would have liked to know how long she'd have to be in his employment, but she didn't dare ask.

"If you leave the house, let someone know, and don't go too far from the harbor. I don't want to have to go looking for you again."

Maren nodded once more and then watched as the captain linked arms with the red-haired woman and walked up a narrow staircase with her. Halfway up, he stopped, put an arm around her hips, and kissed her soundly on the mouth. The woman laughed like she'd been waiting for him to do it. Boyse even slipped a hand into her bodice and kneaded her breasts.

"So, you really did miss me, my salty dog," she whispered so loudly that Maren could hear her, "and I missed you too. Now come on, let's get to bed."

Maren sniffed again, and when Boyse turned to look at her, she put as much scorn into her expression as she could. Then she settled on the bench by the fire and waited. It wasn't long before the first sailors arrived.

"Look, a strumpet!" one cried, and strode toward her. "How much?" he asked.

"What?" Maren said in confusion.

"How much do you want to go to the livery barn with me?"

"To the livery barn?"

The others laughed loudly.

"Oh, a virgin. You're going to have to offer her a lot more, Heintje!" one shouted, clapping his hands against his thighs with glee.

Finally, Maren understood. She gasped. "What do you think I am?" she cried. "Do I look like someone who sells herself for money? I'm a sailor, like you!"

The others couldn't control themselves anymore. They were crying tears of laughter, slapping each other on the shoulder, and even gasping for air in their hilarity. One came to Maren and took her chin in his hand. "That's just the way I like it. Innocent like a virgin and fierce like a wildcat," he murmured. Then he tried to pull her off the bench, but Maren yelled and lashed out, scratching and biting whatever she could reach. But the man was stronger than her. He pulled her up, threw her over his shoulder, and carried her toward the door.

She kicked against his chest and pulled his hair. "Put me down!" she screamed. But the man just laughed and swatted her backside heavily with his huge hand. Maren kicked, screamed, and hit. She couldn't hear the laughter of the others anymore, only her own cries as she fought for her life.

Suddenly a voice thundered through the taproom. *"Put her down. Immediately!"* Then two strong hands gripped her by the waist and set her on her feet. Maren was shaking with fear and anger. She hauled off and gave the sailor such a hard slap that it echoed through the room. A strong hand grabbed her by the wrist. "Stop that!" Only then did Maren realize that Captain Boyse was standing next to her.

The sailor who'd tried to take her to the livery barn shifted embarrassedly from one leg to the other. "Sorry, Boyse. I didn't know the girl belonged to you. Otherwise, I never would have touched her."

"I don't belong to the captain," Maren hissed. She tore herself away from Boyse, smoothed her hair, and straightened her skirts. She felt the blood rising to her cheeks, and her legs were trembling. She would have liked to cry, but she wouldn't do it in front of the men, so she swallowed her tears.

"No one touches the girl!" the captain ordered, looking every man in the eyes in turn until they each nodded. "I hope you've understood me. She's one of my ship's boys, and I need her."

After that announcement, the men slunk away. Boyse regarded her creased dress and sighed as though Maren were a great burden to him. "It's late already. The men won't be sober much longer. Once the Branntwein begins to flow, they'll forget their promises. You'll come with me."

He took her by the wrist and pulled her up the narrow stairs. At the top, he opened a door to a room with a wide bed, a shelf with a pitcher and basin, and a bedside table with a whale-oil lamp. Boyse threw one of the straw mattresses from the bed onto the hard wooden floor, followed by a blanket. "Lie there and sleep," he ordered. "And mind you don't snore."

When Boyse had tossed the mattress, a thin, scanty shift decorated with lace fell at Maren's feet. She lifted the garment with one finger and waved it in front of the captain's nose. "You dropped something," she said with anger. "And I'm sorry you have to spend the night with me instead."

She thought she saw a flash of amusement in Boyse's eyes. "Don't talk so much. Just go to sleep," he said.

At first, Maren couldn't sleep at all. She missed Thies, Finja, and the entire island. Life was hard there, but at least she had known what was going to happen and what was expected of her. Here in this strange city, she felt more lost and alone than she had in her whole life. She knew very well that every day would bring new, unpleasant surprises, about which she wasn't the least bit curious. And when she thought about having to spend the next half year with Captain Boyse, she sighed, and her forehead creased with worry. On the bed, the captain breathed so calmly and deeply that Maren assumed he must already be dreaming. That in turn annoyed her so much that she herself couldn't fall asleep . . .

. . . Something was shaking her. Maren pulled the blanket more tightly around her and groaned, trying to stop the shaking, but then someone grabbed her shoulder, and she opened her eyes. The captain was standing over her.

"What is it?" she asked, annoyed.

Boyse laughed. "You called my name in your sleep," he said, with an undercurrent of amusement. "So I thought I should wake you from your nightmare."

"I wasn't having a nightmare," Maren hissed. "You shouldn't have woken me."

"Fine," the captain said. "If you were sleeping well, I won't begrudge you that. But you woke me up."

Maren could practically hear the grin in his voice.

"If someone calls me, I come."

"I didn't call you," Maren insisted. "You must be mistaken."

"Then everything's fine, and you can go back to sleep. But see that you don't call my name again. As a sea captain, I react instantly to that."

"I didn't— Oh, think what you want." Maren pulled the blanket around her again, but sleep refused to return.

CHAPTER 13

It took over two days for the crew to be signed on, two days which seemed like an eternity to Maren. Captain Boyse had reserved a large table in the taproom, and finally all the men who wanted to work on his ship had arrived. Most came from Sylt and had signed on back on the island, and they had already been at sea with Boyse before. But the whaling ship that the captain was to command this year sailed under a Dutch flag, and it was so large that now sailors from the other North Frisian Islands had a chance to work with him. Most of them knew each other, and that was important because the ship's crew would be a replacement for their families for months on end. The work on a whaling ship was dangerous, so it was also important for them to trust one another and know what they could expect from each other. In total, Boyse hired one hundred seventy-five seamen. That included six officers, eleven boatheaders, three carpenters, four mates, and three bosuns. There were also six cooks and six cooks' drudges, of which Maren was one. Additionally, there were forty-four sailors, forty-one harpooners, forty-two blubber cutters, coopers, able seamen, a barber, a blacksmith, and normal ship's boys. Most of the men whom Maren didn't know from Sylt were different from any of the men she'd known until then. She felt shy around them, and they spoke a language she didn't understand. One wore a black patch over his right eye, another had an anchor tattooed on his lower arm, and another wore his hair as long as a girl's.

Boyse had ordered her to stay put on a bench near him. "I don't want to have to search all of Amsterdam for you," he'd said to justify his decision, but Maren was bored. *What difference would it make if I just peeked around the next corner?* she thought. *There are so many people walking around here during the day that nothing could happen to me. Besides, I remember the name of the boardinghouse and the street, so I can ask if I get lost.* She cast a glance at Boyse, who was just offering to pay a ship's boy eleven Dutch guilders, and snuck out of the room.

When she opened the door to the street, she was struck dumb by the colorful chaos in the alleyway. Carts and carriages rumbled by, and someone was pulling a food wagon which had enticing smells wafting out of it. Water carriers walked with yokes on their shoulders and full buckets dangling from the ends. For a few copper pennies, they'd allow any thirsty person to drink directly from the same ladle, which made Maren shudder with disgust. Nearby, a tailor sat at a table behind an open window, holding numerous pins between his lips. A richly dressed woman strode proudly down the street with her serving maid hurrying behind her with a willow basket on her arm. A few women stood on a corner laughing together. A man who was missing both his legs sat in an entryway, asking passersby if they could spare a piece of bread for him.

All of this was new to Maren. She had barely taken a few steps when her eyes began to burn with all the colors and images. Her ears hummed from the noise, and she felt a headache coming on. When she came to a church, she sat down on the steps to rest a little. How she would have loved to share this experience with Thies! He'd earned his officer's commission, but this year had found no employment. Not even on a merchant's ship.

When the church bell rang its evening peal, Maren got up and went back to the boardinghouse. She opened the door quietly and saw an officer arguing with Captain Boyse. "We still need another good man on the bridge," the officer was saying. "But now they've all been hired." He sounded reproachful.

"Then we'll take one of the Dutch or East Frisian men. They're not bad," the captain retorted.

"You should have taken Thies Heinen. He's a good man, and you know it. I don't understand why you refused him. And not only that, you made sure he wasn't able to get any job at all this year. And now you've got that girl as a ship's boy! No one has done anything like that in all the days of Christian seafaring. I'd like to know why you are doing such absurd things."

Captain Boyse waved his comment aside. "It's personal, and it has nothing to do with you. Besides, Maren won't be the only woman on board. I've decided to bring Zelda."

"What? We're a whaling ship, not a pleasure boat." The officer sniffed indignantly.

"I hired Zelda to keep an eye on Maren. Aside from that, she'll do all the mending."

The officer shook his head. "I'm against it," he insisted. "Women have no place on a whaling ship."

Captain Boyse shrugged. "If you don't like it, go work on another boat. But don't forget we're the ones who come home with the best catch."

Another man walked toward them. Maren could tell by the way he moved that he was a harpooner, a hunter. "The other whalers will call us fools. They'll laugh when they hear we have women on board." He scratched his neck. "Our work is too hard for women."

The officer spoke again. "Some will laugh, I think, but others will be jealous. We won't have to go to whores in every harbor if we have two right on the ship."

He'd barely finished speaking when Boyse leapt to his feet. His face was red, and Maren could see the veins pulsing on his forehead. "There will be no whores on my ship!" he shouted so loudly that the cups on the shelf shook. "Zelda and Maren will work like all the others. And I'll personally cut the throat of anyone who even dares to look at them the wrong way."

The officer shook his head again in disbelief, and then turned away and went to sit with the other seamen whom Boyse had contracted. Every now and then, they peered curiously at the captain, who was sitting again and seemed to have calmed down.

So that's why, Maren thought. *It's his fault that Thies didn't get hired. He didn't* want *me to be able to pay back the loan. He forced me to work on his ship intentionally.* Rage boiled up inside of her again. She would have liked to go straight to the captain and shout directly into his face what she thought about his behavior. But his burst of anger had taken the edge off of her own. *Soon,* she decided. *Soon I will tell him what I think of him. I think he's churlish, mean, and a poor loser.* It was more than clear to Maren now. The captain wanted to take revenge on her for refusing his marriage proposal.

The next morning, the captain ordered Maren to pack her things. "We're boarding the ship today. She's called *Rán*, after the Norse goddess of the sea. Blue peter has already been raised."

"I know who Rán is," Maren answered scornfully. "And I'm sure I'll meet Blue Peter soon enough."

Boyse broke into laughter. "Oh, yes, you certainly will. But 'blue peter' isn't a man; it's a signal flag which is hoisted shortly before a ship sails so the crew knows it's time to get on board. That's also the time the contractors come with their invoices."

Maren's brow creased. "You're making fun of me," she complained. "It's easy to make fun of someone going to sea for the first time."

Then the captain's expression became serious. "You're a ship's boy like all the others. A ship's boy is everyone's scapegoat. The men will often make fun of you. You'd better start getting used to it."

"There are some things I will never get used to!" Maren launched her hairbrush angrily into the sea chest. She was furious at the captain. Not only because he'd made fun of her, but above all because he'd ruined Thies's chances of getting hired. Then she looked up. Captain Boyse was standing directly in front of her in his broad stance with his hands on his hips.

"First, you must learn that you don't talk back to your captain," he said in rebuke. "You are under my orders, and everything I say is law for you."

Maren flinched with shock. She wasn't accustomed to obeying anyone. Her parents had usually let her have her way, and Thies had never been bossy with her.

"I don't like to be ordered around by anyone," Maren said. She would have also liked to tell him what she thought about what he had done to Thies, but Boyse's face had already turned dangerously red, so she resigned herself to glaring angrily at him.

Boyse grabbed her hand and lifted her off the floor with one powerful tug. Then he gripped her chin firmly in one hand and forced her to look at him. "Whaling is more dangerous than you can imagine. You have to obey me for your own safety."

Maren swallowed. She would have liked to nod to show him she understood, but his grip on her chin was as solid as iron. "Let me go," she hissed. When he did what she asked, she added, "I understand, but don't think you can tell me what to do when I'm not aboard the ship. And if others think they can give me orders, then they are sadly mistaken."

"Oh, no, dear child. On board the *Rán* there will be many who have a right to tell you what to do. A galley drudge has the lowest status on the ship. You'll have to obey everyone, whether you like it or not."

Then he sighed. "Whatever possessed me to take you with me? You'll surely be more trouble than you're worth. I should have left you with Thies and not bothered about the money you owe me."

That was just the chance Maren had been waiting for. "I'd be happy to return to Sylt," she said curtly. "You know very well that I'm not here of my own free will."

For a moment, Boyse looked at her with his eyes narrowed. Then he took a step toward her. "Oh, no, my girl," he said in a dangerously quiet voice. "You will work for every copper penny you owe me. And I will see to it. You won't have a single hour to worry about it. You'll work just as hard as all the others. If you behave as impetuously with my men as you do with me, then you'll find trouble for sure. And there's one thing I can promise you. You will be a completely different person when we come back to Amsterdam in the autumn. Your life will be different, and both your heart and your soul will be transformed."

Maren shrank back in fear. Boyse's words sounded like a threat, but at the same time she'd realized that there were different rules here than on Sylt. She believed every word he said. *Yes,* she thought. *I will be a different person. And I can only hope I'll like what I've become.* But there was one thing she didn't understand. Captain Boyse seemed to hate her. Every time he saw her, his gaze darkened. Why hadn't he hired Thies instead? Thies would have been able to earn far more money to pay off the debt faster, and he would have been far more useful. Did he just want to humiliate her at the deepest level? Was it revenge that motivated him? But then why was he bringing Zelda along? Had she done something to him? Did he want to get revenge on her too? Or did he really want her to come along to create a buffer between Maren and all the rough men who would be terribly desperate for a woman?

When the captain left the room in a huff and the door had closed behind him, Maren sighed. She was alone here and had no friends or allies. She understood now that the men would follow Boyse's orders, and there was no one who could protect her from the captain's whims.

She folded her thick winter skirt tidily and put it carefully into the sea chest. She thought of Thies again, and this time a little annoyance slipped into her heart. She knew that Boyse had refused to hire him. Maybe he'd encouraged the other whaling captains not to hire Thies either. But what about the merchant ships? Thies could've found work on one of those. Had he just given up when Boyse refused to hire him? Why hadn't he at least come to Amsterdam to look for another job, where there was plenty of opportunity? He hadn't really fought for what he wanted. She could see that now. Then she realized something and paused in the middle of her packing. No, Thies had done the right thing. He hadn't known that she had to work for Captain Boyse. He hadn't struggled to get another position because he had wanted to be with her.

Maren sighed with relief when that logical conclusion occurred to her. And actually, he couldn't really leave the island. He had to take care of his mother and sister, and now Maren's mother too. At that thought, she was overwhelmed by a feeling of tenderness. *Oh, Thies,* she thought with a sigh. *How I wish I could be with you now.*

CHAPTER 14

The *Rán* had previously been a merchant's ship. The entire hull was about ninety feet long and twenty feet wide, with a band of doubled oak planking at the waterline to protect it from drift ice. The protective band extended one yard above and below the waterline, not quite to the keel. The bow of the ship was strengthened with metal sheeting as protection against the Arctic ice.

Barrels full of saltwater served as ballast on the outward-bound journey, and on the return journey, they would hopefully be filled with whale blubber and oil. She was a square-rigged brig, and the huge top-gallant sail luffed in the breeze as the last provisions were carried on board.

Of course, Maren had often seen large ships in the harbors of Sylt, but rarely so close up. She felt impossibly small beside the wooden giant. The other sailors were already hurrying up the gangplank and disappearing down the main hatch to reserve the best places to sleep. But Maren knew nothing of this custom, and watched instead as the whaling equipment was loaded. There were numerous barrels, gigantic whale ropes, six completely new whaleboats with their sails and oar-locks, fifty harpoon shafts made of hardwood, and sixty harpoons with iron tips and barbs. There were walrus harpoons, ice saws, ice axes, gigantic flensing knives, fish kettles, and three try-pots made of gleaming copper, for rendering whale blubber into oil.

The provisions for the crew were also being loaded and included sixty chickens, a dozen lambs, several sacks of dried grain, barrels filled with sauerkraut and white cabbage, ham, boxes of salt, dried cod, honey, and smoked sides of beef. Additionally, candles, slabs of beeswax, oil lamps, firewood, bales of cloth, and a huge ship's apothecary were loaded.

Maren watched the proceedings with wide eyes. She couldn't believe how much material disappeared into the belly of the ship. Finally, one of the sailors from Rantum called out to her. "Ho, girl! Are you coming, or shall we leave without you?" Maren quickly grabbed her sea chest and dragged it up the steep gangplank. Below her, a coach stopped directly in front of the pier. Zelda got out wearing a dress with a loosely laced bodice. The men on the deck whooped, and Zelda waved to them good-humoredly while the coachman unloaded several wooden chests.

Alerted by the men's calls, Captain Boyse appeared at the rail. He waved to Zelda in welcome and then sent two men down the gangplank to help with her luggage. Meanwhile, Maren almost collapsed under the weight of her sea chest. She'd heard that Zelda was coming whaling, but she only believed it now, when she saw the woman. She rolled her eyes. She already knew that all the men would only have eyes for Zelda. Under the captain's strict orders, they would behave like gentlemen toward Zelda, while Maren could be glad if no one kicked her.

She finally managed to get the sea chest to the top of the gangplank, and then she sank to the deck and wiped the sweat from her forehead with her hand.

"Don't sit there in the way," the captain spoke harshly. "Go find yourself a place to sleep." Maren looked around uncertainly. Where was she supposed to sleep here?

"Below deck. You have to climb down the companionway." The captain shook his head in amazement at her ignorance. "But hurry. You're needed in the galley."

Maren picked up the unwieldy box again and went to the hatch. She pushed back the heavy cover with difficulty and climbed down the narrow ladder into the darkness, not carrying down her sea chest before she'd seen what awaited her. Below, it was almost completely black, and her eyes needed time to adjust to the darkness. It was not only dark, but there was also an awful stench. It reeked of sweaty male bodies, unwashed feet, and stale beer. It also smelled of the smoke that had been used to drive away any lingering vermin from the last voyage. The men had tied their hammocks in two rows, leaving a walkway free down the middle. Along the hull was a row of wooden berths. Some of the sailors had made themselves comfortable on the bare wooden boards. Maren swallowed. She was supposed to sleep here? With all these men? Unimaginable. She almost broke into tears, but she knew there was no one here to help her, so she swallowed her misery. Then one of the men got up from his berth and walked down the corridor to the end, where Maren saw a large barrel. When the man unbuttoned his pants and relieved himself into the barrel right before her eyes, she couldn't help shuddering.

One of the young sailors laughed as he observed her. Another, an old blubber cutter with a long, tangled beard, scolded her. "Don't act so. You'll be seeing the likes of that often, now. Find a place for yourself and keep your mouth shut. And don't think we enjoy having a girl down here either."

Tears sprang into Maren's eyes again, and she blindly sought out one of the wooden berths. The straw pallet smelled of sick, and as much as she wanted to, she didn't dare to look for a different berth with a better-smelling mattress. Then she went to get her sea chest, maneuvered it down the ladder with difficulty, and placed it under the bed. She wanted to ask the way to the galley, but she didn't dare when she realized most of the men were staring at her with malice. Just then, the person in the next berth stuck out a hand toward her.

"My name is Raik," he said. "I'm the cabin boy."

Relieved, Maren offered her hand and introduced herself. She felt as though she hadn't heard a friendly word since she'd left Sylt, and his courteous gesture almost moved her to tears.

"Do you know where the galley is?" she asked. "What will I have to do as a galley drudge?"

At that moment, the captain's voice echoed through the hatch. "Maren!" he shouted, and Maren started with shock, hit her head on the upper bunk, and hurried up the ladder.

The captain was standing at the top, and he held out something made of rough, scratchy fabric toward her. "Here, put these on. You can't go dressed like that. Your rags might catch on fire."

Rags? Maren thought indignantly, and smoothed the floor-length dark-brown skirt she was wearing. Then she took the scratchy bundle and unrolled it, and her eyes went wide. "But . . . but . . . ," she faltered. "These are pants!"

"Of course they're pants. What else would they be? Everyone who works on my ship wears pants."

"Wh-why?" Maren asked, unable to tear her eyes off the offending garment. They were wide-fitting ankle-length sailor's pants, which must have come out of the crew's slop chest. They felt thick and a little damp, and very, very scratchy.

"Because in a skirt you'd always be getting caught on everything. Pants are better. Go ahead, put the things on."

"Here?"

The captain shrugged. "You could go below and let a hundred men watch. It's your choice."

Maren sighed and regarded the captain, who was making no effort to hide his amusement. "All right, but you'll have to turn around," she ordered.

"What?" Boyse broke into laughter. "Do you think I've never seen a woman's legs before?" But when he saw the abashed look in Maren's eyes and the reluctant blush on her cheeks, he turned around after all, and Maren was truly grateful for his small gesture of compliance.

"Ready?" he asked after a moment.

"Ready."

He turned around, examined Maren from top to toe, and broke into peals of laughter. Then he took a sou'wester—an oilskin hat with a wide brim, which had been hanging on the rigging—and slipped it onto her head, laughing boisterously. The other sailors on the deck who had been watching curiously from a distance now laughed with him.

The captain gasped breathlessly between fits of laughter. "You . . . you look like a ship's kobold! Our own little hobgoblin!"

Now the others hooted with laughter, slapping their thighs in amusement, unable to stop. And Maren stood there, her cheeks flaming with fury, her hands balled into fists. She would have liked to scream at Boyse and tell him he was a wretched lout, but she didn't dare to say it in front of the crew. So she took a deep breath, ripped the hat off her head, and launched it over the rail into the sea. Then she walked away with as much dignity as she could with her legs suddenly trapped in pants for the first time. She climbed down the ladder to her sleeping platform and threw herself onto the berth, too angry to cry, and pounded the disgusting straw pallet with her fists. When Raik ventured to ask her what all the noise above deck had been about, Maren continued her pounding. "I hate him, I hate him, I hate him!" she cried.

But she didn't even have enough time to give her anger free rein. She heard the ship's bell ringing, and all the sailors got up.

"What's happening now?" Maren asked.

"There's going to be a prayer service on deck, and then the captain will give a speech before we head out to sea," Raik answered.

Everyone was on deck, and Maren saw a sailor lowering the signal flag, the blue peter. The men were packed closely together, and the captain was standing on a box so he could be seen by all. The prayer service was short. A priest from Amsterdam came on board and sprinkled holy water in several places, delivering a few emotionless prayers. The crew intoned the Lord's Prayer together, and then the unenthusiastic priest shuffled back down the gangplank.

The captain was now standing in front of them with both hands raised for silence. "We sail under a Dutch standard," he said, gesturing at the flag that had just been run up the rigging in place of the blue peter. "That means order and austerity rule aboard the *Rán*. Whoever disobeys this law and order, whoever curses, brawls, cuts or stabs another with a knife, or doesn't attend prayer services without reason of an emergency, will be instantly brought to justice under martial law. The verdict will be reached and punishment executed immediately. The offender will be bound to the mast and lashed with a piece of cord as many times as the sentence demands. If that is not sufficient and the offense is repeated, the wrongdoer will be docked two months' pay or be tied to a rope and thrown several times into the sea."

Maren started with shock when she heard about the draconian punishments, but the men around her just nodded.

"Yes, indeed!" one of them cried. "On a ship like this, there must be discipline." The others murmured their agreement, and the captain continued. "We are Christian seamen. Therefore, there will be a call to prayer every evening. In the morning as well. Meals will come afterward. On Sundays and holy days, one of the officers will read aloud from the gospel."

The men nodded again, and some brought their hands to the crosses hanging at their necks.

"And now, I wish God's blessing on this voyage for all of us. We head to sea." The captain stepped down from his box, the group dispersed, and everyone went to work.

A little while later, Maren finally found the galley. It was in a little wooden house built on deck. There was an open fire for cooking and roasting, and the provisions were stored nearby.

Maren's face was still red with chagrin about her pants. "What do you want me to do?" she asked more curtly than she had intended. "I'm Maren, the new galley helper."

The cook was a fat man with a pale beard and upper arms as stout as trees. He waved a hand at a gigantic sack of carrots. "Scrape them," he barked, and Maren sighed as she set to work. By the time she'd scraped half a sack full, her fingers hurt and her back ached so much she feared it would break. The smoke from the fire stung her eyes, and the fumes made her throat feel sore and raw. She was so relieved when the bag was empty that she lowered herself in exhaustion onto an upturned bucket. But the cook, whom she now knew was called Jakob and was Dutch, shook his head. "You've scraped one sackful, but there are still three more."

Maren could hardly believe her ears. She was tired, her back ached acutely, the pants scratched the insides of her thighs, and the smoke burned so much that she didn't think she'd be able to survive in the galley for another minute.

But Jakob had little sympathy. "If you don't scrape the carrots, I'll have to do it. But that's not my job. So see to it that you finish. The men don't like it when the meal isn't ready on time."

Maren pulled herself up with difficulty and cleaned the second sack full of carrots, and by the time she'd finished the third one, she couldn't feel her back or her fingers anymore. Everything had melded into a single wall of pain. Mechanically, she reached for one carrot after another, scraped it off, and tossed it into a big wooden basin. She felt as though she'd never done anything else other than scrape carrots. After another half a sack, she was ready to sell her soul to the Devil if he would only set her free.

Jakob stood next to her and watched. Maren swayed where she stood. She cut her finger twice. Then Jakob put a hand on her shoulder. "Leave it be, girl. You've done enough for today. Have something to eat now, and then see to it that you get to your berth."

Maren was so grateful to him that she found no words, but she was also too exhausted to speak. She let the evening prayer service wash over her and then staggered below deck to her berth. She didn't even bother to take off her scratchy pants, and she was asleep as soon as she laid down her head.

During the night, she woke to angry sounds. She opened her eyes but couldn't see anything in the thick darkness. Two men seemed to be arguing. Rough words flew back and forth, and then she heard the sound that a fist makes when it strikes a jaw, followed by a cry of pain. Another man shouted for silence. "Do you want me to punch you in the mouth too?" someone asked him. "Just let me know. I'm in the mood for it."

Maren realized that she desperately needed to relieve herself, but could she really feel her way along the small walkway lit only with one dim oil candle? Past all the men? Past the two men who were fighting? And how was she supposed to pee into the barrel anyway? It was too high. Much too high for her to sit on the edge. She tried to ignore the fighting men, the snoring, grumbling, groaning, tossing, and turning, and go back to sleep, but she grew more and more desperate.

When she realized that she couldn't possibly fall asleep again, she got up and decided to go on deck. She'd either find a bucket or squat over the rail.

Slowly, so as not to awaken Raik and the others who were sleeping around her, she snuck to the ladder and climbed up. She struggled to push back the heavy hatch cover, but finally she managed. The cool, fresh night air felt wonderful to her. The ship was still anchored in Amsterdam harbor, but farther away from the shore now, so the lights of the city looked like a glowing sea to Maren. She glanced up at the sailor who was in a crow's nest atop a mast observing the sea. She finally found a bucket that had been used for scrubbing the deck during the day and relieved herself into it. Then she emptied the bucket over the rail, sighed with relief, and went back below deck. She was extremely glad that she'd been alone. She'd learned that the barrel in the crew quarters was used only for making water, and that the men would lower their pants to their ankles without shame and move their bowels over the rail directly into the sea, then pull up their pants again and go about their business. For Maren, this idea was unimaginable, but she knew that she'd have to get used to it. And that probably wouldn't be the worst of it.

The next morning when Maren was on her way to the kitchen, an officer spoke to her as she emptied her bucket over the railing.

"Waste goes over the starboard side," he said. "When the wind blows from this direction, it always goes starboard."

Maren stared at him in confusion. "Starboard?"

"Holy God!" the officer swore. "You're on a whaling ship, and you don't even know the difference between port and starboard?"

Maren swallowed and shook her head shyly. All at once, the officer reached out and slapped her in the face.

"Ow!" Maren cried in outrage and held one hand to her cheek.

"Where does it hurt now, left or right?"

"Right," Maren said quietly.

"Good. I slapped your right cheek. And now your right cheek hurts so much that you see stars. Do you understand?"

Maren shook her head again. She had no idea what the man wanted from her, or even what he was talking about. She only hoped that the captain didn't happen to be on deck at the moment.

"Right. Seeing stars!" the officer shouted. "Do you understand?"

Maren was having difficulty holding back her tears. The officer was raising his hand to slap her again when it dawned on her.

"Right is starboard!" she shouted, and threw up her arms to protect her face. "The right side hurts, and I see stars. That means right is starboard."

The officer let his hand fall. "So, you're capable of learning something, after all," he said. "Just don't forget it." Then he walked away.

CHAPTER 15

The next morning at first light of dawn, the wind changed. Captain Boyse gave the order to weigh anchor. Maren woke dead tired and feeling as though she'd been beaten. All of her limbs hurt, and she had no idea how she would be able to survive working in the galley again. The lumbering brig turned northward, and as exhausted as Maren was, she still found it impressive to see the heavy ship slowly set in motion with its sails snapping and its rigging creaking.

Raik was standing next to her.

"How does the helmsman know which direction to go?" she asked him.

"*Shhh,*" he whispered. "You shouldn't ask questions like that when anyone else is listening, unless you want to be the laughingstock of the entire crew."

"I already am," Maren answered, and she pointed at the pants.

"The sailors know the direction by the position of the sun, by their nautical charts, and by using their instruments. With compass, octant, and plumb line, they can find out where they are and where they need to go. When you have a little time, you can go ask an officer if you can look at his chart."

Maren snorted indignantly. "I live on Sylt. I've seen more than enough nautical charts." She was about to add something, but just then, the men tossed their hats and caps into the air.

"Greenland, ho!" they cried. "Off to the whaling grounds!" Then they all cheered, and Maren got carried away by their enthusiasm and cheered along with them.

A little later, everyone dispersed and went about their work, and Maren was just about to join Jakob in the galley when Zelda suddenly appeared.

"So," the older woman asked, "did you sleep well?" Then she yawned loudly and stretched, like someone who'd just slept in a soft feather bed and had good dreams.

"Thank you for asking," Maren replied curtly. But then her curiosity got the better of her. "And where did you sleep, madam?" she inquired formally.

Zelda smiled at her. "Call me Zelda. We'll be spending months together, and as the only women on this goddamn brig, we'll have to stick together."

Maren was taken aback at the crudeness of her words, and she decided Zelda was a vulgar creature, whether she was the only other woman on the ship or not.

"Why do you ask? I slept in the captain's cabin, of course. Where else would I sleep?"

"In the captain's cabin? But then, where was the captain?" The thought that Zelda had slept in a proper bed, undisturbed, while she herself had had to share the space below deck with a hundred men made her scowl.

Zelda shook her head in amazement at Maren's question. "The captain slept with me, of course." She laughed. "Where else should he stretch out his weary limbs?"

Maren's mouth fell open. "But . . . but . . . ," she stammered. "You aren't married. Or are you? Or at least engaged?"

"Heavens, no!" Zelda laughed again. "We're not a couple. At least, not the sort of couple that set up a home together and have children. I'm his mistress."

"His what?"

Zelda laughed yet again, and Maren was gradually starting to feel like a complete idiot.

"His mistress. That means I'm his lover. We share a bed. Nothing more and nothing less."

"Then . . . then . . . he pays you for it?" Maren couldn't believe she was standing there talking to a whore. On Sylt there were women who were rumored to have secret lovers as long as their men were at sea, but as far as she knew, there was only one who actually sold her body for money.

"Of course," Zelda replied, as openly as if she were sharing a cake recipe. "Otherwise I wouldn't be here."

Maren was dying to ask a question. Even *she* didn't understand why it was so important for her to know the answer. But her entire being burned with the desire to ask. "Do you love him?"

Zelda's forehead creased. "No, I don't. In my profession, it would be the worst misfortune to fall in love. Love is a luxury for girls who don't have to earn their own money."

Maren swallowed again. There was another question which needed an immediate answer. "And the captain? Does he love you?"

After stopping to consider for a moment, Zelda shook her head. "No, I don't believe he does."

"Does he love someone else?" Maren just couldn't stop asking the questions, even though she was certain she wouldn't care about the answers in the slightest.

"I don't know," Zelda answered a little hesitantly. "He doesn't talk about his feelings. But sometimes I get the sense that there's a girl who means more to him than any other."

Who was this girl? Maren had thought that when Zelda told her about Boyse, it would satisfy her curiosity. But the opposite was true. Now she desperately wanted to know who the captain was in love with.

"Do you know her?"

"No. No one knows her. He doesn't talk about it. Just like he doesn't talk about what happened to him in the past."

"What happened to him?" Maren asked. She sifted through her thoughts, trying to remember if she'd heard anything about the captain on Sylt, but there was nothing.

"No one knows," Zelda said. "But one thing is clear. Whatever happened made him prefer being on his own. He may be captain, but he has no friends on board."

Zelda was silent for a moment, and then she asked a question of her own. "Tell me, you come from the same island. You must know what happened to him."

But Maren didn't know. "I'm only half his age. I know nothing about it."

Zelda nodded thoughtfully and sighed. "He's a sad and lonely man, and most of the time he's angry too. I wish I understood him better." She spoke so pensively that Maren wondered if Zelda actually did feel more for the captain than she admitted. Suddenly she felt sorry for the woman. *It must be terrible to love someone and not be loved back,* she thought.

With her next breath, she remembered Thies. She hadn't thought about him all of yesterday. But now she missed him even more. If Thies were only here with her on the ship, she wouldn't have to be afraid of the snoring, or fighting, men. If only Thies were with her, everything would be fine.

Come evening, Maren was so exhausted again that she had only one thing on her mind. Sleep, and more sleep. She couldn't care less that she had to sleep among a hundred men; she just wanted to rest. She'd had to cut onions all day, and her eyes burned like fire. She felt as though she didn't have any tears left inside her. Her throat was sore, and her fingers stung from countless tiny cuts. The day before, Jakob had been kind to her and had sent her away when she was tired.

On this day, though, he seemed to be in a bad mood. He had been cursing like a carter all day, insisting that she hurry. When she was finally finished with the onions, he'd handed her a gigantic skillet that was so heavy she could barely lift it, and he'd ordered her to wash it. Maren tried to clean the skillet, but it kept slipping out of her hands and crashing with a loud clanging to the floor. It happened again just as Captain Boyse was inspecting the galley. If it had fallen even a handsbreadth closer, it would have landed on his toes.

"Forgive me!" Maren cried immediately and bent down to retrieve the pan, groaning as her back threatened to break.

Boyse ignored her and spoke directly to Jakob. "The crew wasn't satisfied with yesterday's meal," he said severely.

Jakob nodded. "The carrots weren't scraped properly, were they?"

"If you knew that, why did you serve them that way?" Boyse asked, and Maren could hear the aggravation in his voice. Jakob would tell the captain that she had scraped the carrots carelessly. And then, oh, God, he would take his belt to Maren's backside in front of the crew. She began to tremble thinking about it.

But Jakob just shrugged. "What do you want, Captain? I can only work as hard as I can. Send the men who complained to me. Then we'll see if they can do any better themselves."

Boyse's forehead creased with annoyance. "That's not a solution that satisfies me. I need the crew to be in good spirits. Excuses like that won't work on this boat." He considered for a moment and then pointed a finger at Jakob. "You'll give up your ration of Branntwein this evening.

The men have to see that I take their complaint seriously. And if it happens again, you'll have to bleed for it."

Jakob nodded as though he didn't care, but Maren was terribly glad and extremely grateful that he'd covered for her.

"Thank you, Jakob," Maren whispered earnestly after Boyse left.

"Well enough," the cook grumbled. "But that's the only time that I take the blame for you. In the future, when you make your bed, you can lie in it."

Maren swayed dangerously as she climbed down the narrow ladder below deck and threw herself into her berth, dog-tired.

"So, what did you do all day?" asked Raik, who'd spent the day scrubbing the upper deck.

"Onions," Maren whispered with her last bit of energy. "I don't think I'll ever be able to smell anything else, so long as I live." She closed her eyes and tried to fall asleep as quickly as she could in order to forget the trials of the day.

As he did every Sunday, the captain had given the crew their weekly ration of Branntwein. And there wasn't one among them who hadn't seized the moment and gotten thoroughly inebriated. The brig was in calm waters, and Maren had heard an officer say that Boyse could afford to make do without part of the crew the next day. Moreover, only those who had completed their tasks and had a free shift due to them had been given a ration.

Maren wasn't interested in all that. She, too, had received her ration of Branntwein but had immediately given it to Jakob. Partly because he had lost his ration for her, and partly because she'd never drunk anything strongly alcoholic in her entire life, and she couldn't imagine starting to do so here aboard the *Rán*.

But now a deckhand came toward her. He was already swaying a little and had to lean against her berth for support.

"Ho, sailor girl," he slurred. "Don't you want to try some?" A bottle swung back and forth slowly over Maren's head.

"No, thank you," she replied politely. "I don't think I'd like it."

A few men laughed, and that seemed to encourage the drunken deckhand. "Don't be so contrary! What's wrong with trying? Then at least you could find out if it tickles your fancy."

"No, thank you," Maren repeated, and turned onto her other side so her back was toward him.

Things quickly began to get out of hand. He shook her by the shoulder. "You shouldn't even *try* to sleep! Tonight, no one will sleep. Come, have a swig by your own free will, or I'll pour the swill down your throat."

"Leave her alone," Raik said, butting in. "She said she didn't want any."

"Bah! Why should I care what a woman wants? She has to obey. And now I want her to drink Branntwein."

Raik had gotten up and tried to pull the flask out of the drunk's hand, but the man held it tightly and hit Raik in the center of his face, so the cabin boy fell to the ground and lay there, unmoving.

"What are you doing?" Maren screamed at the man. "You've hurt him!" She wanted to get up to take care of Raik, but the heavy hand of the sailor pushed her back down onto her berth.

Then he forced himself on top of her, holding her down with the weight of his body. He pulled her arms over her head, grabbed her roughly by the wrists, and held the flask to her lips with his free hand.

"Drink!" he demanded.

Maren pressed her lips together and hoped someone would come to help her. But no one did. In fact, just the opposite. Gradually, other men gathered round and encouraged the deckhand with claps and shouts.

"Go on, sluice her gob, Sven! She's working with men now, so she can drink like one."

She heard coarse laughter, and another man bent over her and pried her jaw apart with strong hands. "Pour it down her gullet now!" he shouted, and the deckhand didn't have to be told twice.

At the first swallow, Maren felt as though her throat were on fire. She had to cough, but the deckhand kept pouring alcohol into her mouth. She couldn't breathe, and the Branntwein ran out of her lips, down her neck, and pooled between her breasts. She didn't want to swallow; she wanted to spit it into the man's face. But she couldn't. She had to drink, otherwise she would drown.

So she swallowed the fire, which seemed to burn a hole in her stomach. It set her throat aflame and numbed her tongue. When the deckhand briefly took the bottle away, Maren coughed so hard she feared her soul would fly out of her body. The men whooped and jeered, and all at once, the entire situation seemed very funny to her. She looked into the man's face and had to laugh when she saw his nose, because there were suddenly two of them. Everything seemed comical. She glanced over at Raik, who was slowly getting up from the floor with a bloody nose, and she began to laugh hysterically. All her tiredness and exhaustion disappeared in an instant, and Maren sat up and shoved the deckhand lightly away. "If . . . if . . . you—*hic!*—thought that I . . . was going to let you tell me what to do, then—*hic* . . ." Then she'd already forgotten what she wanted to say.

Another sailor stood close to her, holding his flask out in front of him. She took the bottle from his hand and drank deeply. Then she spread her arms and spun in a circle. "Now we shall be joyful and celebrate!" she cried. "Let's sing!" And she began to sing an old song, linked arms with the sailors, and swayed to the music as the men raised their rough voices with hers.

"Can you dance too?" one of them asked, and Maren threw her head back and laughed loudly.

"Of course I can dance. Do you want to see how my skirts fly?" She had forgotten that she was wearing pants. She spun in a circle, twirling down the long aisle between the hammocks, and stumbled. She pulled herself up and continued, singing all the while at the top of her lungs. Every now and then, she stopped, accepted Branntwein from one of the men, and took great swallows of it. But then she became dizzy. She swayed and could barely keep to her feet. All the men stood around clapping and encouraging her, but Maren could barely stand.

"I suddenly feel ill," she exclaimed in amazement, and had barely gotten the words out when she bent forward and ejected everything that had been in her stomach. Then she tried to stagger to her berth, but her legs collapsed under her like stalks of wheat. She was sick again, but it didn't seem to bother anyone. They were out of control now, stomping so the entire ship vibrated. Two of them had linked arms and were dancing in a wild spin, two others were bickering, and another reached into a barrel of drinking water and was spraying those who were trying to sleep, to loud yowls of protest.

Everything spun around Maren. She tried to hold on, but every time she tried to hold something, it spun away. The entire room seemed to blur, and she just couldn't get her feet under her. She grinned, but then she was so nauseated again that she threw up on the floor. *No, that wasn't the floor.* Everything was whirling, and Maren had misjudged and thrown up on her pants. She wanted to laugh about it, but then someone held Branntwein under her nose again, and she wanted nothing more than to wash away the terrible sour taste in her mouth, so she drank and kept on drinking until everything around her went black. She fell backward and hit her head on the hard planks, but she didn't feel a thing.

CHAPTER 16

When Maren awoke, she didn't know where she was. A blacksmith had opened up shop in her head and was pounding away, her throat was as dry as dust, and a terrible storm was raging in her stomach. She groaned and wanted to close her eyes again immediately, but then she was grabbed by the arm and pulled into a sitting position.

"Leave me be," she murmured, batting weakly at the hand that held her.

She immediately received two powerful slaps, which droned in her skull like church bells. Her eyes went wide. "What in the . . . ?" But then she saw the captain's angry face.

"Get up!" Boyse roared at her. "Move!" Then he tugged at her again as though she were a rag doll. Once he'd pulled Maren up from her berth, he let go briefly, but she swayed and fell back onto the straw pallet.

"Get up, I say!" he shouted louder. He pulled her out of her bed and dragged her forcefully by the arm up to the forward deck.

"What . . . what . . . ," Maren stammered. "Oh, God, I feel *sooo* sick."

"That serves you right, you little drunkard. No one drinks himself insensible on my ship!" Then he let her go and poured a bucket of ice-cold seawater on her.

"No!" Maren cried, holding her arms protectively over her head. But the captain seemed to think that one bucket of water wasn't enough to cure a hangover, and he proceeded to empty a second and then a third bucketful over her.

Maren finally managed to get her eyes open. She wiped the water out of her face and looked down at herself. *Oh, God!* The pants, the shirt, everything was sullied. And now she could even smell herself. She'd never felt so ill in her entire life. She was terribly homesick, and she longed for Thies and Finja. She longed to be with someone who had her welfare at heart; someone who'd make her a strong herbal brew against the pounding headache and nausea. She wanted to lie on a soft straw pallet in her box bed, close her eyes, and only open them when her head and her stomach had calmed down again. She wanted fresh clothes, and mostly, she wanted to forget what she could only dimly remember. Had she really danced in front of all the men? Had she laughed and sung? She wanted to shake her head, shake away the dreadful memory, but, oh, it made her head ache. She was so nauseated that she broke into tears.

Captain Boyse put a hand on her shoulder. "What's wrong?" he demanded. "Why are you wailing like that?"

Maren buried her face in her hands, because she was strangely embarrassed to be in his presence with filthy clothes and tangled hair and without her boots. "I want to go home," she said with a sob. She knew she sounded like a small child, but she couldn't stop crying. Everything was terrible here. The hard work, the horrible quarters, the loneliness, and her homesickness for Thies and the island. "I want to go home," she whimpered, and sobbed so hard that her entire body quaked. She didn't care what the captain thought of her anymore. He could think she was weak if he wanted. She just couldn't stand it any longer.

She sank to the deck with her hands still covering her face and cried like she hadn't cried since she'd been a child. She felt inconsolable, as desperate as it was possible for anyone to feel. The homesickness almost broke her heart, and just the thought of having to spend months on end here on the ship made her want to die.

"I want to go home," she whimpered again.

Then she felt a hand gently pushing a strand of hair off of her forehead. The gesture was so tender that for a moment Maren believed Thies had miraculously appeared.

"Get up," a rough male voice said quietly, and to her amazement, Maren recognized the voice as belonging to the captain. But that was impossible. Ever since she'd left Sylt, Boyse had spoken to her only harshly, or had yelled at her. It must be the alcohol still playing tricks on her senses.

She looked up at the captain in confusion. What she saw in his eyes confused her even more. His eyes were very dark, and the taunting gleam in them had disappeared. Instead, he looked worried. She sniffed again, and when the captain used his handkerchief to gently blot the tears from her cheeks, a warm tingle went through her that almost made her forget her homesickness.

"Is it really so bad here?" Boyse asked softly.

Maren nodded but then shook her head. "I . . . I don't know."

He took her hand. "Come," he said. "I'll find you a new place to sleep. It's my fault. I never should have left you alone with all those men." His words were gentle, and Maren almost believed that Boyse had finally stopped hating her and might even give up on the horrible plan of revenge that had made him bring her aboard the ship.

But that hope only lasted for the blink of an eye. Zelda appeared on deck, and Boyse released Maren's hand. His expression became closed again.

"What happened?" Zelda asked.

"She got drunk as a lord," the captain replied.

"Oh, dear," Zelda said, smiling sympathetically. "And now your head is pounding, isn't it?"

Maren wanted to nod, but the motion brought back the smithy in her head.

"Take her with you," the captain ordered his lover.

"With me? Where?"

"To the cabin."

"To our cabin?" Zelda looked at him in disbelief.

"It's my cabin. Do as I say." Then he turned and walked away.

Zelda sighed as he left. "Fine. Let's go, then."

She led Maren halfway across the foredeck and then down wide steps into a small room fitted with several comfortable hammocks. At the end of the walkway between them, she opened a door, and Maren stared in amazement. So this was the captain's cabin! In the middle of the room was a broad wooden platform that held two feather beds and even a proper pillow. A candelabra with beeswax candles made a soft light, and a brazier spread a pleasant warmth.

Maren realized only then that her entire body was shivering. Zelda noticed too. "You're cold? No wonder. You're soaking wet. What did you do?"

Maren's teeth chattered. "The c-captain . . . He emptied a few buckets of water over my head."

Zelda laughed. "Typical. He wanted to sober you up."

"I'm sober," Maren whispered, and actually, her headache wasn't so bad anymore, and her stomach had calmed too.

"Do you have anything else to wear?" Zelda asked.

"In my s-sea chest." Maren's teeth chattered harder.

"Well, you can't expect me to go down there and get it. You'll just have to wear some of my things. Now take off those wet clothes."

Maren obeyed, glad to get the soiled, sour-smelling garments off of her body.

"There's a pitcher and basin with warm water over there, and the soap is next to it. Help yourself while I find something for you to wear."

Maren did as she was asked, relieved to be able to wash properly again. She enjoyed the warm water and the gently perfumed rose-scented soap, and when Zelda helped her wash her hair, she almost felt human again.

"There, put that on." Zelda pointed at a dress that was spread out on the bed.

"That?" Maren spluttered. She went closer and rubbed the soft fabric between her fingers. She'd never felt anything so fine. Not even the most elegant formal wear on Sylt had been so soft. "What kind of material is this?"

Zelda shrugged. "Velvet," she said curtly. "A suitor from Genoa brought it to me." She said it as though it were nothing special, but Maren couldn't stop running her hands over the material.

"Do you plan to stand around half-naked much longer?" Zelda inquired.

Maren quickly slipped into the dress, but the bodice was much too big for her. She glanced at Zelda's breasts, which were twice the size of her own. She tried to lace the stays as tightly as possible, but she still felt half-naked.

Then she brushed her hair, set her sailor's cap on her head, and turned to leave. "I think I'm needed in the kitchen. Jakob will be waiting for me."

Zelda nodded, smiled, and pointed to the cap. "You certainly can't go wearing that thing."

"Why not?"

"The cap doesn't match the dress," Zelda explained, as though it were the most normal thing in the world. "Here, take the bonnet if you don't want to wear your hair loose." She handed Maren a bonnet made of delicate lace, but Maren shook her head.

"I'll just ruin the dress and the bonnet. Sparks fly in the kitchen. It might get a few burn holes and stains."

Zelda waved off her concern. "Keep the dress! I have enough dresses. I only brought that one so I'd have something to trade with if we meet people on the coast of the Arctic sea."

Maren nodded and thanked Zelda with a curtsy. "I'll repay you somehow, I promise. As soon as I can."

"It's not worth mentioning," Zelda said. But Maren had already noticed Zelda wasn't pleased that Maren had been given access to the captain's cabin.

That evening, Maren was about to return to her berth below deck, but Zelda grabbed her by the arm as she passed. "The captain has ordered that as of tonight you must sleep in our cabin."

Maren's forehead creased. "Why?"

"Well, I think he doesn't want to leave you alone with all the men again. Last night they got you drunk. Who knows what they'll think of next?"

Maren nodded, uncomfortable about being so close to the captain. That morning she had seen a completely different side of him, but sharing a cabin with him and his lover was far too intimate for her. Still, she didn't dare argue, so she went to the cabin with Zelda.

Zelda pointed to two straw pallets stacked against the wall, covered with a blanket along with a feather quilt and a pillow. "That's where you'll sleep. I hope you're happy with it."

"Happy? It's the most wonderful bed I've ever seen," she cried. Of course that was an exaggeration, but at that moment it was true for her.

"You can lie down now," Zelda said, and although she'd spoken kindly, Maren heard it as an order. "The captain and I will sit in the wardroom for a while."

Maren nodded and lay down as Zelda left the cabin. The wardroom. Maren knew that was where the officers, mates, harpooners, and blubber cutters dined and drank. The rest of the crew ate wherever they could find a place: on an overturned bucket on deck, on the bare planks, simply standing, or below deck in their berths or hammocks. She herself had never been in the wardroom, but those who had rhapsodized about its grandeur.

She instantly fell into a deep, dreamless sleep. But in the middle of the night, she was awakened by a noise. It sounded like moaning, and Maren wondered if she should get up and see who was in pain.

It was Zelda's voice; she recognized it. The whimpering and panting sounded absolutely dreadful, but then she heard the rough voice of the captain.

"Come, open for me. I know exactly what you need."

"Yes, you do know," Zelda answered. Then her moaning became louder. The bedstead shook rhythmically, and it sounded as though two naked bodies were falling on each other.

Maren sat up and peered into the darkness at them, and after a while, she could make out Zelda's slender body twisting under the captain's. In that moment, she understood. The two of them were doing what only married people should do, what she herself had done just once with Thies. Maren felt a wave of shame and indignation. But there was another feeling. A tingling between her legs. Just there, where . . . She groaned softly and turned over to face the wall, the blanket clamped firmly between her thighs. She squeezed her eyelids tightly shut. But then she became too warm. She would have liked to shake off the blankets to cool her overheated body, but she didn't dare to do that either. What was wrong with her? And why did the captain's quiet, hoarse laughter send a shiver down her back? And why did she suddenly hate Zelda as deeply as she'd otherwise only hated Grit? She wanted to stuff that seductive laugh and sultry moaning right back down her throat.

She lay there that way for a long time, with a burning lap and overheated limbs, until she finally heard the captain's snoring, became calmer, and slowly found sleep.

CHAPTER 17

The days began to blend into one another. Every morning, Maren got up and went to Jakob in the galley and worked until her back and feet hurt, her hands were rough and dry, and her eyes stung from the smoke. Then she got her meal and devoured it while sitting on a coil of rope or an overturned bucket on deck. When it rained, she pulled an old piece of sailcloth over her head. In the evening, after all the galley work was done, she returned to the captain's cabin. Some mornings she was so nauseated she could barely keep down the piece of dry hardtack she was given for breakfast. In the galley, too, she felt more and more unwell from day to day. She couldn't bear the smell of sauerkraut without having to be sick. She became nauseated when cutting salt pork, but now when she cut onions, her mouth watered.

Jakob observed all this with skepticism. "It doesn't seem right," he said. "You should've gotten over being seasick by now. It's usually that way, in any case." He scratched his chin. "Well," he said quietly, more to himself than to her, "but the others were all men. Who knows how women react to seasickness?" He gave her a rag dipped in vinegar to place on her neck, but that made her feel worse.

Jakob shrugged. "I'm sorry that you're not feeling well, but I can't do without your help. At least, not until we've reached the whaling grounds."

"Don't worry," Maren replied. "I'm not sick. I'm doing fine. I feel healthy. Maybe I just need to get used to the food here on board. And the sea air." She continued to work efficiently, but every evening she was desperately tired, so tired that her bones hurt.

As soon as she lay down on her pallet in the captain's cabin, she closed her eyes tightly so she'd be deeply asleep by the time the captain and Zelda came in. She didn't want to hear what the two of them were doing—but at the same time, she didn't want to miss a moan. Every time she listened to their amorous play, her body began to glow. Blood flowed hotly through her veins and pulsed in her arteries, her heart pounded swiftly, and her mouth became dry. She felt a pleasant tingling between her legs that lingered long after the captain and Zelda had fallen asleep.

Tonight she lay awake again with her eyes squeezed shut as they entered the cabin. Maren heard Zelda giggle.

"Quiet. We'll wake her," the captain ordered.

"Why must we always take heed not to wake her? Why is she sleeping in our cabin? I thought it was just for one night, but she's been with us so long I can't enjoy myself anymore. It's time for her to go back below deck."

"No." His voice was harsh and stern.

"Why not?"

"I explained that to you already. She's not safe there."

"So she's to live with us in the cabin for the entire voyage? Why did you bring her anyway?"

Maren breathed as flatly and quietly as she could. She didn't know why she was suddenly so nervous, but she was desperate to hear the captain's answer.

"She's under my protection," he growled. "You don't need to know any more than that."

You don't need to know any more than that? Maren thought. Hadn't Boyse told his lover that he had intended to marry Maren? No, obviously not. And now that she knew Zelda a bit better, she knew that it wouldn't make her friendlier if she found out. But why hadn't Boyse said anything? Was he so ashamed of her rejection? But why? He had Zelda, and he had been with her for a long time. Why hadn't he married *her*?

"I thought I was somewhat more to you than a harbor whore," Zelda complained, her voice unusually emotional.

Maren heard Boyse swallow. "I like you; you know that. And I've always treated you well. But you don't have the rights of a wife."

His words were calm, almost kind, but Maren shrank away from them as from the crack of a whip, even though they hadn't been intended for her.

She could feel Zelda stiffen. Then the woman spun around so fast that her skirts swished. "Well, then, you don't need me here," she said, and she left the cabin.

Maren carefully opened one eye. She saw Boyse standing in the middle of the cabin, scratching his neck. Then he glanced toward her, and she quickly closed her eyes. A little later, she finally fell asleep.

It got colder every day, even though it was the end of May. They had been traveling for over three months toward their destination, the waters between Greenland and Newfoundland. The blows of coopers' hammers as they built barrels to hold the whale blubber had been echoing through the ship all day. Harpooners and blubber cutters sharpened harpoons and flensing knives with huge whetstones, smiths forged harpoon tips in glowing fires, and sailors made space on deck to process the blubber, while the ship's boys mended sails and scrubbed planks. Everyone had his tasks, and Captain Boyse saw to it that they were done properly.

The closer they came to the expanse between the seventy-fourth and seventy-seventh degrees of latitude, the faster life on board changed. They practiced for the whale hunt even though it was so cold that water froze overnight in buckets on deck and frost stiffened the sails so that they rattled loudly. The captain had already chosen the whaleboat crews that would leave the brig to go on the hunt. Every whaleboat had a harpooner, four oarsmen, and a boatheader to steer the boat and lead the crew.

They practiced again and again. First, they practiced lowering the whaleboats from the brig, then boarding, steering, and the motions of the hunt. The harpooner cast harpoons, and the sailors practiced pulling the unimaginably huge whale back to the mother ship. Then it was left to the blubber cutters, the try cookers (the men who rendered the blubber into whale oil in the huge try-pots), ship's boys, and everyone else aboard the brig. The blubber cutters would stand atop the whale to flense it, and helpers would sit in a small boat nearby to hand them tools. Others waited on deck to cut the blubber into smaller pieces as quickly as possible and stow it in barrels. They practiced until the boatheaders were satisfied with their crews and Captain Boyse could find no fault with their work either.

Some got injured during practice and had to be replaced. And so it happened that young Raik became part of a whaleboat crew. His job as cabin boy was filled by a galley drudge, and, thanks to the rotation of tasks, Maren ended up as part of the team helping the blubber cutters. As long as she was only practicing, Maren found the work fun. She didn't have to hunch over all the time anymore, and her back and feet no longer ached so terribly. The men she worked with sang bawdy sea shanties and made jokes.

Captain Boyse watched the sea carefully. He stood at the rail for hours on end, watching his crew practicing, and staring at the water. Every now and then, he lowered a bucket down to the sea, filled it, and pulled it up. Then he sniffed the water and even stuck a finger in to taste it.

"What's he doing?" Maren asked.

"The captain is looking for krill," an experienced blubber cutter replied.

"What's krill?"

"It's what whales eat. When the sea has a certain color, smell, and taste, it means there is krill in it. And where there's krill, there are whales."

"Is there krill here now?"

The blubber cutter bent over the rail. "It's not enough for a whale yet, but it won't be much longer."

Two days passed. Two days during which the men, clad in warm coats and caps against the cold, stood on deck and gazed at the sea, stretching gray as lead before them. Occasionally, they passed icebergs or saw another ship on the horizon. Few spoke. They sometimes pointed into the distance when they thought they'd seen something moving and believed it might be a whale. But so far, it hadn't been.

When she wasn't practicing handing flensing knives to the blubber cutters, Maren scrubbed pots and pans in the galley, cut bread into chunks and vegetables into pieces, and watched the sea too. The entire brig seemed to be holding its breath. There was a certain tension in everyone, from the captain to the lowliest ship's boy. None of them wanted to miss the sighting of the first whale. And even though the wind whipped over their unprotected faces and tore at their coats and hair, and the icy waves cast spray into the air, everyone watched and waited. Captain Boyse had put a ship's boy into a bosun's chair and had him hoisted up the mast to the crow's nest. Every hour he called, "What do you see?"

"Nothing in sight, Captain," the boy would reply.

After three days, the color and smell of the water had grown stronger, and the whalers were growing impatient. It wasn't just the captain who called to the lookout, but everyone else as well, so the boy didn't have a moment of peace.

"It's time," the men said to each other and nodded.

The harpooners checked and rechecked their harpoons and lines, the blubber cutters sharpened their knives, and the officers bent over their charts, observed the stars, and consulted the compass. But nothing happened.

That evening, Maren was already lying in her bed when the captain entered the cabin. Zelda hadn't slept there since she'd left in anger, but that didn't seem to bother Boyse. Now he was lying in his bed, and Maren could hear from his restless, shallow breathing that he was still awake.

"Will the whales come tomorrow?" she asked. She had let herself become caught up by the men's enthusiasm for the hunt a long time ago.

"Maybe," Boyse answered.

"And if they don't?"

"Then they'll come the next day. Go to sleep now."

For a little while, all was quiet, until Maren was overwhelmed by curiosity. "Zelda . . . Is she angry at me?"

"Why should she be angry?"

"Because I'm sleeping here, and now she doesn't come anymore."

"Let that be my concern."

The captain turned to face the wall to indicate that he wanted to sleep, but Maren continued anyway. She used the cover of darkness to finally ask the question that had been burning in her mind. "Why did you want to marry me if you have Zelda?"

"That's none of your concern," the captain grumbled.

"Is she . . . I mean . . . Does she also have a debt to you?" Maren had asked the question softly, so she was even more startled when Boyse leapt out of his bed and grabbed her hard by the shoulder.

"Don't ever say such a thing!" he ordered her. "I would never sleep with a woman just because she owed me something. Zelda is no whore to me, and I'm no whoremonger. Is that clear?"

Maren nodded apprehensively. She realized that her question had irritated the captain more than she'd expected, but she couldn't understand why.

"Please forgive me," she blurted. "I didn't realize you were in love with Zelda."

This time, the captain grabbed Maren by both shoulders and shook her as though she were a feather bed.

"I don't love Zelda. She's only my bed partner. My affairs are none of your business. Is that clear? Do you understand?"

Maren swallowed and then nodded. She'd rarely seen Boyse so enraged, and she didn't understand why her questions seemed so inappropriate to him. After all, he'd asked her only a few months ago if she would be his wife. But since Boyse was already angry, she decided to risk repeating her first question.

"But if you had Zelda, then why did you want to marry me?" She prepared herself to be shaken again, but surprisingly, the captain remained calm.

"Zelda isn't the kind of woman who's interested in marriage. She loves her freedom too much. We've known each other for years, and we like each other. But we're not in love. A man should feel more than friendship for the woman he marries and wants to have children and a home with."

Maren lay still, barely daring to breathe. Did that mean the captain felt something for her? No, that was something she couldn't possibly imagine.

She was just opening her mouth to ask when he growled, "Go to sleep now. Your questions are wearing on my patience."

CHAPTER 18

The crew spent two more days in tense expectation. The weather had calmed somewhat, and every now and then, the sun broke through the clouds. The light was clear and so bright it made Maren's eyes water, and the wind was icy and sharp as needles. Icebergs drifted in the distance, but they were much too small to cause any trouble for the *Rán*. The men lingered on deck. Some of them whittled gifts for their wives and children. Others slept, and still others smoked their pipes and stared at the water. It was quiet on deck, and only the clattering from the galleys and the rolling of dice tossed on an upturned barrel could be heard.

Maren ambled over the deck, her hands bracing her sore back, and held her face to the sharp sunlight.

"Be careful," Jakob the cook warned her. "Smear a little butter on your skin. The sun here will burn you very fast."

But Maren laughed, shook her head, and went to find Raik. "Are you excited about the whales too?" she asked.

"Of course. Everyone is."

"But aren't you afraid of the hunt?"

Raik shook his head. "I want to be a boatheader someday. It'll be easier if I distinguish myself by showing courage and bravery now. Besides, my family needs the money." Raik came from Amrum, the island closest to Sylt. Maren knew that his father was dead and his mother alone with his four younger siblings. Now he was the provider for his family. And she? Was she not the provider for her family? Wasn't she here to pay off her family's debts? Her father was dead too. And she, too, was now responsible.

Finally, after hour upon hour of waiting, the lad in the crow's nest cried out with excitement. "Thar she blows! She blows!"

The sky was strewn with thick clouds that promised rain or snow. The wind blew briskly, but too weakly to be a storm. It was glorious whaling weather.

Everyone who wasn't working on something vital ran up on deck and gazed in the direction the lookout had indicated. It was true. On the horizon, a black mountain rose out of the waves and sprayed a gigantic spout of water into the air.

"There!" the sailors cried. "And there!" The spout appeared again and again. "There's an entire pod of them!" the men declared.

Captain Boyse was standing ready on the deck. "Prepare to lower the whaleboats!" he cried.

Maren stood at the rail, and Zelda stood beside her, seemingly harboring no grudge against her.

The brig slowly approached the gigantic creatures. Whaleboats were lowered, and the harpooners stood ready with their harpoons in hand and shouted orders to the oarsmen.

"Lay into your oarlocks, you fiends! Pull the oars! Dead ahead!"

Maren watched in fascination. She'd never seen such immense animals in her entire life. One was just rising up out of the water. She noted the grayish-black coloring of the creature, the huge head with the arched lower lip that was higher than a man was tall, and the white area under the animal's mouth. The massive tail flukes whipped the water into high swells, making the whaleboats rock dangerously. But nothing happened. The boats slowly closed in on the whales, and the whales glided unhurriedly through the water. Every now and then, they blew spouts into the air, rose up, and dove down again. The crew had been practicing for this moment for weeks.

Maren glanced at Zelda, remembering her nighttime conversation with the captain. Was Zelda waiting for Boyse to propose? Did she love him? She must, otherwise she wouldn't have given herself to him so shamelessly and joyously in the darkness of the cabin. She opened her mouth to ask, but suddenly the captain hurried past behind her. He glanced at Maren, and his dark eyes pierced her. Boyse's look was a silent question: Could he trust her? Maren nodded almost imperceptibly. As much as she wanted to know whether Zelda loved the captain, she wanted him to trust her more. She almost had to laugh at the thought of it. She, the lowliest of all the sailors, was the captain's confidante.

She wouldn't mind if he didn't hate her anymore. But she wasn't completely certain that he didn't. Of course, she'd noticed that the captain's eyes followed her as soon as they encountered each other. But his gaze, which smoldered like a dark fire, was inscrutable. Was it a look of annoyance? Or of—oh, no, she didn't want to think about it.

Someone shouted from one of the whaleboats. "See the huge one there? That would be a feast! Straight ahead!"

The waves had grown higher and were now topped with whitecaps. In comparison, the whaleboats looked no larger than nutshells in the distance. They rode up the crests of the waves, and just when it looked like the sea had swallowed them, they reappeared in the trough before the next swell. The oarsmen bent low and pulled on their oars, while the harpooners stood straight and true as though anchored in position and held their harpoons ready.

The first two whaleboats set their sails as they approached the whales, coming so close they had to maneuver around the huge gray tail flukes. The boats flew through the water, and Maren was amazed at how the harpooners managed to remain upright and keep shouting their orders to the boatheaders over the sound of the foaming, roiling sea.

Finally, a whale rose so near to the bow of the brig that his spout sprayed the deck. Maren cried out, but not because she got wet. She cried out because the whale was so huge, the most unimaginably gigantic creature that she had ever seen.

"Look, look!" she shouted, tugging excitedly on Zelda's sleeve. The animal, a bowhead whale, was a good twenty yards long and had gray flukes that were almost as big as one of the whaleboats.

The whaleboats circled the creature, and the harpooners threw their harpoons, which hissed through the air. One of the harpoons tore off its line, and the harpooner cursed loudly. The harpooner in the second whaleboat missed his mark, but the third harpoon sank deeply into the flesh of the gigantic animal. Blood flowed, and the sea turned red. The whale twisted wildly and the boat rocked, but the harpooners held the lines. Then the whale pulled away, towing the whaleboats behind it like hapless toys. Shouts went from boat to boat, and Boyse stood at the rail and shouted orders, which were swallowed by the sound of the churning sea.

Maren had her hands in front of her mouth. She didn't know whether her heart was breaking for the gigantic creature or she was afraid for the men. Zelda stood next to her, pale and tense. More harpoons flew through the air, stopping the whale's escape. Blood spurted from its body. The rest of the whaleboats had surrounded the injured animal, and more and more harpoons were thrown. The whale reared up in one last effort to escape, and then it became calmer. Two whaleboats closed in. Maren held her breath. And then it happened. The whale struck out with its gigantic tail and hit the narrow stern of one of the boats, which pitched dangerously. But the other boats were already there. The harpooners struck their killing blows, and finally the animal was still and silent in the blood-red sea.

"The poor creature!" Maren truly felt pity for the whale. Tears pooled in her eyes, but Zelda grabbed her sleeve.

"This is no time to start sniveling. You should be thinking about the fact that every dead animal means hard coin for you." She turned around and disappeared below deck.

Maren wiped away her tears. Zelda was right, but the death of the whale still affected her deeply. Such a huge animal—the king of the ocean! Hunted and killed by humans who weren't even a tenth the size. She sighed and gazed over at Boyse, who stood a few paces from her, looking very pleased. The oarsmen in the whaleboats were towing the dead creature through the sea toward them, leaving a wide trail of blood. They approached slowly, and Maren could see that the oarsmen were reaching the end of their strength.

Finally, they managed to bring the carcass astern the brig. They secured it, and the rest of the crew's work began. The harpooners boarded, their eyes glowing with the satisfaction of a successful hunt. Boyse clapped them on the shoulders, and they nodded silently and went about coiling their lines and cleaning their harpoons, while the others drew the gigantic carcass alongside and tied it to the starboard side of the ship.

The blubber cutters descended, walking along the whale as though it were a boardwalk. They began by cutting giant "blanket pieces" of blubber. With block and tackle, the crew hoisted the blubber directly onto the deck of the brig. There, another team carved the huge pieces into smaller ones and stowed them in barrels.

Everyone aboard the *Rán* was busy, and Maren, emptying a bucket of peelings from the galley over the rail, paused for a moment to watch. Zelda stood next to her, but she wasn't half as impressed as Maren was. Maren's curiosity didn't last long, though, because the smell of the blubber nauseated her. She felt so sick that she had to throw up over the rail several times. Zelda stroked her back, filled a cup from the drinking-water barrel on deck, and handed it to her.

"Move on, womenfolk! You're standing in the way there!" the head blubber cutter said, glaring in annoyance at both of them. "Go below deck or somewhere else!"

Zelda took Maren by the arm and led her to the center of the ship, directly under one of the masts.

"Tell me, do you have a suitor?"

"A suitor? What makes you say that?" Maren realized that during the last few weeks, she'd spent less and less time thinking about Thies. Yes, she missed him, especially during the hours when she had a little time for herself. But her mental picture of him was already fading a little, and she hadn't smelled his scent in so long that she could barely remember it. She wondered if he missed her.

"Do you have one or not?" Zelda insisted.

"Yes, I do. We're engaged. We'll be married in November."

"I thought so." Zelda regarded Maren as though her words had changed everything. "And he let you go off with these whalers alone?"

Maren shrugged. She realized that she was annoyed at Thies, angry at him for sending her to Greenland. Well, he hadn't really sent her; he hadn't even known her plans. But he probably wouldn't have tried to stop her if he'd known. Or was she being unfair? What could he have done? He had his mother and sister to care for. *He should have gone to the mainland to get a loan,* Maren thought, and she was suddenly so upset at Thies that she groaned. No, he never should have let her go! He should have gone with Captain Boyse in her place. And if Boyse hadn't wanted him, then he should have . . . Oh, she didn't know. She knew that her anger wasn't fair, but at the moment, she felt lonely and abandoned. But what could Thies have actually done? He'd tried to get hired on a ship but hadn't been successful. Yes, she was irritated, but she didn't want to make Thies look bad in front of Zelda.

"We had no choice," she explained. "I have debts with the captain, and I'm here to work them off."

"Really?" Zelda narrowed her eyes as though that was impossible for her to believe. "Boyse brought you because of your debts?"

Maren nodded, and Zelda's eyebrows pulled together in consternation. "Is there anything else between you and the captain?"

"No. We've known each other for a long time, but that's not any wonder because we're both from Sylt." Maren didn't know herself why she didn't tell Zelda about Boyse's marriage proposal.

"And he knows about your fiancé too?"

"Yes, he knows him. Thies is also a sailor. Last winter he studied with Boyse for his officer's commission."

"And the captain still didn't want to have him aboard his ship?"

"No."

Maren stared stubbornly at the blubber cutters, who were making a huge amount of noise with their shouting and cursing, but she couldn't avoid Zelda's question that way.

"So you have a fiancé with an officer's commission, and you're still here to work off your debts?"

The way Zelda said it, it sounded cruel, as though Thies had sent her on this journey purposefully. But it hadn't happened like that. But then, how had it happened?

"It's none of your concern," Maren finally said, sounding a little petulant. "Stop asking questions! I don't know anything about you either. Not even why you're here on this ship."

For a while neither woman spoke, the silence between them broken only by the cursing of the blubber cutters. Behind them, men were cutting the blanket pieces apart with huge knives and layering smaller pieces into the barrels. Their arms and hands dripped with blood, and the smell of the dead animal hung over the *Rán* like a cloud.

Then Zelda put a hand on Maren's arm. "You're right. I shouldn't ask you. And if you'd really like to know why I'm here, I'd be glad to tell you."

Maren shook her head. What use was it? Nothing tied her to Zelda. She didn't care if she was here or somewhere else.

"Why are you here?" she heard herself ask.

Zelda sighed, and all at once, her face became earnest. "I'm growing old, you know. As a whore, you're only desired as long as you're young. Two years ago, I bought the house in Amsterdam, and I can afford to let my girls do the work alone. I still feel too young to retire, but there are weeks when I earn next to nothing. Boyse offered to take me on the trip and pay me for it. He's never done that before, even though we've known each other for a long time. Sometimes I think he did it out of pity, you know?"

"Boyse? Pity? Never!" Maren shook her head.

Zelda shrugged. "I could hardly believe it either, but he paid me, and now I'm here."

The women were silent again. Maren stole a glance at Zelda from the side. She noticed a few wrinkles around her eyes. Her hair, too, had a few strands of gray mixed in. She appeared young with the kohl around her eyes, her red cheeks, the ribbons in her hair, and her tight bodice. But she wasn't. Not anymore.

Suddenly Maren felt pity for Zelda. Maren would return to the island, marry, bear children, and have a respectable life. She would never be rich, but it didn't matter. Thies and she were destined for each other, and that alone was enough for happiness.

"Have you lain with him yet?" The question took her so much by surprise that Maren gasped.

"What?"

"Have you lain with your fiancé?" Zelda repeated her question.

Maren would have liked to leave, but something in the other woman's voice made her feel obliged to answer. "Yes. I did. One time, right before we left. One last proof of love, you understand?"

Zelda nodded. "I understand more than you think. You're sick almost every morning, and your breasts seem to have grown larger. You're with child, Maren."

Maren stared at her disbelievingly, her eyes wide with terror. "That . . . that can't be true. You can't get with child the first . . . first time."

But she looked so scared that it was clear she didn't believe her own words.

"Well, I don't know for certain, but all the signs are there. When did you leave Sylt?"

Maren's brow wrinkled as she counted back. "It was four months ago. First, we went to Amsterdam, and now we've been at sea for weeks and weeks."

"That means you're in your fifth month," Zelda explained. "As far as I can tell, you'll have a baby in about four months."

CHAPTER 19

The days and weeks went by in a rush, and the crew caught a whale almost every week. Even though the creatures were slow, they often managed to get away, and the whalers returned to the ship empty-handed. Maren had meanwhile learned more about the animals. She learned that they communicated with each other through sounds, mysterious sounds that made her think of a gathering of witches. They squeaked, whistled, howled, and grunted enough to terrify anyone, and many seamen believed that whales were sea demons, and prayed as soon as they saw a spout of water on the horizon. Once the whaleboats had chased a mother whale and her baby, and then it was Maren who prayed, prayed that both of them would escape the harpooners.

She also learned what their gigantic "beards" were for. The comb-like beard was called *baleen* and hung on the whale's upper jaw like a curtain. The animal used it to filter the water, catching the krill in it. The baleen grew between one and four yards long and was used by people to make corset boning, riding crops, umbrellas, walking sticks, and baskets. Once, Maren had touched a piece of baleen and had been amazed. The baleen plates were solid and smooth but also flexible. She remembered the feel of corset boning against her ribs.

When she wasn't busy in the kitchen, she helped to cut up the large pieces of blubber and pack them in barrels. On land, the blubber would be rendered into oil, which would be used as fuel for lamps and to manufacture soaps, paints, and gelatin. Blubber was also used aboard the *Rán*: the leftover scraps were cooked in the try-pots to make enough oil and soap for their own use, and the seamen rubbed their bodies with the fat to protect their skin against the cold.

The days flew by, and the nights were shorter than Maren could believe. They went farther and farther north, and as they traveled, the temperatures dropped. Almost every morning now, the drinking water was frozen, and the *Rán* got closer and closer to the solid Arctic ice pack.

At the beginning of the voyage, Maren had lost track of the days of the week, and now she barely knew what month it was. Zelda had returned to the captain's cabin and had hung a curtain made of old sailcloth between Maren's straw pallet and the bed. Maren didn't mind at all. Just like she didn't mind being with child as long as she didn't have to think about it. According to Zelda, she was now in her seventh month, but thanks to the loose men's clothing she wore, no one had noticed. She'd made Zelda promise not to tell anyone. But Maren realized that as her time approached, she would no longer be able to hide her condition. What should she do? If she were very lucky, they might reach land in time for the birth. And if she were even luckier, no one would notice her condition until then. But it wasn't very likely.

The *Rán* drew near to the island of Spitsbergen and had almost reached the Hinlopen Strait. The crew, encouraged by Captain Boyse, was in hunting fever. They had not yet filled all the barrels with blubber, and the water still had the color and smell of krill. Now their goal was to take in the best catch that a whaling ship ever had and earn so much money that every man and his family would get through the next winter comfortably. No one could predict how good the conditions would be next year, so they went out in the whaleboats every day. Maren stood in a dinghy and handed the blubber cutters their flensing knives. Almost every time, she got soaked to the bone, and the smell of the whale blood made her nauseated. She often had to bend over the side of the dinghy to throw up. While she was emptying her stomach, she could hear the blubber cutters shouting.

"The serrated knife! Quick, give it to me!"

She didn't even have time to rinse her mouth. She just reached for the knife and passed it along.

At night, she lay on her straw pallet in complete exhaustion. Sometimes she found time to stroke her belly, but she just couldn't believe that a little person was growing inside. Occasionally, when she was half asleep, Maren heard Zelda's lustful moaning, but she hadn't been interested in what was going on behind the sailcloth for weeks. She managed to do what was asked of her, and the rest of the time, she lay on her straw pallet, too exhausted even to think about Thies. Her days were defined by work and sleep. She even stopped worrying when the men were given their rations of Branntwein, since she was practically falling asleep on her feet.

Sometimes, when she had a short break, she sat on a coil of rope on deck and closed her eyes, sleeping while the rest of the crew milled around her and cursed loudly. Sometimes she didn't even hear the bosun's whistle, which called the crew to evening prayer and otherwise served to draw attention to the officers' commands.

Zelda helped her when she could. She brought Maren meat and eggs from the wardroom, made sure her clothing was loose enough and let it out when necessary, and helped her to wrap her ever-expanding belly with cloth compresses for support. Zelda kept urging her to tell the captain the truth so she wouldn't have to keep working as a helper for the blubber cutters. It was a job in which one got injured sooner or later.

Maren knew she had to think about what would happen when she returned to the island with a baby. Would Thies be happy? Even though the child would be illegitimate? It wouldn't be for long. Only until they married. Maren had optimistically suggested to Zelda that perhaps they would be back before her time came, but the experienced woman had shaken her head. "Imagine the worse possible outcome, and then try to come up with a solution. Then you'll be all right. And if it turns out better, then you can be happy."

And then one day, everything changed. A powerful wind mixed with snow and sleet blew over the sea. A blizzard raged, shook the masts, tore at the sails, and threatened to wash everything on deck over the rail. The wood of the hull creaked and groaned. There was no time to think about whaling. It had grown so cold that the drinking water on deck was frozen during the day, and one had to cut out a piece of ice and melt it in order to drink. Some of the sailors got sick. They coughed and glowed with fever. In every protected place, pullovers and vests hung to dry. The men had stuffed their boots with straw and wrapped rags around their feet. Whoever had warm stockings or a sweater made of women's hair was a king. Maren could hardly remember a day when she hadn't been freezing. After dark, she could barely get warm at all. The cold had crept through to her bones, and at night she often wrapped herself in every piece of clothing she owned to keep the baby in her belly from freezing. Once, she'd talked about the baby with Zelda.

"Are you happy about it?" the older woman asked.

"I don't know. It's wonderful to have a child, especially with the man I love. But the timing is not especially advantageous."

"Of course you're right about that. You must prepare yourself for the fact that the child may die. Or that you may die yourself. You know that, don't you?"

"Why do you say such things?" Maren recoiled in horror from Zelda's words.

"I say it because I always prepare myself for the worst and then look for a solution. Many women die in childbirth. You're young and strong, but you should still prepare yourself. You have to write down who the child's father is, what its name should be, and where it should be taken if something happens to you."

Maren hated to think about it, but at the same time, she knew that Zelda was right.

"And think about what would happen if your fiancé won't acknowledge the child."

Maren made a face. "Why shouldn't he? I've never had anyone but him."

"Well, you don't know what's happening to him now. And you've been away a long time. Sometimes things change."

"Our love will never change!"

Now Maren thought about this while standing at the rail watching the icebergs drift around like fat gray ghosts.

"It's time for us to head for home," Jakob said, coming up beside her and tipping a bucketful of galley waste over the rail.

"I'd be glad to," Maren replied, pointing at the icebergs. "It's getting colder. And we haven't seen a whale in weeks." That morning, she had been woken before dawn as the ship groaned terribly. Maren had believed that it might even break. She got up and went on deck. It was still pitch-dark, broken by the light from a single lantern. She leaned over the rail and saw that big pieces of drift ice were beginning to obstruct the progress of the *Rán*. Again and again, the brig creaked and strained against the press of the ice.

"Isn't the ice dangerous?" she asked Jakob. "It sounds like the whole ship is breaking apart."

Jakob shook his head. "There's still enough space for us between the floes, and it wouldn't be bad to catch one or two more whales. There are still a few empty barrels. Most of the other ships have already turned for home, but I believe the captain won't turn around until the last barrel is filled to the brim. He's never been satisfied with anything less."

Maren didn't answer. What could she say? She'd been on the whaling ship for months, but she still didn't know if the trip would be worth her while. She only knew that it was in her interest to catch as many whales as possible. That's why she partly didn't mind that they were still out on the icy sea, but on the other hand, she wanted nothing more than to go home and have her baby there.

The wind grew stronger overnight. Icy gusts howled over the sea. The men couldn't stand to be on deck for more than a few moments because their beards froze almost immediately. The clouds hung so low that Maren believed that she could almost touch them, and the icebergs seemed to be larger and closer together. Maren saw that the ship's boy in the crow's nest had brought up a brazier with a few glowing coals to warm his icy fingers. When his cry rang out, she'd seen what he had at the same moment. "Thar she blows! She blows!"

The men always appeared on deck within a few seconds of hearing the call and lowered the whaleboats immediately. But this time it took a little longer. Their excitement was diminished too. The men seemed exhausted and listless. They got in the boats, the oarsmen took the oars, and the harpooners stood ready with their harpoons as they always had, but Maren could see that their eagerness, their bloodlust, and their passion had become frozen too. Boyse shouted to his men from the deck, but the storm tore the words from his mouth.

The whaleboats slowly approached the whale. It was an especially large animal, and it thrashed in the water and threw spray into the air on all sides, soaking the men. The first harpoon flew wide and missed its target. The second one hit, but the whale twisted so wildly in the roiling, foaming water that the line broke.

"Ho! Are you all blind?" Boyse shouted angrily from the deck. "Go catch that creature!"

More harpoons flew, and blood ran down the gigantic animal and turned the sea red. But the whale didn't surrender. It twisted and pounded with its tail, capsizing one of the boats. Two others came about to rescue the men in the water, leaving no opening for the harpooners. Then the whale, still bleeding from its wounds, splintered the capsized boat and sent the planks flying. The other boats turned back, but Boyse blustered. "Have you all lost your minds? Get that whale! Hurry! Don't come back without it!"

Despite his rage, the boats continued back toward the ship. The whale, which was badly injured and obviously reaching the end of its strength, drifted in the bloody sea. Then the first boatful of soaked, exhausted men arrived at the ship, but Boyse wouldn't let them aboard.

"Go!" he cried. "We're going to catch that damned creature! Go, men!" He pushed the strongest man back into the boat and tore the spear out of the harpooner's hand. "You're all lily-livered cowards!"

Boyse had been transformed by the fervor of the hunt. He shouted wildly at his men.

Finally, the whaleboat was occupied by five men and the captain. He drove the oarsmen mercilessly, and the men gave all the strength they had left.

"It's madness," one of the men who'd just returned to the ship said. He was soaking wet and had a bleeding wound. "One whaleboat alone! How are they going to catch the whale? They'll all perish."

The whale had gathered its strength, and it floundered in the foaming sea again, rearing up and crashing back into the water, making huge waves that rocked the whaleboat dangerously. But Boyse stood solid as a rock, threw his harpoon, and let the line run through his hands. He drove the oarsmen on and threw a second harpoon, but the creature was still twisting in pain and batted at the boat with its massive flukes, hitting it on the pointed stern. Even though no one on the brig heard the wood crack, everyone flinched. One of the oarsmen went overboard. Two others reached for him and pulled him back into the boat, but Boyse seemed not to notice his men's distress. Tirelessly, he cast one harpoon after another at the dying animal, which was writhing in agony.

One of the officers put his hands around his mouth to project his voice and cried, "Turn back! Turn back. You won't be able to do it!" But the storm blew his words away, and Captain Boyse threw his last harpoon. And the whale, fighting for its life, reared up once more and created huge swells as it fell back in the water. Blood ran down its powerful body and stained the sea red.

The whale fought to the last, swimming toward the tiny whaleboat. When it had almost passed them, it raised its tail and slapped the water so the boat simply tipped over. Maren screamed, and then she saw the men's heads bob to the surface in the distance like tiny pins, while the dying whale distilled all the pain of its torture into its final twitches.

"Lower the last whaleboat. Hurry! All men to the boat!"

But there *were* no more men. The exhausted oarsmen had dragged themselves below deck. The only ones left on deck were Maren, old Jakob, and two or three sailors.

"Hurry! Get in the boat or they'll all drown!"

Drown! The word shook Maren awake. *The captain! No, he mustn't drown! No, never!* Pain and a nameless fear tightened around Maren's chest. She didn't think about the child in her womb; she only thought of Boyse. How could she live without him?

Faster than she could think, and faster than her thoughts would have allowed, she sprang into the whaleboat. She didn't realize what she was doing. She reacted instinctively, the way animals do.

The officer wanted to send her back, but there wasn't time. It was terribly cold, and the sea was an icy grave. Time was pressing. There was no one else there to help. So the officer, the sailors, and old Jakob sprang into the whaleboat after her. The mate ordered Maren to take the rudder. She had never done it herself before, but she had watched. Her heart and mind were filled with terror. But without thinking, she did what was necessary.

The oarsmen leaned into their work, breathing heavily under the strain. They gave all they had, but to Maren, everything seemed to be moving in slow motion. It felt to her as though heavy weights were hanging on the back of the whaleboat, dragging against their progress. The roiling sea sent the boat hopping from wave to wave like a leaf. Water slopped over the sides again and again, and Maren gasped every time the cold spray hit her. She kept her eyes focused straight ahead on the men bobbing in the blood-red sea. Clumps of ice rammed the boat with loud crunching and cracking sounds. One of the oarsmen lost an oar from sheer exhaustion.

"We have to turn back. There's no point," the officer cried.

"No!" Maren cried. "We've almost made it. We can't let them drown!"

With their last strength, the men strained at the oars, pale with exhaustion, cold sweat running down their foreheads.

They finally got close enough. One sailor was pulled aboard, and then another only half-conscious. One sank before her eyes in the tossing sea, and another was floating facedown in the waves, drifting farther and farther away from them.

"Where's Boyse?" Maren cried. She searched on all sides, her heart racing painfully. She was dizzy with cold, but still she searched the waves. And finally, finally she saw him. He was floating and sometimes sinking, reappearing, and sinking again. "There! There!" Maren shouted, directing the oarsmen.

They couldn't do it. They couldn't get close enough to Boyse. Every time it seemed like they would reach him, he sank again and reappeared a little farther away. Blood flowed from a wound on Boyse's forehead, and the officer tried to pull his almost-lifeless body closer to the boat with a harpoon, but he couldn't reach.

"Someone has to get in the water!" Maren shouted.

"That would be certain death," the officer replied.

But then Maren jumped. She didn't think about not being able to swim. She didn't think at all, at least not of herself. But she had to try. Her past disappeared instantly, and she lived only in the present moment, lived only to rescue the captain.

Her heavy boots pulled her downward, and the ice-cold water robbed her of her breath, but she fought for her life. The icy wetness numbed her limbs, and her clothing became waterlogged, making her heavier and heavier. She gasped for air and saw dark stars burst behind her eyes. But then finally Boyse reappeared in front of her, and she reached for him. She grabbed him by the sleeve, and then the mate's whale iron was there for her to hold on to, helping her pull the weight of the unconscious man to the whaleboat. And the oarsmen, who had grown almost apathetic with exhaustion, now sprang up and heaved the unwieldy body of the captain on board, and then they reached out to Maren and pulled her out of the icy water too.

CHAPTER 20

It felt as though she were floating up out of the depths of the water, as soft as mist.

For a blink of an eye, she saw a woman's face hovering over her. She knew the woman, but she couldn't remember her name. And then she sank back below the surface. She rose again, the face was suddenly clearer, and she recognized Zelda.

"What . . . what happened? Where am I?"

"Hush! You mustn't get excited. You have a dreadful fever."

"Fever?" Maren looked around her in confusion and then recognized the captain's cabin.

"Yes, you have a fever. Do you remember what happened?"

Maren tried to remember, but it was hard. It had been cold. Unbelievably cold. And there had been a whale. The whale was bleeding from countless wounds and was pounding its tail flukes as though it were possessed by demons. But how did she get here? Why was she so sick? She automatically put a hand to her belly. She was with child. Yes, she remembered.

"Is the baby all right?" she asked worriedly.

Zelda shrugged. "I don't know. It's moving; I can feel it. But you had cramps that seemed like birth pangs to me. The child may come too soon."

Maren stroked her belly protectively and smiled as she felt the baby move. Not powerfully. It was more like a gentle caress from the inside. Now that she'd felt her child move, she wanted to know about everything else.

"What happened exactly?"

"The whale, do you remember? We were standing on deck when the men lost a whaleboat."

Maren's brow creased. She was hot and cold at the same time. As sweat collected on her upper lip, her teeth chattered. "Yes, I remember the whale," she said. "And then the men returned. The captain went back to get the whale with a single boat."

Zelda nodded sadly. "We lost ten men altogether."

"What happened?"

Zelda's face twisted into a painful smile. "Then the captain's boat capsized, and an officer put the last whaleboat in the water. There was hardly anyone here to crew it, so you got in the boat." She sniffed and dried her eyes with her hand. "You saved his life."

"His life? Whose?" Try as she might, Maren couldn't remember anything else about what had happened.

"You saved the captain's life. He went overboard. You jumped in after him and kept him from drowning in the waves."

"Oh." That was all Maren could say. "How is he now?"

Zelda laughed softly. "Like you. He has a fever, but yesterday evening he was able to eat something. He'll survive. See for yourself."

Zelda pointed to the other side of the cabin. Maren pulled herself up onto her elbows. It was true: there lay the captain. He was unshaven and his hair was matted, but his chest rose and fell evenly as he breathed. Maren felt an incredible wave of relief wash over her. She didn't like Boyse. She had never liked him. But she still thanked God that he was alive.

"The entire crew thinks you're a hero," Zelda continued. "They send you greetings and good wishes for your recovery."

Good wishes, Maren thought. She was simultaneously hot and cold, but nonetheless, she felt strong enough to get up.

Zelda pushed her back by the shoulder. "You must rest. And above all, you have to eat. Don't move. I'll get you some hot soup."

Zelda smiled at her again, pushed a strand of hair off her forehead, and disappeared. Maren lay back, hands folded over her curved middle. She felt a powerful tightening that faded away and then returned even more strongly.

All at once, she heard a voice. "Thank you." She turned her head and saw that Boyse was awake and looking over at her.

"You're welcome," she answered and smiled. Yes, it really made her happy that she had saved the captain's life. But she also knew he probably would have preferred it if he had been rescued by one of his men instead of a delicate girl.

"Your debts are settled now. They would have been settled if I had drowned. But now you will be paid for the voyage like the other ship's boys." Boyse practically growled the words, and Maren couldn't repress a smile.

"Thank you," she said.

"Now don't go thinking you're special. At sea, everyone has to be there for everyone else. The others would have done the same for me. Or for you."

Maren laughed softly. She knew that it wasn't true. After all, she had been the only one willing to jump in the water after him. But she also knew that the captain wouldn't want to be reminded of that.

"You don't have to work anymore either," he grumbled. "Everyone saw that you're expecting a child. No one shall say that I took advantage of a woman who was with child."

Maren smiled again and put both hands on her belly.

"You can have the cabin until we reach Amsterdam. As soon as I've recovered, I'll move into the wardroom with Zelda. And I hope by God that it won't be for long."

"Aren't we on the way home?" Maren asked.

"No. The sea has frozen around us. That idiot of a first mate was focused on caring for the sick, and in his concern, he ignored the approaching storm front. Now we're caught in the ice."

Shock went through Maren's body like a bolt of lightning. She was a Sylt girl. She knew what it meant for a ship to be caught in the ice.

Then Zelda returned with the hot soup. Maren studied her as she approached. She was pale and had dark circles under her eyes, and her cheeks seemed hollow.

"The provisions!" she said fearfully in realization. "There aren't enough, are there?"

"Don't worry about that. There's enough for you and your child," Zelda replied, and Maren knew immediately that Zelda was suffering from hunger.

She drank a few sips of the hot broth and then gave the cup to Zelda. "You should have some too. You need it just as much as I do."

Zelda glanced at the cup covetously, but then she swallowed and shook her head. "If you can't finish it, give it to the captain. He's still very weak."

Maren nodded and was about to hand him the cup, but the captain shook his head determinedly. "You're with child. If anyone must eat and drink, it's you."

Maren swallowed. She knew very well what it meant to be hungry. She had often been hungry, but never so much that it had been a question of life and death. And although neither Zelda nor the captain mentioned it, she knew how the crew was feeling.

"Will the ice melt soon?" she asked quietly.

Zelda shook her head. "No. It's gotten colder. Our only hope is that another ship will find us."

"But how will they get to us through the ice?"

She shrugged, and Maren realized how demoralized the older woman was when she saw the gesture of futility.

"You're scared, aren't you?" she asked.

"Yes, but this isn't about me. I've lived my life. But you and your child . . . I'm worried for you."

All at once, a wave of pain rolled over Maren's body, and she felt a flood of wetness between her legs.

"Something . . . something's happening to me!" she stammered. Zelda lifted up the blanket and saw a greenish fluid. She smiled, but there was sadness in her expression too.

"Your baby is coming," she whispered.

Another wave went through Maren. She grimaced and reached for Zelda's hand. "Please don't leave me alone," she said.

Zelda gently extricated her hand. "We need hot water and clean cloths. Don't be afraid. I'll be right back." She squeezed Maren's hand and then left the cabin, and Maren, rigid with fear, didn't dare to move.

"Is it his?" An annoyed voice broke her paralysis. "Is it Thies Heinen's child?"

"Who else's could it be?" Maren hissed, and let out a muffled cry because it felt as though her entire lower body was being squeezed.

"Then you truly love him?"

Maren hesitated. In the last weeks, she hadn't thought about Thies very much. But that was surely because she hadn't had a single peaceful moment on this damnable ship. "Of course I love him," she declared in a steady voice. "We will be married as soon as I return to Sylt."

At that, the captain turned toward the wall. "If you prefer, I can leave," he said. "I'm sure I can find a corner somewhere."

"No!" The word was out faster than Maren's thoughts. "No, please, stay with me." She didn't know exactly why it seemed vital for him to stay, but it was doubtlessly so.

"Why? I won't be much help."

"But . . . but somehow I feel . . . safer . . . when you're around."

Captain Boyse laughed. "So far, I haven't had that impression. You saved my life, and not the other way around. If anything, *I* should be the one to feel safer in *your* presence."

"That's nonsense," Maren said with her teeth clenched. "When you're here, nothing can happen to me."

Then Zelda returned. She turned back the covers and pushed Maren's clenched knees apart. "It will take a while," she said, sounding sure.

"How do you know that?" Suddenly Maren was afraid. Afraid that her child would be born dead, afraid that she herself would die, out here on the icy Arctic sea.

"In my profession, it's easy to get with child. And there's usually not enough money for a midwife. Believe me, I've delivered more babies than you can imagine."

Zelda felt Maren's round belly, mopped the cold sweat from her brow, and held her hand during each contraction. The captain, still shivering with fever, asked how she was doing every now and then.

They passed many hours that way, with Maren's cries coming at regular intervals and shaking them out of their reveries. And then Maren felt as though she would be torn apart from the inside out.

Zelda sat between her spread knees. "It's coming," she said. "I can see the head. It won't be long now."

But then the child turned: the head disappeared, and a tiny foot became visible. Zelda reached for the foot gently and moved it carefully, but Maren screamed as though she were being stabbed.

"What's wrong?" Captain Boyse asked. He sat up and looked at Zelda.

"The baby. It's in the wrong position. I have to try to turn it."

"No, no," Maren whimpered. "I'm going to die. I won't survive it." Her body stiffened and she screamed, and Zelda wiped the sweat off her brow with her lower arm.

"You have to help me, Captain. You have to hold her."

Boyse got up and came to the straw pallet, and put Maren's head in his lap and held her by the shoulders.

Zelda took a deep breath. "You have to be strong now, Maren." Then she put one hand on Maren's lower abdomen and the other at the top of her belly. She pushed and pulled, kneaded and tugged, and sweat ran freely down her face. Maren was stiff with fear and horror.

"Help me!" Zelda cried. "You have to push now!"

The captain held her by the shoulders and encouraged her. "I'll count to three, and then you push. One, two, three!"

Maren tried, pushed as hard as she could, but nothing happened.

"And again," Zelda said, and once more the captain counted for her. Maren had no more strength; she'd been suffering terrible pain for so many hours.

"Do it! One more time!" The captain urged her on as he had the oarsmen on the whaleboat.

Maren gathered her last bit of strength and pushed, and she felt something slide out of her.

"Yes, yes! Good!" Zelda cried. She caught the baby and slapped it once on the bottom to make it cry.

Maren sank back in exhaustion.

Boyse rubbed her shoulders. "Good girl," he said.

Then Zelda washed the baby, swaddled it in a warm blanket, and laid it on Maren's chest. "She's so small and delicate," Zelda said.

"Will she live?" Maren asked fearfully.

Zelda didn't answer her. The captain spoke instead. "Yes. She will live. I'll see to it."

With a smile, he put on his boots as he gazed at the little girl sleeping calmly at Maren's breast. "First, we must christen her," he said. "I'll get something for the young mother to eat."

CHAPTER 21

Maren would never have imagined that the tiny baby would melt the hard hearts of the sailors. The news of the birth had spread through the ship like wildfire, and they were overwhelmed by a flood of visitors. Jakob came and brought her a piece of smoked meat.

"I . . . I thought you'd need something for your strength," he stammered.

Maren knew that he'd practically had to cut the meat from his own ribs, and she accepted it gratefully.

Then Raik came, bringing a pullover made of woman's hair. "You can wrap the little one in this," he said. "My sister made it for me out of her own hair."

Maren was grateful for this too and thanked him warmly. Then the first mate came, accompanied by two sailors who were carrying a brazier full of coals.

"This is to keep the little one warm," they said, and Maren knew that the brazier was from the pilothouse, and those who worked there would be even colder now.

Most of the time, Zelda was at her side. "The baby arrived too soon," she repeated. "We have to help her drink. She might not be able to nurse by herself."

It was true. Maren held the baby to her breast, but she fell asleep immediately. Zelda gently stroked one of Maren's swollen nipples, caught a few drops of milk on her fingers, and gave it to the child. Otherwise, the baby slept. Maren squeezed her tightly against her body to warm her, and although she was very delicate, she seemed to be at peace in her arms.

Sometimes Zelda bathed her and rubbed her with whale oil afterward. It stank, but it helped to protect the baby's skin against the cold.

Then, when the child was a week old and had finally learned to nurse, Captain Boyse called everyone on deck on a very cold, sunny morning. Maren and the baby were summoned too. Before they left Amsterdam, Boyse had asked a priest to bless the brig. He still had a bottle of holy water on board. It was intended for giving last rites to the dying, but this was an important occasion.

Right before the christening, the captain returned to the cabin. He stood undecidedly by Maren's bed, and then kneeled down by the straw pallet and peered thoughtfully at the little one. How gentle his face had suddenly become! He even smiled as he carefully stroked the baby's cheek with one finger.

"Do you have everything you need?" he asked Maren.

"I have more than I need," she replied. "Everyone has been so kind to me." She paused and swallowed the lump in her throat. "No one has been cruel or complained. Even though she is illegitimate, and I am a woman who lost her virtue."

Boyse nodded. "What name do you intend to give her?"

Maren had been thinking about it carefully. At first, she'd wanted to name the baby Finja, after her mother. But then she'd changed her mind. Her mother surely wouldn't want to have an illegitimate child named after her. She had deliberated and had settled on the name Angret. She had no relatives with the name, so no one would feel as though they had been dishonored. And yet, Angret was a respectable name on Sylt.

"Angret," she said. "Just Angret."

Boyse grimaced.

"You don't like the name?"

He took a deep breath. "That was my mother's name."

Maren flinched. "I . . . I didn't mean it that way."

"What didn't you mean?"

"I didn't mean to name my illegitimate child after your mother."

All at once, the captain seemed to be annoyed. "I forbid you ever to call that child illegitimate again. You said that Thies is her father and that you love him. That means she's a love child." He paused. When he saw the look of shock on Maren's face, he forced a smile onto his lips. "It would be lovely if your daughter had the same name as my mother."

Now Maren smiled too. She smiled hesitantly, but she squeezed the little girl against her and kissed her delicate head.

"And the godparents? Who have you chosen?"

Maren didn't have to think long about that. "Zelda. I'd like to have Zelda as godmother."

The captain made a face again. "She's a whore; you know that."

"She's a friend. That's what I know," Maren replied.

"You need two godparents."

Maren nodded. She had also deliberated about a godfather. She had thought about asking Raik, and then Jakob. But something inside her resisted those thoughts. She would have preferred Boyse himself to be the godfather, but she didn't dare to ask him.

"I don't have a godfather for her," she said instead. "Maybe Zelda will be enough."

"No, she's not enough. You know that yourself. Godparents are there to care for a child if you can't do it yourself. Think about how Zelda lives. And then think about who you would like to choose as a godfather."

"I'd like you to be the godfather."

The captain took a deep breath. "You didn't want to marry me, but I'm good enough to be your child's godfather?"

Maren lowered her eyes. She knew without looking at him that he was still hurt by her rejection. But why? It couldn't be because he loved her. If he did, he would have been nicer to her during all their months at sea. Although he'd been kind to her at times . . . He'd given her a place to sleep in his cabin and had helped to deliver her child.

"That's completely out of the question!" His words sounded harsh and determined. And Maren also heard the words that the captain hadn't said but which echoed through the air between them anyway. *I won't be the godfather of an illegitimate child.*

She sighed. "Well, then I'd like to ask someone who lives on Sylt. Maybe old Piet." She said it defiantly, wanting to provoke the captain, but he just nodded.

"If Piet doesn't want to, I'll order the first mate to do it."

Order? Maren broke into tears. She was still weak from the birth, and she longed for home, longed for Thies and Finja. She didn't know how she was going to make a living with her little girl. Her body hurt and her emotions were intense—and they made her cry. Now she wept all the tears she'd been holding in for months. She wept all the tears that were left inside her because Thies hadn't been able to protect her from going on the voyage. She wept because her father was dead and because she was homesick. She wept and sobbed, and her shoulders quaked. The captain stood in front of her and observed her dispassionately, and Maren wished very much that he would take her in his arms and comfort her, but of course he didn't.

"Stop your weeping," he said. "It won't help." Then he pointed to the little one. "It was your own choice. No one is responsible for your unhappiness but yourself."

Maren knew that what he said was true, and she cried all the harder because of it. The captain left the cabin, and she buried her face in her pillow, holding the small child tightly. Then Zelda came and helped her to get up and dress.

"Hurry, the crew is already on deck, and a storm is coming."

A little later, Maren stood on the foredeck with the baby in her arms. First, Raik read Christ's call to baptism from a battered Bible, warped from being soaked with seawater and drying out again. Then everyone on deck spoke a creed. There should have been a sermon, but who besides the captain could have given one? And he said nothing, only regarded the baby for a moment and then glanced at Maren's eyes, which were puffy from crying. Then he asked Zelda and old Piet, who was delighted, if they would agree to be the godparents. Both godparents affirmed they would, and then the christening candle was lit. In this case, it was a beeswax candle from the wardroom.

Then the captain opened the small bottle of holy water and dripped a little over the baby's head. "I christen thee Angret, and give thee into the care and protection of God."

Afterward everyone congratulated Maren, and the first mate gave her a roll of parchment upon which he'd written Angret's baptismal verse in his best calligraphy: *Fear not, but speak and do not remain silent. For I am with thee, and no one shall dare to do thee any harm.*

Maren hesitated a moment before taking it. The baptismal verse didn't sound like it came from the Bible, but more like something the captain might have said to the child. But the first mate added that God had spoken the words to the apostle Paul during his ministry to the Corinthians, and that Zelda and Piet had chosen it.

Finally, those who had gifts came forward. Raik had whittled a wooden rattle for Angret, Jakob brought a quart of yogurt, and Zelda offered a blanket made of soft wool, which she had been sleeping under herself every night. One sailor brought a jar of whale oil, and another brought a wooden comb, and another brought a ball made of rags. But the most beautiful gift of all on the christening day came from the men themselves. Maren saw their glowing eyes and their tender glances at the tiny baby, and one of them spoke the words that all the others were thinking. "Now that we have the little one, God can't possibly let us perish in the ice. The child is hope. All shall be well."

CHAPTER 22

They were stuck in the ice for two months, one week, and four days. The men became bored and would fight every now and then. They fought over the scarce drinking water and provisions, but whenever they saw Angret, they were calm and kind. In the meantime, the little one had grown strong enough to nurse normally. Her mother's milk and the fresh sea air made her hardy, and she bloomed despite being born prematurely. But Maren herself had fallen into a kind of melancholy. As much as she wished to be at home on Sylt again, she was also afraid about what might be happening there. Christmas was coming, and she would miss it. She wondered if Thies still thought about her. She didn't know.

At last, one day the lookout in the crow's nest shouted, "Ship ahoy!"

All at once, the men came back to life. A few of them ran to their berths and packed their sea chests with clothing and blankets. Then they dragged the chests onto the deck, ready to throw them overboard onto the ice and abandon the *Rán,* seeking refuge on the other ship. Some men were already making their way over the ice to the unknown ship, which had a bow made of iron and was therefore safer among the floes. The others stood on deck, waiting, and then Captain Rune Boyse appeared.

He stood with his legs planted wide on an overturned box and shouted at the men who were just about to throw their sea chests onto the ice. "What kind of yellow-bellied dogs are you?" he cried, so loud that the crew flinched. "Do you think you have to save yourselves? Don't you trust me?"

Jakob grabbed one sailor who was just about to climb over the rail by the collar and forced him back on board.

Another very young sailor cried back, "I don't want to die or freeze! That ship is our only hope!"

Then the captain leapt from his box, grabbed the man, and gave him a half dozen powerful slaps in the face, which made the sailor stagger backward.

"No one on my ship gives up!" Boyse cried. "I accuse any man who tries to leave of mutiny." The others who had dragged their sea chests up on deck stiffened. They glanced back and forth between the captain and the other brig. But Rune Boyse didn't leave them any time to think about it.

"Strike the sails!" he yelled. "Hurry, get the sails down!" The men did as he ordered. Some members of the crew had raised the sails in panic when they had seen the ship, and now the *Rán* was groaning and creaking against the pack ice, threatening to break.

Then the captain ordered the first mate to keep an eye on the crew, climbed over the rail himself, and hurried toward the other ship. He skidded on the ice, bracing himself against the wind with his hat pulled low over his face. When he finally returned a few hours later, he had less than good news.

"They've given up on us," the captain said, after the first mate had called the crew to deck. "In Amsterdam, no one believed we might still be alive. They say our brig was lost, and they said a mass for our souls in church. And the ship there can be no help to us. It's caught in the ice and can't go farther now either."

He paused for a moment, looking each man intently in the eyes. Then he smiled. Yes, he'd found the right words. The crew was starting to feel angry about the situation. Now that they'd been declared dead, they wanted to live that much more.

One of the men even laughed, but it didn't sound joyful. "Then they'll see how alive we are, once the other ship has given us provisions and water."

Another pursed his lips in thought. "They think I'm dead? Well, then they'll all be wild with joy when I return. And if I'm lucky, my wife will have already married the neighbor."

The banter flew. A few days later, the weather finally cleared, and the boy in the crow's nest called open water for the first time in weeks. Then the wind turned from west to east, and the ice finally opened enough that the brig could set sail for home.

PART 3

1765

CHAPTER 23

The closer they got to home, the grayer the sky became. They'd left the ice and bitter cold behind, but the clouds hung low over the mast and emptied so much rain onto the brig that the ship's boys barely needed to swab the deck.

Maren still spent most of her time in the captain's cabin. The baby was now two months old and getting stronger every day. Zelda came several times a day to enjoy Angret's company.

"The child is truly a miracle," she said. "I don't know what I'll do when you're back on Sylt. But she's my godchild, and I will come to visit her."

As she spoke, she regarded the other woman carefully, but Maren was glad for her words. "Come whenever you wish. I'll always be happy to see you."

"But I'm a whore. You don't regret that you chose me, of all people, to be her godmother? On land, people sometimes think differently than they do at sea."

Maren shook her head. "You're my friend, and you always will be. I don't care what people think. The captain can vouch for that. You're the best friend I've ever had. God strike me down if I am ever ashamed of you."

When seagulls appeared and circled over the ship, the men shouted and cheered and threw their caps in the air. Some sank to their knees and thanked God for saving them.

The next day, they saw a Dutch smak in the distance, and two days later, they sailed into Amsterdam harbor.

A crowd had gathered on the quayside, awaiting their homecoming. Maren saw a gray-haired woman throw her arms around old Jakob, and he picked her up and spun her around, laughing. She saw the first mate standing next to his sea chest, his eyes scanning the crowd, and then he was greeted with joyful cries by two little girls.

Zelda walked next to her with tiny Angret in her arms. "You can come with me now," she said. "And when you've found a smak that's going to Sylt, I'll come with you."

Maren took Angret from Zelda and held her tightly against her body. *Will it always be this way?* she asked herself. *Why isn't Thies here? Why didn't he wait here in case the brig arrived after all?*

The sailors' wives had found quarters at the inns which surrounded the harbor. Mothers and sisters were at the quay and were grinning as tears streamed down their cheeks. Even Zelda was greeted by a woman in a brightly colored dress. Maren alone had no one waiting for her. So she went with Zelda and slept in a room with her and the baby. Sometimes she saw Captain Boyse in the mornings as he ate his breakfast. She always asked if he had heard about a smak going to Sylt, but he only shook his head.

Finally, one morning he said, "There's a ship leaving for Sylt the day after tomorrow. You should be on it so the child can finally meet her father. It may take me longer to sell the cargo and return the brig to the shipping company."

"Can't I travel with you?" she asked hesitantly, but Captain Rune Boyse shook his head.

"You'll leave as quickly as possible. We're back on land. I'm no longer responsible for you. We're squared and even. It's time our paths part."

Maren stiffened in shock. The captain's face was closed. He gazed at her indifferently. Somehow she'd thought they'd become friends. No, not friends. But somehow connected to each other. Close. She had obviously been mistaken. Maybe the captain didn't hate her anymore, but he was far from liking her. Only Angret managed to get a smile out of him. Maren was disappointed. She was so disappointed that she could barely hold back her tears. At the same time, she felt incredibly foolish. That was the plain truth: she had rejected him, and a man like Rune Boyse couldn't forgive something like that.

"Here!" The captain broke through her musings and tossed a leather purse full of coins onto the table between them. "This is for you."

"For me?"

"Yes. It's fair payment for your work aboard the ship."

"But I thought—"

"Don't think. You saved my life, and now I pay you your wage. Take the money. You'll need it. The baby surely doesn't have everything she needs. And now, farewell. I have things to do."

Maren took the money and went to the market the next day. She walked among the stands, looking for warm wool and knitting needles, soft fabric, and some leather for baby shoes. She bought a small hairbrush and a little spoon, just the right size for the baby's tiny rosebud mouth. While she was shopping, she wore Angret in a sling against her chest and held her tightly. She bought a little goat's milk, some honey, and some herbs for tea. While she was asking the herbalist for dried blueberries, someone came up behind her and cried out her name.

"Maren? Is that really you?"

She turned around. There stood Maike, her friend from Rantum. She grinned at Maren, spread her arms wide, and moved to embrace her, but she stopped abruptly and stared at the little bundle on Maren's chest. She let her arms fall. "It's . . . it's you, isn't it?"

Maren smiled, because she was glad to see a friendly face. "Yes, it's me. What are you doing here?"

Maike cleared her throat. "Well, I just got married. My husband is from Amsterdam; that's why we came. I arrived two weeks ago." She sighed and gazed at the child again, looking into its face. Then she pointed tentatively. "Is that your baby?"

Maren smiled and stroked the baby's head. "Yes. She's my daughter. Her name is Angret."

Maike frowned a little. "Well, then it's not so bad for you, is it?"

"What isn't so bad?"

Maike went pale. "Oh, nothing. I was just talking too much."

"What isn't so bad?"

Maike took Maren's hand and pulled her into an entryway where they were more protected from the wind. "We thought you were dead," she said. "When all the other whalers had returned, no one knew anything about your ship. Later, when the last ship had returned to Sylt, they said you had all drowned in the North Sea. Your mother was inconsolable. Her hair went completely gray overnight."

Maike stopped and stroked Maren's arm for a moment. Maren swallowed. "What else?"

"Well. There were masses. Like there always are when sailors don't come home from the sea." She stopped, but Maren knew that Maike was still holding something back.

"Did Thies have a mass read for me too?"

Maike sighed. "Well, it wasn't really the right time for that."

"What do you mean?"

Maike sighed deeply again and then took Maren's hand. "Thies married. When he heard that you were dead, he found another to be his wife."

The moment Maren heard the news, the sky turned gray. The colors of the cheerful market stands faded, and the sounds became shrill. She began to shake, and she held the baby more tightly against her.

"He married? But why?"

"He thought you were dead, and so did everyone else on the island."

Everything swam before Maren's eyes. She had difficulty holding back her tears. But there was one thing she had to know. "Whom did he take to the altar?"

Maike sighed and shook her head. "Does that matter now? Now that you have a child, I mean."

But Maren grabbed her arm and shook it. "I have to know!"

"Grit." Maike spoke the name quietly, but it rang in Maren's ears like the strike of a gong.

"It *would* be Grit!" she whispered, numbed by the intensity of the pain. Then she pressed Angret more tightly against her. "I have to go," she said, and she left without turning back. She walked aimlessly through the streets of Amsterdam like someone who wasn't in her right mind. She crossed alleys and squares she'd never seen before. Everything in her pressed her onward, as though she could walk away from the pain. She couldn't feel the bleeding blisters on her feet. She barely heard when Angret began to cry from hunger.

Somewhere she stopped to nurse the child without really paying attention to what she was doing. Then she walked on, leaving her anguish and tears behind. Only when it was dark did she come to her senses. She had no idea where she was. But she had money, and she stopped a hackney coach and asked to be driven back to the harbor.

She found herself standing in front of Zelda's house, but she didn't dare enter. Whatever had happened on the whaling ship, Maren realized now, had happened because she knew she still had Thies. As long as she had been sure of his love and support, it didn't matter if Angret had been born out of wedlock. Once she was back on Sylt, she could marry him, and Angret would be recognized as the love child that she truly was. But now this! Maren was not only alone and fatherless, but she would perhaps also be abandoned by her mother because she was a girl without her virtue. She had been at sea so long that it didn't matter anymore if Thies was the father or not. She could already hear the gossip: *"She brought a child from the whaling expedition! What was she doing on a ship with all those men? Who knows who the father really is? Didn't she kiss Captain Boyse here on Sylt, even though everyone knew that she was already promised to Thies Heinen?"* Maren wouldn't be able to do anything but hold her child close and know the truth. Now Captain Boyse had his revenge, and it was a much more terrible revenge than he could possibly have planned.

The next moment, Maren considered simply walking into the water. The idea grew in the back of her mind and slowly pushed aside all other thoughts. What reason did she have to remain in this world? Her debts were paid, Finja would be able to live more peacefully without her, and Thies, her darling Thies, was the last person who would be happy to see her. If she walked into the water, she would find deliverance. She wouldn't have to prove what couldn't be proven, and she would be doing the others a favor. The shameful child would be gone, Thies would be able to live happily with Grit, and even Finja would be better off having a dead daughter than one who had thrown away her virtue.

The weight of her pain was no longer quite as heavy on her shoulders. A few tears ran down her cheeks and fell on the baby's head. Then Maren pulled herself together and walked toward the water. It was now dark, but the moonlight made the waves gleam like precious silk.

Maren stood on the beach for a while. She felt calm. Soon she would have her peace, peace and quiet. And even if she went to hell, anything would be better than remaining in the world as a burden and shame for everyone she knew and loved. And who could love her now? Thies had married Grit, and that meant that his love for her had died. And Finja? She had buried her husband and had always led a pious life.

Now her only daughter had an illegitimate child. No, Finja wouldn't be able to love her anymore either. She was completely alone.

Maren removed her boots, setting them tidily next to each other on the sand, and hoped that someone who needed them would find them. She also removed her cloak and her warm vest. Then she said a short prayer, kissed Angret on the forehead, and walked into the water with the little one pressed tightly against her. She took a step and felt the cold water first on her ankles, then her knees and thighs. The icy cold crawled through her flesh to her bones, but Maren ignored it. She walked onward, putting one foot in front of the other, moving deeper and deeper into the tide. Maren had her eyes focused on the horizon, which was inky with darkness. She took one step after another, and as the water rose up around Angret and the child cried, she said, "Now it's cold and wet. But soon you will be warm. You won't have a happy life, but you will have a happy death. You will play at the feet of Lord Jesus, and you will never know hunger or fear."

Then Maren kept walking, step after step. The water reached her chest. Her teeth chattered, and she was colder than she had ever been in her life. She hoped that the hellfire that was waiting for her would thaw her limbs, and the thought gave her the strength to continue.

CHAPTER 24

All was quiet and warm. Maren wasn't freezing anymore. She lay somewhere soft. For a moment, she asked herself where Angret could be, but then she realized that the baby must be in heaven and she herself would certainly be in hell. But she had imagined hell differently. Not so quiet, or pleasantly warm. Loud and unbearably hot instead.

Everything is as it should be, she thought, and she smiled with relief. But then she heard someone call her name.

"Maren? Maren!"

She opened her eyes slowly and saw Zelda's face above her. "Where am I?"

"You're in my house, in Amsterdam."

Her brow creased. "Not in hell?"

Zelda smiled. "Not hell, just a harbor brothel."

Maren turned her head and saw her wet gown hanging over a chair. She worriedly touched her body and realized that she was wearing a soft nightdress.

"Where is Angret?" she asked, and her fear for her child made her voice come out in a raw, stiff squeak.

"Don't worry, she's with Arja."

"Arja?" Maren briefly wondered if Arja was another name for hell or the Devil.

"Arja. She's one of my girls. She recently bore a child, and now she's taking care of Angret. She nursed her and was amazed at how hungry the little one seemed to be. Now Angret is sleeping beside Arja's son in the cradle."

Then everything came back to Maren. The beach. The glittering waves. Her joy that she'd soon be free. And now she lay here, in Zelda's house.

"How . . . how did I get here?" she asked.

Zelda swallowed. "I saw you standing in front of the house. You looked distraught. Your shoulders hung down, your back was hunched, and tears were running down your face. Then you left, and I feared the worst, so I followed you. I was too late. He'd already gotten you and the baby out of the water and had carried you most of the way here in his arms."

Even though Zelda hadn't said his name, Maren knew whom she was talking about. Captain Boyse.

"Oh!" She was suddenly so ashamed that she would have liked to close her eyes and never wake up again.

"Why?" Zelda asked. "Why did you walk into the water with the baby?"

Maren swallowed the lump in her throat and had to close her eyes. She could see Maike in front of her, telling her about Grit's happiness.

"Thies, my fiancé. He married someone else," she mumbled.

"On the island? On Sylt?"

Maren nodded and felt the tears escaping her closed eyelids. "And not just anyone. He married my rival."

She sighed deeply, then opened her eyes and looked at the other woman so forlornly that Zelda was overwhelmed with pity. "My baby, my little one. She will always be illegitimate. I have no home anymore. I can never go back to Sylt. The people there would despise me, and Angret would suffer for it too. Oh, if you had only let me die!"

Now she cried again, sobbing so her shoulders shook, unable to calm herself. Zelda sat next to her and held her hand, but she found no comforting words.

After a long time, Maren finally quieted. She wiped the tears from her cheeks, looked at Zelda desperately, and asked, "What shall I do, now?"

Zelda cleared her throat. "He married another when he believed you were dead. I've heard that under such conditions, one can annul the marriage. After all, the two of you were engaged."

"We were secretly engaged. Not officially."

"Well, I think it might work anyway. What do you think? Would Thies accept Angret as his own child?"

Maren thought about Thies. Would he believe that Angret was his daughter? If he could, then she was sure that he would accept her and take care of her. But he wasn't alone anymore, and he certainly wasn't in charge of his household anymore. Grit was there. And she would sooner hang herself than let him accept Maren and her child.

Was Thies strong enough to stand by Maren? She didn't know, and she couldn't think about it now if she didn't want to fall into a bottomless pit of despair.

"Where is the captain?" she asked. He had saved her, and Maren thought it would be right to thank him even though she would rather have died.

"He's not here," Zelda said without elaborating.

"Where is he? When is he coming back?"

Zelda sighed. "He packed his things and moved somewhere else."

Maren's eyes went wide. "But why? He likes being with you."

Zelda gave a pained smile and didn't speak.

Then Maren understood. "He doesn't want to see me anymore. He can't stand me, is that it?"

Zelda shook her head. "No, I wouldn't say that, exactly," she said placatingly. But Maren had heard enough.

"Leave me for a while," Maren begged. "I have to rest, but then I, too, will go. The next ship for Sylt leaves early tomorrow morning, doesn't it?"

Zelda nodded. "But you can stay as long as you wish," she promised. "We'll provide for you and Angret somehow."

Maren was so grateful for those words that tears sprang to her eyes again. "Sometimes I think you're the only person in the world who cares about me."

"No, that's not true. And I think it's good for you to go home, at least at first. Maybe everything will turn out differently than you think right now."

Maren frowned. "What if it doesn't?"

Zelda spread her arms. "Well, if it doesn't, you can just come back here."

"How shall I make a living?" Maren didn't mean to ask the question out loud, but it slipped off her tongue faster than she could think. "Shall I become a whore?"

Zelda flinched a little, looking hurt. "It's a good profession," she said, sounding defensive. "It would help you to get by. And if you go about it cleverly, then by the age of thirty-five, you can be set for the rest of your life. Look. I bought myself this house and hired girls. I don't need to work myself anymore." She stood up and gazed down at Maren and couldn't hide a hint of disdain. "There's no right to happiness in this world and no right to love," she said softly. "Learn to love yourself and to provide for yourself. Then not much can happen to you."

Maren watched her leave and close the door behind her. *She's right,* Maren thought. *You can't depend on anyone. I have to take care of myself. Myself and Angret.* All at once, she was glad that she wasn't dead. She longed for her daughter, wanted to breathe her warm scent and hear her happy noises. She would take her to the island. Maybe Maren would be an outcast there, but at least she would be home.

For the first time in her life, Maren didn't feel just the weight of responsibility on her shoulders but also the desire for it. She would make sure that Angret grew up to be a strong, independent girl. She would become a young woman who wasn't indebted to anyone. And if Thies wouldn't help, then she would have to provide for Angret herself. *I'm strong too,* Maren thought. *I proved on board the ship that I'm not afraid to work and that there are a lot of things I can do.* Then she got up and packed her belongings.

CHAPTER 25

Maren stood gratefully at the rail with Angret at her chest and took a last look at Amsterdam. It was a beautiful, brilliantly sunny day. Single white clouds blew across the blue sky, and the air was fresh and smelled of salt. A cool wind blew, turning the passengers' cheeks red and tugging at their caps and hoods. The ship cut through the water, and whitecaps danced on the waves. Most of the travelers were on deck, watching the city of Amsterdam getting smaller and smaller until it finally disappeared into the distance.

They would soon be at home on Sylt. She felt alone, but her child filled her with strength. She thought back over the previous months and reflected on all she had experienced. Maren had changed without knowing it. But now she realized that she had become braver. She was definitely no longer as weak as she had been. Zelda had helped her to see that. And that wasn't the only thing she was endlessly grateful to Zelda for. The future was unpredictable, but Maren would deal with it as it came. Now she had Angret, and for Angret, she would do anything. It didn't matter to her anymore if Thies would accept her or not, because Angret had a mother who would fight for her whenever it was necessary.

"I didn't think that you'd be back on your feet again so quickly," she heard a voice say behind her.

Maren turned around. There stood Captain Boyse, regarding her intently.

"Oh, I . . . I have to thank you," she stammered.

Boyse waved her thanks aside. "If I'd actually believed you wanted to die, I would have let you."

"But . . . I did want to die. Then, at least."

"No, you didn't. You wanted to live. You just didn't want to live the way you lived before."

Maren stared at him. He was right: She wanted to live. She wanted to live for Angret, who needed her. She wanted to see the sun and feel it on her face, taste the snow on her tongue and hear the rushing of the sea. But how had he known that? She herself had only just figured it out.

"Thank you," she said again. She had an urge to take his hand, but she didn't do it. She felt so close to him. That was no wonder, considering they'd saved each other's lives, but he obviously felt less connected to her than to his men on the brig. After all, he'd left Zelda's house because he couldn't stand being around Maren anymore.

So she asked, "Will you, too, scorn me on the island because I lost my virtue?"

Boyse laughed. "Do you believe that of me?" He reached for Angret, took her in his arms, and stroked her delicate cheek with his thumb. "I helped bring her into this world," he said softly. "That was one of the most beautiful experiences of my life. She can count on me whenever she needs me."

Maren was touched by his words, but a little bell of warning sounded in her head. "But you didn't want to be her godfather."

Boyse shook his head. "No. I didn't, and I still don't. I want to be more than a godfather to Angret."

With those words, he put the child back into her arms and left. Maren watched him go. What he just said . . . What had he meant?

Over the next few days, she barely saw him. He spoke with other men who'd sailed with merchants and were now returning to the islands for the winter and also with men who'd come to Amsterdam to make purchases.

Maren was alone most of the time. She often stood at the rail and showed Angret the sea. The little one followed Maren's finger with her eyes when she pointed out a seagull. She cooed in her arms, reached for Maren's hair, and touched her mother's face with her tiny hands. She had become a little stronger, but she was still a delicate thing, with such thin skin that her bluish veins shimmered through. Sometimes, old Piet from Rantum joined them. He smiled at the child and made silly noises that made Angret laugh and otherwise stood silently next to Maren.

Only once, when the neighboring island of Amrum appeared on the horizon, he put a hand on Maren's shoulder. "You can do this. And if you can't, I'll be right there too."

Then he shuffled away. But those few words gave Maren a little more courage. She needed courage. She realized it as the Dutch smak arrived in the harbor of Sylt, and many of the islanders had come to celebrate the homecoming of those they believed had died.

Maren saw her mother, who was standing next to Old Meret. For a little while, they just watched the ship, and then Finja raised her hand and waved to her daughter. At that moment, a huge weight fell from Maren's shoulders. Her mother. She had waved to her. She wouldn't reject her. Then her gaze slid to the left. There stood a man with his hands in his pockets. Maren recognized Thies immediately. He looked at her, but she couldn't make out the expression on his face. But he, too, had come.

Then the ship arrived at the quayside, and the passengers streamed out. Maren held Angret in her arms, her heavy sea chest at her feet. In the sea chest was the leather purse with the payment she had earned. It was a goodly amount of money for Sylt. It was enough to repair the house and buy enough wood for the winter. Maybe even enough to begin a new life.

Piet approached her. "I'll take your sea chest," he said, lifting the box onto his shoulders. "My wife came with the wagon. I'll bring the chest to your mother's house. Take your time."

Maren nodded gratefully. She was the last to disembark. She didn't dare look left or right. She was afraid to feel the disdainful stares of the islanders. With her head down and the baby pressed against her, she took the final steps and finally stood once more on the soil of Sylt.

"Maren!" Finja hurried toward her daughter with her arms spread wide. She embraced her, took her face between her hands, and kissed her again and again. Tears rolled down her cheeks. "I thought I'd never see you again! God be praised for bringing you safely home!"

Maren risked a tentative smile. "As you can see, I didn't come alone." She searched her mother's face for a sign of disapproval, but there was only the purest joy to be seen there.

"May I?" Finja asked, and she reached out to take the baby.

"Of course. After all, you're her grandmother." Maren passed the child to Finja, and Finja hugged the little one to her, kissing her so thoroughly that Angret began to fuss.

"She's so beautiful," Finja said and stroked the child's cheek gently. "She's enchanting."

"Her name is Angret," Maren said. "Angret Finja."

"How wonderful!" Finja still regarded the baby with amazement. But then she said, "Come, let's go home. You must be exhausted, and we have a lot to talk about."

Maren nodded gratefully. The women made their way through the crowd, but suddenly Maren was poked roughly in the side. She looked up and saw Grit's furious face.

"I wish that you'd stayed dead!" She practically spat the words in Maren's face. "No one here missed you. Not anyone." Then her gaze fell on the baby who lay contentedly against Finja's chest. She pointed a finger at the child and laughed shrilly. "Ha! I thought so. You couldn't get your legs apart fast enough, could you? You'd already tasted the captain's kiss long ago!" Then she spat at Maren's feet. "Whore!" she shrieked.

"Come!" Finja pulled her daughter behind her, out from the throngs of people and toward the path that lead to Rantum and their home. For a little while, the women walked silently, until the noise of the harbor had died out behind them.

"Does everyone think the way Grit does?" Maren asked.

Finja shrugged. "They can think what they want. The important thing is that you are both home."

They walked the rest of the way in silence, and when Maren saw the crooked house with a white puff of smoke coming out of the chimney and smelled the familiar scent of sea air and heather, she felt a wave of relief. "We'll be all right, won't we?" she asked her mother.

"Of course we will. People will get used to it. I'll just get the cradle out of the barn. I kept all your other baby things too." She smiled. "The little one will want for nothing."

"You aren't angry at me?" Maren asked when they had finally arrived in the house and were drinking a hot cup of herbal brew. Angret lay protected by pillows in the alcove and slept, while Maren and Finja sat across from each other at the kitchen table.

"No. Why should I be angry at you? Your life didn't turn out the way I'd thought, but you're alive. And your daughter is amazingly beautiful."

"You aren't ashamed of me?"

"Do I have a reason to be?"

Maren shook her head. "Thies is her father. I only lay with a man once, on the night before I left for the whaling voyage. The child was born at sea, when we were surrounded by ice."

"Is she christened?"

Maren nodded. "Captain Rune Boyse christened her. He was there at her birth."

"Does she have godparents?"

Maren swallowed. "Piet from Rantum is her godfather. Zelda is her godmother. She's . . . she's . . . a whore from Amsterdam." Maren straightened her shoulders and chin and then added, "And she's the best friend I've ever had."

Finja nodded and was quiet for a moment. Then she said, "She's welcome in my house. And Piet as well." Then she got up and went to the barn to find everything that Angret would need.

Maren was alone and let out a long breath of relief. In her deepest heart, she had known that Finja would greet her and Angret warmly. She had her home again and would be able to stay with Finja. The three of them could live here, just like the other women on Sylt did when their men went to sea in February for their long voyages. But Finja had asked no questions. Maren had told her mother that Angret was Thies's daughter, but Finja hadn't said anything about it. What about Thies? He'd stood there at the quayside, but he hadn't greeted her. She had to meet him, had to talk to him. She looked over at Angret, who was sleeping peacefully.

She wrapped herself in her warm cloak and was about to leave the house when Finja returned. Her dress was dusty, and a thin piece of cobweb was caught in her hair. She wiped her brow with her sleeve. "I wouldn't do that, if I were you."

"What wouldn't you do?"

Finja sat down. "Please bring me some water, won't you?"

Maren obeyed and put a full cup in front of Finja. "What wouldn't you do?"

"Well, I wouldn't go to Thies."

"Why not?"

Finja sighed. "You left in February. Now it's December. You returned with a child in your arms. She's so delicate that she doesn't look like she's more than a few weeks old."

Maren sat down again too. "What are you trying to say?"

"Everyone will say that you got with child on the voyage. I'd wager that people are already getting hot heads over it, trying to figure out which member of the crew could be the father. Leave it be. No one here has forgotten that Rune Boyse proposed to you."

"Leave it be? But Thies really *is* Angret's father."

Finja pursed her lips. "In the eyes of the others, she's illegitimate. If you go to Thies now, everyone will say you're trying to destroy his marriage."

"But Grit didn't marry him for love!" A pain surged through her chest, as though her heart were being torn into pieces. "We were promised to each other. He broke his promise. How can anyone point a finger at me?"

"You were gone. Too long. Thies waited. He was only married in November. Only after we'd heard that you and the others were dead."

Maren's shoulders sank. She had known all of this, but in her heart, she'd had a glimmer of hope that Thies would still be true to her. Yes, she had even dreamed that she'd leave the ship and fall directly into his arms. Did Thies believe what the others did? That was even more reason he had to know that Angret was his child.

CHAPTER 26

The next morning, Maren walked along the beach. It was a clear day with a blue sky. The wind drove countless shredded clouds away ahead of it. Maren had wrapped Angret warmly and climbed the dunes with her. The air smelled of salt and seaweed. Before she'd been to sea, she had believed that the sea everywhere must smell the same way, but it wasn't so. Here on Sylt, the smell of the sea was mixed with the smell of heather. At Spitsbergen, the sea had smelled of krill, and every now and then, she'd thought it had no smell at all. In Amsterdam, the smell was mixed with pitch and smoke, and on the Dutch smak, it had smelled of fish.

As she stood at the top of the dune watching the North Sea shimmering silver gray in the distance, she sighed with relief. Finally. She was home again. A few seagulls squealed overhead, and two fishing boats lay on the beach above the high-tide line. From afar, Maren recognized an old woman who was collecting driftwood. Home. She turned the baby so she faced the sea.

"This is where you're from," she told her little daughter. "This is your home."

But Angret had no appreciation for the meaningful moment, and she began to fuss. Only when Maren had pressed her closely to her chest again did the little one quiet down and go back to sleep. Slowly, with one hand supporting the small back, Maren climbed down the dune to the beach. Far out on the water, she saw a ship that was probably on its way to Scandinavia. She sat down on an overturned fishing boat and gazed at the sea. A few clouds drifted across the sky, the wind tugged playfully at her dress, and the waves wore whitecaps that looked like pointed hats. Finja had advised her to think about her future. A future without a man. But Maren was much too happy about finally being home on the island again to ruin the beautiful day with dark thoughts. Yes, she would think about it, but she actually didn't have very many possibilities. She had to earn a living. Maybe she could pluck ducks again, but the money she made wouldn't be enough to live on. She could knit, but she couldn't make a living that way either. Maybe she should listen to her mother and buy a flock of geese. The geese could graze on the dike in spring and summer and be slaughtered in the winter. But Maren had no idea how to keep geese.

At the moment, she had money. Now it was up to her to use it in a way that would support them for a few years. There were several women on the island who had to depend on themselves. Their men had died at sea. One was said to sell her body to men, but everyone avoided her like the plague. One widow ran a shop that sold food, oil, and a few other everyday necessities. But Rantum didn't need more than one such shop. Then there was the midwife who earned her living independently, and of course, Old Meret. She collected healing herbs and made tonics and powders from them, and people came to her to have their palms read and to cure their afflictions. A few women collected bird eggs in the salt marshes, and others near List tried their luck at oyster harvesting. The rest of the women had to live from what good people would donate to them and from what was washed up onto the beach. A widow couldn't usually hope to be remarried, because there were more women than men on Sylt.

But then, what could Maren do to provide for Angret, Finja, and herself? If she found nothing else, she might be able to buy a piece of land somewhere where the island was a little wider, plow a little field, and at least make sure that they wouldn't go hungry.

She found a shell at her feet, and she bent down to pick it up. The sea-polished shape fit perfectly in the palm of her hand. Maren ran her thumb over it and remembered the beautiful things made of shells she'd seen at the market in Amsterdam. There had been bowls and vases decorated with shells, wooden combs with mother of pearl, carved boxes, and little chests. Maybe she could make such things? But on Sylt, no one had use for them. Maybe making such luxuries would help to while away the long dark winter afternoons, but she wouldn't be able to earn anything with them.

Maren was so lost in thought that she only heard the footsteps behind her when they were very close. She turned around. Thies was there. He had his hands in his pockets, and he had forced a thin smile onto his lips. The wind tore at his hair, and his eyes looked lifeless and flat with dark circles under them.

"God's greetings," Thies said formally, his voice rough.

Maren nodded. She had imagined her reunion with Thies a hundred times over, but now everything was different. Her heart beat only a little faster than usual. She regarded his face. At sea, she had believed that she'd kiss him right away, but now she just looked at him. She wasn't completely indifferent, but she wasn't excited either.

"What do you want?" she asked and was startled by her own voice, which sounded harsher than she had intended. Yesterday, she had hardly been able to wait to see him and tell him that Angret was his daughter. But today, everything was different. Today, she realized, she was starting to plan her life without him. Yesterday she had been hoping for the impossible, and today she had admitted the reality of the situation to herself.

She gazed at Thies, and nothing moved in her—no longing to be touched by him, no longing to touch him.

"May I sit with you for a while?" he asked.

"I won't forbid you."

Thies sat down next to Maren and tried to get a look at Angret's face. "I thought you were dead."

"Well, as you can see, I'm safe and sound."

For a while they were quiet. Maren's heart did a light drumroll. She barely dared to breathe because soon she would know how he felt about Angret. She glanced at him furtively from the side. He, too, was breathing quickly, as though he were truly stirred.

"I wish you happiness for your marriage," Maren said softly. It took her an effort to get the words out.

Thies nodded. "I thought you—"

". . . were dead. I know. But I'm not. Although some people would be glad if I were."

"Don't talk that way. I'm happy that you're alive." Thies's words were gentle, but to Maren's amazement, they didn't touch her. It was as though this were a different Thies. Was it because he belonged to someone else now? Or had the love that Maren had felt for him disappeared? She saw that his hands were no longer rough, but rather soft and well cared for. She saw he wore a new shirt of the finest linen, decoratively embroidered. She also saw the deerskin breeches, which must certainly have come from the mainland. She smelled a fine, herbal, lemony soap, which didn't fit with her memories of Thies.

"You've changed," she said.

Thies shook his head. "No. I'm the same. Only the situation has changed."

Maren smiled and waved a hand at his shirt. "Well, the situation obviously hasn't gotten worse."

"Let's not argue," Thies begged her. "I'm truly glad that you're alive."

Now Maren turned directly to face him. "So? What does your gladness bring me? What do you want here? Why aren't you with your wife?"

"I heard . . . People say . . ."

"What do people say?"

Thies took a deep breath. "Some people are saying that the child is mine, and others say you brought her back from the whaling voyage."

"And you? What do you think?" Maren wanted to know.

"Well, you were away for a long time. Grit said it was impossible. That the child is mine, I mean."

"Does she also say that the baby I brought with me from the icebound sea is illegitimate? Does she even know who the father is?" Maren's words were sharp.

"You know how the people here talk." Thies picked up a thin twig and scratched in the sand with it.

Maren felt anger rising inside of her. She stood up and looked scornfully down at Thies. "I never knew you were such a coward," she said in a hard, ice-cold voice. "The child is yours. Angret is your daughter. I shared my bed with no other man."

"But, the long time that you were away . . ." Thies broke off, and still didn't dare to look Maren in the eyes.

"Believe what you want. I don't need you in my life. Go to Grit! I'll wager it won't take long before you have a child with her." She turned and began to climb the sandy dunes.

"Wait!" Thies hurried after and grabbed her by the sleeve. "That's exactly what this is about."

"What is this about?"

Thies swallowed. "Well, Grit was married for a long time and didn't have a child, although she wanted one. She even went to the mainland to see a doctor. It's possible that she can't have children."

Maren hearkened. What if Grit was barren? It would make it easy for Thies to annul his marriage to her, but he hadn't said a word about that, and Maren didn't want to put the idea into his head. It was strange. She had believed in Thies, in his love, and she had believed that they would be happy together. But it occurred to her that the longer she had been away from Sylt, the less she had thought about him. He, who had seemed to be the only man in the world to her, hadn't survived the distance. She had met other men. Men who could be depended upon. Men who were strong and courageous. And Thies's memory had faded. She had thought that at the sight of him, all her love for him would flare up again, like the Biikebrennen, but it hadn't. She looked at Thies and felt . . . nothing. It was actually difficult now for her to believe that Thies was really Angret's father.

"So, because Grit is probably barren, you must know who Angret's father is?"

Thies nodded. He was pale, and there was pain in his gaze. But Maren had no pity for him. "Well, she's yours. And if you don't believe it, ask my mother. The baby has a birthmark on her right shoulder. Just like you."

She held the child more tightly and was about to leave, but Thies held her back. "If what you say is true, and she's really my daughter, then . . ."

"Then what?" Maren glared at him. "I'll tell you what happens then. Nothing. She's my baby. Mine alone. She doesn't need you."

Thies opened his mouth as though he wanted to say something, but Maren wasn't listening to him any longer.

A visitor came in the afternoon. It was Old Meret. She brought some herbs and a baby blanket that she had knitted herself. "To keep the little one nice and warm," she said and kissed Angret on the forehead. So far, no one else had come, but Maren hadn't expected them to either. After all, Angret was a child without a father. That made Maren all the happier about Old Meret's gift. The three women sat in the kitchen by the warm fire while the baby slept.

"She's a love child. At least, she was when she was conceived," Maren began, but Old Meret stopped her with a wave of her hand.

"You don't have to explain yourself to me. A child is always a gift."

"Yes, but I want you to know that I didn't just throw away my virtue."

"I would know that even if I didn't know who the father was."

"You know who the father is?"

The old woman nodded. "Just look at the child. She's the very image of Thies. It doesn't matter what Grit says. He can't deny he's the father. Does he want to?"

Maren shrugged. What could she say?

"I don't know what Thies wants. Now I believe I never knew," Maren explained.

Old Meret stroked her hand gently. "Everything will be all right, child. I know it will."

"I . . . I didn't think . . . ," Maren stammered in sudden desperation. "I didn't think he was such a coward. I truly believed . . ." She was so shaken by sobs that she could barely breathe.

Finja came and took her daughter in her arms and rocked her as if she were still a little girl. "Thies is what he is. Grit has the power in their marriage. It's a wonder that he even spoke to you today. He must have had to sneak away. Forget him."

When Maren heard her mother's words, she knew that Finja spoke the truth. But all at once, she had to release everything that had been weighing on her soul. The hardships of the whaling voyage, the pain of the birth, her fears about the future. She needed to get it all out. Only then, Maren knew, could she start thinking about her future. And so she wept, wept for the loss of her great love, wept because she had come home again at last. When she was finally done, Finja's apron was soaked with Maren's tears.

Old Meret had sat there the entire time saying nothing, asking no questions. But now she covered Maren's hand with her own. "You alone can determine whether or not your child will be an outcast. Ask the minister for a proper christening. Look for respectable godparents from

Sylt. You are a diligent, clever, brave girl. Most of the people of Sylt have known you since you were little. They know that you're not the kind of girl who would give away her virtue for a few pennies. But you'll have to get used to other people's gossip." She hadn't quite finished speaking when there was a knock at the door. Piet was there holding a basket.

"This is from my wife and me," he said. "A gift to welcome the little one." He unpacked a thick bundle of sheep's wool, a smoked ham, and a colorful rag ball. "It's not much, but it comes from the heart," he said. Then he reached into his pocket and pulled out a gold coin. "This is from Jakob. He asked me to bring it to you. He was afraid that you wouldn't accept it, so you are receiving it today, from me, so you have no way to refuse it." He smiled so kindly as he said it that Maren again had tears in her eyes.

He patted her awkwardly on the shoulder. "If you need me, you know where I live." And with those words, he left the house that sat at the foot of the Rantum dunes.

CHAPTER 27

The Sunday of the christening dawned gray and cold. A thick fog hung over the island, so dense one couldn't see even a ship's length ahead. The wind rose every now and then in strong gusts, but it had no effect on the mist. A few ravens croaked, and the dunes were covered with a dense layer of hoarfrost. The fog made everything quiet; the only sound was the rushing of the sea. Together, Finja, Maren, and Angret made their way to the church. The little one was wrapped in the soft blanket that Old Meret had made and wore the christening dress that her mother had worn. Maren wore the gown that she'd been given by Zelda, and Finja wore her traditional formal wear.

When the church bell rang for the service, Finja told her daughter to hurry. "Walk a little faster, otherwise we'll be late."

But Maren stopped. "I don't know if this christening is right. To be honest, we know that the minister only agreed to do it to appease Captain Boyse. There may be ill feeling."

"Don't be silly! People know you. They don't wish you any harm. You're not the first to have a child out of wedlock, and you won't be the last. And yours is not the first or the last child born out of wedlock to be christened in the church. Of course the minister will record her birth in the church registry upside down, the way it is always done, but that's the only difference."

Finja smiled at her and stroked Angret's cheek, and then she continued walking along the sandy path. It was covered with a thin layer of frost that crunched quietly underfoot.

They walked at a slightly quicker pace, and soon the path in front of them was filled with others who were also on their way to the church. People had even come from the neighboring villages of Keitum and Hörnum in wagons and coaches. Maren saw Piet and his wife and waved to them, and both of them waved back. Old Meret waited at the end of the path, and even Antje, Thies's sister, nodded to Maren.

The Church of Saint Sebastian was full, fuller than might be expected in such weather. Someone had decorated the pews with bouquets of gorse and rosehips and had laid a wreath of ivy on the altar. Sweet-smelling beeswax candles stood in the polished silver candelabras, and even the baptismal font had been freshly polished. Everything was prepared as though it were a normal christening. At the sight of the child, the congregation stood, and most of the women were smiling. As Maren entered the church, a man stood up in the first pew and beckoned to her to come forward. It was Captain Rune Boyse. Maren hadn't seen him since she'd left the Dutch smak. She approached the pew and then sat down next to him. Finja took a seat at her other side.

"So, are you excited?" he asked, watching her trembling fingers flutter over the leather-bound hymnal. Rune Boyse put his warm, heavy hand atop her shaking fingers, and soon Maren felt calmer.

"I want to thank you."

"What for?"

"Well, I'm sure I have you to thank for the church being decorated."

"That's normal at christenings."

"Yes, that's true. But everyone knows that this is no normal christening. So far, I've never seen an illegitimate child be christened in a decorated church."

At those words, Rune Boyse squeezed Maren's hand so tightly that she almost cried out. "Never say such a thing again," he hissed.

"What?"

"Never call your child illegitimate again!" His voice was raw with annoyance, but Maren couldn't understand why. She pulled her hand away.

"What else shall I call her?" she asked brusquely. "Or rather, what do you think the others call her?"

"Angret. The child is called Angret. That's her name."

Maren gazed at the captain in wonder. Why couldn't she figure him out? Mostly, he acted as though he didn't care about her at all, but he also got angry with her, and he was occasionally so kind to her that she was moved to tears. He had saved her life, he had helped bring her child into the world, but at the same time, it was he who had made her go on the whaling ship in the first place.

At that moment, the sexton began to play the cembalo, which stood to the right of the altar in lieu of an organ. The congregation went quiet. Then the minister spread his arms wide and glanced at Captain Boyse, who nodded, and he began to speak in a loud, clear voice.

"O Lord, thou hast searched me, and known me.

Thou knowest my downsitting and mine uprising, thou understandest my thought afar off.

Thou compassest my path and my lying down, and art acquainted with all my ways.

For there is not a word in my tongue, but, lo, O Lord, thou knowest it altogether.

Thou hast beset me behind and before, and laid thine hand upon me.

Such knowledge is too wonderful for me; it is high, I cannot attain unto it.

Whither shall I go from thy spirit? Or whither shall I flee from thy presence?

If I ascend up into heaven, thou art there; if I make my bed in hell, behold, thou art there.

If I take the wings of the morning, and dwell in the uttermost parts of the sea;

Even there shall thy hand lead me, and thy right hand shall hold me."

"Who chose that psalm?" Maren asked the captain softly. She was so touched that tears sprang to her eyes.

"Well, I did. Normally, the parents choose the psalm, but you had enough to do, so I did it for you. It's psalm 139. The sea is in it."

Behind her, she heard a commotion. A woman was muttering, and even without turning around, she knew that it was Grit. But the sexton began playing again, and the congregation started singing, and then the minister continued to speak. "Lord, thou who hast created all life and called us to thee through Christ, we thank thee for this child."

"Stop!" A woman cried out, and in the sudden silence afterward, the sound of her voice echoed through every corner of the church. The minister lowered the Bible from which he had been reading. The sexton looked up from the cembalo.

Captain Boyse stood and turned around. He pointed a finger at Grit. "Did you just say 'stop'?"

"Yes. It was me. Someone has to speak up. We do not thank the Lord for this child. This christening is not right. Not in the eyes of God, and not in the eyes of the congregation."

Maren, more distraught than she'd ever been before, began to cry quietly, and she held Angret so tightly that she began to cry too.

"Oh?" Boyse replied, scoffing. "And you know what's right in the eyes of God and the congregation, do you?"

"I know how it should rightfully be. That's an illegitimate child. And if she's being christened here like a child from a decent Christian marriage, then the entire church and its congregation is sullied. It's contempt of God to decorate the church and polish the font. But the worst impertinence is that the sinful mother is sitting proudly in the first row at the christening of her bastard. It's the custom that the mother of a bastard isn't present at the christening. And if she is, she sits in the last pew. But she's sitting right at the front. Sylt has never seen the likes of this before."

Grit stood and turned around slowly so everyone in the church could see her and cried shrilly, "A sullied church and a sullied congregation! Do you believe that God will hear our prayers after this? Do you believe he will lend an ear to our supplications, to our woes and hardships?" She raised a finger and paused dramatically. "Oh, no. God will abandon us and punish us all for the sinfulness of the one among us. You all have to decide now. It's either her"—and at this she pointed a finger at Maren—"or us!" Then she turned around and spoke directly to Captain Boyse. "Must we all be punished by God because one of us has sinned? One of us is damned, but the rest of us who have been God-fearing and pious should not be made to suffer."

A plump woman with a red kerchief on her head stood up in the back row. "She's right. We don't want a whore and her bastard in our congregation."

Then the usually quiet Piet stood. "The child is as innocent as any other newborn child. We know the mother. She is not sinful even if she once sinned," he said.

Old Meret stood. "If we scorn the mother, then we must also scorn the father."

And Grit shouted, "What does the father have to do with the sins of the mother? He allowed himself to be tempted by the eternal evil of a woman. She is the temptress. She alone is at fault."

The minister laid the Bible on the altar and shifted from one foot to the other. "Quiet, now. Keep your calm," he begged, but his voice was overwhelmed by the commotion that had taken hold in the church.

But Grit wasn't finished. She pointed a finger at Captain Rune Boyse. "You! You're a panderer—or worse! You shared a cabin with her on the ship. And everyone here knows that you kissed her. There are witnesses!"

Boyse went pale. He looked at the minister, who was paging through his Bible, looking for a verse to match the situation. The sexton had crossed his legs comfortably and was watching the congregation with curiosity.

"No!" Boyse roared, and his thundering voice echoed off the walls of the church. "That's not what happened."

"Then what happened?" Grit screeched, windmilling with her arms as Thies attempted to pull her back into her seat. "Swear here at the altar by the likeness of our Lord that you didn't share your cabin with Maren."

Boyse said nothing. He tried to silence Grit with an angry stare, but it didn't work. "Swear on the Bible that it's true," she insisted, and several members of the congregation murmured in agreement.

Then Boyse turned to the minister, strode to the altar, and laid his hand on the Bible. "Yes, we shared a cabin. But only to protect Maren from the rest of the crew. I swear by God and the Bible that we did not lie together." He regarded the congregation scornfully, and then he sat down next to Maren again. "Minister, you may continue."

The minister cleared his throat, glancing at the sexton and then back at Boyse. Then there were noises from the back pews. Feet scraped; clothing rustled. Maren didn't dare turn. She knew what was happening anyway. Part of the congregation was leaving the church in disgust. The rustling and shuffling ebbed away, and then it was quiet again.

Maren turned to look. Fewer than a third of those from Rantum had left the church. Most of them still sat there watching the minister impatiently, waiting for him to continue.

As old Piet held the child over the baptismal font and his face glowed like the sun with pride, tears filled Maren's eyes.

CHAPTER 28

"I don't understand why Captain Boyse went to so much trouble for Angret's christening. He knows the islanders. He should have realized that there would be resentment. Why did he bother?" Maren asked.

"He's a good man. And he cares about you. Besides, he needs to keep law and order on the island. That's his job. After all, he's part of the council."

Finja patted Maren's shoulder. "Don't take it so hard. People here have nothing against Angret. And they've known you long enough to know that you aren't a frivolous person."

"Yes, Mother. You keep saying that. Old Meret and Piet say so too, but there are others who think differently." She didn't say it, but she was thinking about Thies. It was well and good that he was Grit's husband. She hadn't spoken to him again since he'd found her on the beach. She was surprised that Thies, whom she had thought she knew well, had shown no interest in Angret. He hadn't even asked to see the birthmark on her shoulder.

"I always thought that a man could sense if a child was his," Maren continued. "How could Thies possibly think she might be someone else's? He's known me all his life. He should know that Angret is his child. He should have protected her."

"Protected her? From whom? From his own wife?" Finja shook her head. "You expect too much of him."

Maren nodded. "Maybe." Then she took the laundry basket and put on her cloak so she could hang up the washing outside. It was the beginning of February. Over the last few days, the island had been covered in fog, as though everything were wrapped in gray blankets. The laundry had been damp for days, but now the sky was clear and the sun was shining. An icy wind still blew over the dunes, reddening noses and cheeks, but the island was a bit more colorful now. The sand was yellow again, and tiny purple blossoms of heather showed on the dunes. The sea no longer reared up into mountainous gray waves, but instead lay smooth and blue in front of the island.

Maren hung Angret's clothes on the line along with a few of her own things and some table linens and bed linens. In a few weeks, she would get her own flock of geese. She had spoken with an old fisherman from Tinnum, and he was willing to sell her a few goslings in spring so that she could feed them over the summer and sell them for Saint Martin's Day. Maren's days were full, but something was missing.

She wasn't missing a man; she was missing excitement in her life. Every day was like the one before, and the next would be the same too. She was happy to be with her mother, and she loved her little daughter. And yet, she sensed that life couldn't continue the way it was for very much longer. There were no signs of change, just a deep certainty that change would come.

The next day, shortly before sunrise, Piet came. He knocked on the door and accepted a hot cup of tea. He sat down at the kitchen table, but he was hesitant to speak.

"Now, tell us why you've come," Finja said. "Your wife needs you at home. And you never come just for a chat. So out with it!"

Piet shifted in his chair. When Maren sat down with them, Angret on her lap, he smiled at the little one, touched her tiny fingers, and sighed deeply. "Then you haven't heard yet?"

"What? Tell us." Finja's impatience was clear as she shifted in her own chair.

"Grit and Thies."

Maren's heart beat faster when she heard the two names. "What do they want?"

"They called a meeting of the council. You will soon be visited by one of the chancellors, Maren."

"Why?" Maren could actually feel the color ebbing from her face. She slid her chair a little away from Piet, as though he, too, posed a threat.

"Thies wants to acknowledge his paternity."

"Oh!" That was all Maren could think of to say. It wasn't bad news. If she were lucky, Thies might even take care of Angret every now and then. And if she were very lucky, Angret might even get a father.

"Yes." Piet took out his pipe, filled it carefully, and blew a few clouds of smoke into the air. "But that's not all."

Finja's brow creased. "What else could he want?"

"He wants to take Angret to live with him and Grit. The council shall make the decision."

"No!" Maren sprang up and pressed the child against her. "He wants to take her away from me?" She stared at Piet in disbelief.

The old man nodded and looked very sad about it himself. "You know the council has the right to decide with whom the child will be better off. It will be difficult for you."

"But why? Grit has always hated me. She would hate Angret too. No, I will not give up my child. I'd die first!" Maren was so upset that red blotches appeared on her face and neck.

Finja went pale. She reached across the table for Piet's hand. "That can't happen," she said. "You have to stop it. You're her godfather and a village elder. You sit on the council yourself."

Piet blew another blue cloud of smoke. "How can I stop them?" He shook his head. "If I knew how, I wouldn't hesitate for a moment."

Maren looked desperately around the small kitchen, and then pressed Angret into her grandmother's arms and dashed out the door. Finja and Piet watched her worriedly.

Maren raced across the dunes. She hadn't even taken the time to put on her shoes, and the sand made its way into her wooden clogs. She hadn't remembered her cloak either. The wind tore at her dress and whipped it so high in the air that her thighs shone in the sunlight. Her hair lashed across her face, her cheeks were red from anger and fear, and her eyes glittered with a fierce light.

"I will not give up Angret," she murmured to herself. "She's my child, and I am her mother."

The sand crunched in her clogs, but Maren ignored it. She hurried along the path and paid no mind to the neighbors who called to her over their fences. With her shoulders straight and her chin jutting forward in defiance, she hurried through Rantum, blind and deaf to everything around her. Her thoughts were only for her child. She was convinced that she'd only find the women at home: Grit, Antje, and Thies's mother. Three against one. But she would fight the way that mother whale fought for her baby.

Then she stood at the door, trying to catch her breath. Her cheeks were flaming red, her heart raced, and not even the cold wind could cool her glowing face. She pounded with the door knocker as hard as she could. Then she crossed her arms over her chest, ready to do battle, when she heard steps in the hallway.

The door opened—and there stood Thies.

"You?" Maren let her arms drop in surprise.

"Yes. I live here."

Maren peered over his broad shoulders to the interior of the house. "Where are the others?"

"Antje, Grit, and my mother went to Tønder."

Thies didn't say what they were doing there, but Maren knew by the look on his face.

"Oh, no!" She raised a finger and waved it angrily in front of his nose. "No, that's not going to work. They can buy as many baby things as they want in Tønder, but Angret is staying with me."

Thies stood rooted like a tree trunk, unmoving. His gaze swung back and forth like a fen fire. "That's not ours to decide, Maren," he said softly.

Then Maren was gripped by rage such as she'd never known before. She practically leapt on Thies, grabbed him by the shoulders, and shook him. "She's *my* child!" she screamed as loudly as she could. "Do you hear me? *My* child!" Then she suddenly let him go, sank to her knees, and began to wail and sob so her entire body shook. "No!" she wailed. "No, Thies, you can't allow this to happen. She's all that I have."

She felt Thies's hand on her shoulder. "Get up. You'll catch cold. It's no longer in our hands. The council will decide."

She looked up, and her eyes were so full of hatred that anyone else would have been horrified. "I never would have believed you capable of this," she said. "You betrayed me. And now you want my child too. Do you have no heart at all?"

It didn't occur to her that the captain had once asked her the very same thing. She was just a mother who was fighting for her child. Thies stood there motionless, saying and asking nothing, with no expression on his face.

"Why?" Maren demanded.

Thies shrugged. "It's not to hurt you. Grit will never be able to have children, and our line has to be continued. Angret is my daughter. She will have all she will ever need with us. A mother, a father, and a good future. Because of Grit's wealth."

"It's about money, is it? Thies, I have money too. I earned it on the whaling voyage. Take the money, and let me keep Angret."

Thies shook his head. "I don't want your money. I want my daughter to be raised properly."

Maren sank to the ground again. The dampness seeped through her clothes, but she didn't notice it. She felt more alone than she ever had in her life. She didn't know what to do. She gazed up at Thies's impassive face. Then she clung to his leg and pressed her face against his hard knee. "Thies, I beg you. For the love we once shared. Leave me my child."

Thies pulled himself away from her. He did it carefully, but still forcefully. "I only want what's best for the child. She should have a respectable name and come from a respectable household."

"Don't you feel anything at all for me anymore?" Maren asked.

"I do. I feel pity for you. Truly! But I must also think about myself and my own future."

Maren jumped up again and grabbed Thies by the collar, shaking him back and forth with all her strength. "You want my child because your wife can't have children? You're trying to take away the only thing I have. I love Angret!"

Thies let her tear at him, offering no resistance. "It's not as though she'll be gone from the world. You'll be able to watch how she grows."

"I don't want to just watch. I want to be part of her life!" Maren cried, beside herself. She felt such hatred that she saw white flames shooting through her vision. She wanted to grab Thies, wanted to hit him and kick him—but she didn't have the strength for it.

"Please, Thies!" she cried desperately. "Please!"

He swallowed. "I can't help you, Maren. Believe me, I, too, wish that things had happened differently. But this is the way it is. She deserves to have a proper family."

"What about me?" Maren asked. "Did you ever once think about how I would feel, even for a moment?"

Thies looked past her into the distance, but after a while, he nodded. "Yes, I thought about you. You tried to walk into the water with her. You wanted to end both of your lives. It would be easier for you without her."

Maren shook her head. She had no idea how Thies had found out about what had happened in Amsterdam, but it didn't matter. She was defeated. She was on the ground. There was nothing left to say.

One last time, she gazed at the man she had once loved. "You didn't just break my heart," she said softly, "you're about to tear it out of my body."

Then she left. She moved away slowly with shuffling steps, her head hanging almost to her chest, her shoulders hunched. She put one foot instinctively in front of the other. She didn't turn around and didn't see Thies watching her.

CHAPTER 29

Maren didn't know how long she'd been sitting at the top of the dune, staring at the leaden sea. *If I'd only walked into the water faster,* she thought. *Why did Boyse rescue me? Things were bad then, and I didn't believe they could get worse, but they have.* She sighed. Tears ran down her cheeks, but she ignored them. She also ignored the cold that crept under her clothes and turned her feet to ice.

A few seagulls cried and dove sharply toward the beach below. Otherwise, all was quiet; not even the sea made a sound. There were no breakers on the beach, and not one whitecap on the water. The day was dull and gray, and it matched Maren's despair perfectly. However bad it had gotten before, there had always been a spark of hope somewhere. Even in Amsterdam, when she had tried to walk into the water. She never admitted it, but she had been happy, until today, that Boyse had saved her. But now there was no hope left. She would lose Angret. Maren thought about taking her daughter and fleeing to Amsterdam, to Zelda. She could begin a new life, find work as a serving maid. But she had fought so hard in the last months that she had no strength left. Besides, the island was her home. Her roots were here, and her mother, who needed her, was here as well.

She felt as empty as an upturned barrel, and in her head, there was nothing but a huge gray hole. She had no idea how she would be able to go on living without Angret. She only knew that she couldn't bear the thought of seeing her daughter in Grit's arms. She didn't even think about Thies. Had it ever been about him? Or had the fight between her and Grit made her want him? She didn't know.

She slowly began to feel the cold that had seeped into her bones, and she thought she might shatter like ice as soon as she moved. Her teeth chattered, her throat was raw and dry, and yet, she still didn't want to go home. The frost inching through her bones was like a blanket that numbed the worst of the pain. She thought of Captain Boyse and how often he'd helped her. But she couldn't go to him now. She couldn't ask him for help, because he had made it clear that he wanted nothing more to do with her. She thought about his strong arms, how he had carried her, and how safe and protected she had felt with him. She remembered the kiss that had made her blood rise, and she thought about how kindly and tenderly he had treated Angret. And then she thought about how it might have been if she had married him.

The thought sparked a flame inside of her, but she realized immediately that she had lost him. Forever. The darkness inside her became blacker and blacker, and it mixed with the darkness of the winter evening. Unaware of what she was doing, she stood, staggered down the dune, fell, got up again, lost one of her clogs, and finally arrived home, blue and stiff with cold.

"Child!" Finja cried. "Where have you been? I was so worried about you."

Maren couldn't answer. She shrugged and fell listlessly into a chair. Finja gave her a cup of hot tea, put a blanket around her shoulders, and threw a log on the fire. But none of that was enough to drive away the cold that had settled in Maren's bones. It was as though her soul had frozen out there on the dune. Not even on the dune, but at the threshold of Thies's house. She sat by the fire, holding the teacup in both hands, and stared into flames that couldn't warm her.

"The baby is sleeping already," Finja told her. "Imagine, she ate solid food for the first time today! I grated an apple for her."

Maren didn't react. Finja sighed, swallowed the tears that rose as a lump in her throat, got out her knitting, and sat silently with her daughter.

At some point, she went to bed, and Maren still sat there as though paralyzed.

When Finja awoke the next morning, she saw Maren sitting exactly the same way she had been sitting the night before, having only set the teacup aside. Finja was shocked by the sight of her. Her hair hung in matted strings, and her eyes were dark circles. Her face was as pale as gruel.

Finja touched her shoulder lightly, but Maren didn't react. Then she put a hand on Maren's forehead. "You have a fever, child. You have to lie down." She took Maren under the arms and pulled her to the box bed. She noticed that Maren's feet were still ice cold, and she was missing her clogs. She pulled off Maren's heavy skirt and heated a stone, which she wrapped in a cloth and put under Maren's feet. Then she covered her daughter with two down quilts and pulled the curtains on the box bed.

Finja tiptoed to the parlor, kneeled in front of the cross on the wall, and prayed. "Dear Lord, I beg you, please don't take her from me. I know she is trying to reach you, but she's still so young. Please let me keep my child, Lord."

In the afternoon, Maren became delirious. "No!" she cried out. "No!" She pounded on an invisible opponent with her fists, as though someone were trying to take something from her. "Go away!" she cried. "No, no, no!"

Finja put a hand on her forehead again and realized that the fever had risen. Then she wrapped herself in her cloak, tied a scarf over her head, and went to find Old Meret. The weather had changed. A winter storm had begun. Sharp needles of sleet blew into Finja's face and made her eyes water. But she took no heed. She hurried over the slippery path and pulled open Old Meret's door without knocking.

"You have to come. I think she's dying."

Old Meret asked no questions. She grabbed a basket and loaded it with jars of salves and linen bags of dried herbs and hurried out of the house with Finja.

She observed Maren, who was sleeping restlessly, limbs thrashing as she murmured broken sentences in her delirium. Then she told Finja to soak three cloths in ice-cold vinegar water. She folded back the quilts to expose Maren's calves and wrapped them with two of the vinegar cloths. She placed the third cloth on her forehead.

"What's wrong with her?" Finja asked as she took Angret in her arms.

"We'll have to wait and see. How long has she been like this?"

Finja shook her head. "I don't know. When she discovered that Grit and Thies wanted to take Angret, she ran away. She was out all day, and when she returned in the evening, she wasn't herself anymore."

"Did she go to Thies?" Old Meret asked.

"I think she must have. She probably begged him to let her keep the child. And he . . . he . . ." She was so worried she didn't know what to say.

Old Meret nodded. "He doesn't dare to stand up to Grit. He's a weak man."

"He broke Maren's heart!"

As Old Meret changed the poultices on Maren's calves and brewed a strong healing tea, Maren became a little calmer. She stopped fighting against her invisible opponent and fell into a quieter, more restful sleep, though it didn't seem to be very deep.

Old Meret kept an eye on her while she sat at the table with Finja. "What will you do?" she asked.

Finja bit her lower lip. "What *can* I do?"

"If you want to keep Angret, the two of you will have to fight for her," Old Meret said.

"But how?" Finja shook her head. "Maybe it's God's will because Maren bore the child out of wedlock."

"Nonsense!" Old Meret slapped her hand on the table. "You know very well that she loved Thies, and that in her heart, she was married to him already."

"But what can we do?" Finja said with a sigh.

"Only one person can help," Old Meret said. "You know that very well."

"You mean Captain Boyse?"

"Of course I mean Boyse. He's on the council, just like Piet. Their opinions are taken seriously. The others will listen to them on the day of the hearing. Their voices have great weight in the decision."

Finja nodded and then began to trace the grain of the wooden table with her finger.

"What's wrong? Why haven't you left?"

Finja looked up. "He wanted to marry her. She rejected him, as you surely know. He won't want to help her now."

Old Meret bent forward and looked deeply into Finja's eyes. "You have to try. You have to fight. Your daughter and your granddaughter need you now."

Finja sighed. "I can't."

"Why not, for goodness' sake?"

"Many years ago, something terrible happened that divided our families forever."

"What happened?"

Finja shook her head. "I can't tell you. I can't speak of it." Then she raised her head and looked around the kitchen as though she were seeing it for the first time. She saw the glowing fire and smelled the sheep's dung. Every time a strong gust of wind shook the shutters, a little smoke blew into the small kitchen. The floor was covered in tiles that in two places bulged slightly upward. The kitchen table was scratched from being scoured with sand so many times, and the chairs were old. There was an oil lamp on the table with five wicks, but it had been a long time since they had all been lit at once. They had to be frugal with lamp oil, so they only used two wicks at a time. Only at Christmas did they light all five. She glanced at the stack of driftwood by the door, which dwindled a little every day.

Finally, her gaze fell on the alcove where her daughter slept, restless and moaning. Behind Maren slept her little granddaughter, with whom she had fallen in love at first sight. Finja didn't care at all that she had been born out of wedlock. Next to the alcoves was a cupboard full of pottery dishes and a single cup made of porcelain, which she had received as a wedding gift from her godmother. Finja realized that she was looking at everything as though it were for the last time. She was saying good-bye.

"It doesn't matter what happened years ago. You must act now. Boyse could make all the difference." Old Meret had spoken in a whisper, but Finja took in every word.

"He will demand a very high price," she replied.

"No price is too high for the lives of your daughter and granddaughter."

Finja sighed. She wrapped her arms around her, as though she were cold. "I will go," she said. "I will go to Rune Boyse. But I don't know if I'll be coming back."

Old Meret stood up. She took Finja tightly in her arms. "Whatever happens, I will take care of Maren and Angret. I promise you that." She took Finja's face between her hands and wiped away two tears with her thumbs. "And now, go!"

CHAPTER 30

Finja carefully put one foot in front of the other. The path was frozen and slippery, and she had to be cautious. The snowflakes still blew straight into her face, pricking her skin like needles, turning her cheeks red, and making her eyes water. But perhaps the wetness on her face wasn't really coming from the snow. Perhaps it was her tears. She reached a hand into the deep pocket of her skirt and felt for the gold pendant with the image of the sea goddess, Rán, and the signet ring that also bore Rán's likeness. The path was difficult not only because of the weather. It was difficult because at the end she would have to talk about a secret that had been well guarded for the last nineteen years. If it had been up to her, the secret would never come out, but now the lives of her daughter and granddaughter depended on it. Finja didn't know if she'd be able to go on living afterward, once everyone knew.

But at the moment, she didn't care. The last twenty years had been good for her. She'd had a good marriage with Klaas. They'd had Maren, and they'd been poor but happy. At least Finja had felt that way most of the time. Sometimes she had even been able to forget her terrible secret for a while. But now the past had finally caught up with her. No, that wasn't true. It was more like history was repeating itself. The first time, she hadn't even tried to fight. This time she would.

As she made her way down the long path from Rantum to Keitum, her past rushed by in her mind's eye. She recalled her own youth, thought of the Biikebrennen, and what had happened almost nineteen years ago. She'd never spoken about it to anyone. How could she? Only one person on the entire island knew, and she was on her way to see him now.

When she finally arrived at his gate, her heart was racing—and not only from her long walk. Finja paused and pressed both hands against her chest. She could still turn back. But no, she *had* to speak to Rune Boyse. *Maybe,* she thought, *maybe I can still keep my secret. Maybe he's forgotten.* But she knew well enough that Rune Boyse never forgot anything.

She knocked and was let in by the kitchen maid. Finja unwrapped her warm cloak with difficulty and unwound the scarf slowly.

"May I offer you a cup of tea?" the maid asked kindly.

Finja shook her head. "Tea won't help me. I'd much rather have a cup of strong grog, if I may."

The maid nodded and disappeared into the kitchen, while Finja knocked at the door of the study.

"Come in."

Finja took a deep breath and then pushed down the door handle and walked in. Captain Boyse was sitting at his desk, quill in hand with a ledger open in front of him.

When he saw her, he returned the quill to the inkwell and stood up. "You're a rare guest in my house, Finja," he said, and pointed to a comfortable armchair near the fireplace. Finja sat down, crossed her ankles, and put her hands in her lap. But she couldn't sit still, and she began to fold her fingers together and then release them, and finally to knead her hands.

"I can see you're distressed." Boyse slid a chair forward and sat across from her.

The maid came in with the hot grog on a silver tray, and next to the cup was a silver sugar box. Finja thanked her and took a few desperate swallows, burning her mouth. Boyse watched her. He leaned back, stretched out his legs, and rested his arms comfortably on the arms of the chair.

"What can I do for you?" he asked. "And first, of course, how are you?"

Finja put the cup down. "I am not well, Captain."

"I'm sorry to hear that. What is causing you dismay?"

"I suppose you already know."

Boyse nodded and stroked his beard. "You mean the issue which Thies Heinen intends to bring before the council?"

Finja nodded. "He wants to take my daughter's child away. My granddaughter."

Boyse nodded again. "An ugly affair. But how can I help?"

"You sit on the council. You could speak against it."

The captain's brow creased, and he shook his head. "You know I can't do that. They will want to consider who will better provide for the child. Maren has no husband. Even if I vote against Thies Heinen, I can't change anything."

Finja stared at her hands in her lap as she balled up a handkerchief. "I can't believe that you don't know a way to help."

"That's the way of it. I wanted to marry your daughter, and you alone knew the reason. I wanted to make reparations for what my family did to yours. But she didn't want me. My hands are tied."

Finja looked up. "I'm ready to reveal my secret. You would benefit from it; you know that. At the council meeting, one more case could be heard."

"After so many years? What sense would that make?"

"You know the sense of it. If I reveal what happened to me, then your parents' fortune will belong to you alone."

Boyse crossed his legs. "I'm not concerned about the money. I was never concerned about it. God knows, I have enough."

"Then what concerns you, Captain?"

He was silent for a moment and looked out the window at a straggly bush dusted with snow. It was still snowing hard, and the sky was thick with clouds, indicating that it wasn't likely to stop soon.

"One should receive what one has earned," Boyse said quietly. "Justice is a precious thing. I've always fought for justice. And for a peaceful coexistence."

Finja sighed. "That's why I've come. So you will have justice. So you can restore justice."

Boyse leaned his elbows on the armrests of the chair and pressed the fingertips of both hands together. "You don't want justice, Finja. You want to protect your grandchild. But it's not as easy as you think. You want to reveal your secret to restore justice to me, and you expect me to do something in return. You want me to speak to the council for you so you can keep Angret. But I believe that every child needs both a father and a mother. If the little one stays with you, the father will be missing."

"What are you trying to say?" Finja narrowed her eyes.

"Can't you figure that out?"

"Then you think Angret should live with Thies and Grit? That Grit, of all people, should raise Angret?" She shook her head in disbelief.

"There's another possibility," Boyse said, looking down at the tips of his fingers.

Finja looked questioningly at the captain, and then her expression cleared. "I know what you mean. You mean my daughter should marry? And the faster, the better. Then she would have a father for the child, and the council would have no reason to take Angret away from her. Is that true?"

"Well, it's a possibility."

Finja waited for Boyse to continue speaking, but he didn't. She had to risk impertinence. "You once wanted her, my Maren."

Boyse nodded. "Yes, a year ago I would have taken her. But much time has passed, and many things have changed. I've learned that certain things can't be forced."

Finja nodded sadly. "And if I help you to restore justice? Will you help me then?" She simply couldn't give up.

Boyse stood up and paced uneasily back and forth across the room. His expression was thoughtful. Then he stopped in front of Finja. "It's time to reveal your secret. Not for me, but for your own good."

"Why? I had a good marriage with Klaas. Why, after all these years?"

"Because there must be justice."

Finja took the cup, drank the rest of the grog, and cleared her throat. Then she stared at her hands in her lap again. "Your older sister's husband took me against my will almost nineteen years ago, and nine months later, Maren was born. I never told Klaas anything about it. Not even a hint. Until his dying day, he believed that Maren was his child. And he loved her as only a father can love his daughter. Your sister killed herself because of it, and her husband inherited what was hers: half of your parents' home. He sold it and left the island, leaving you with nothing. If people had known what he had done, you would have been able to keep the inheritance from your parents. Back then, you asked me to speak out about what your brother-in-law had done to me. But I couldn't do it, because Klaas would have learned that Maren wasn't his daughter. And you, Rune, suddenly had no home, and you left to go to sea. And eventually, after about ten years, you returned a wealthy man. You built the most beautiful house on the entire island and were respected and successful, but in your heart, you still had the knowledge of having been denied your inheritance."

"I never cared about that. Not about the house or the money. The man raped you and is guilty of the death of my only sister."

"I know that, Rune. But one needs to be strong for justice. And I wasn't strong enough. You wanted to marry Maren last year. I know why you wanted to do that. You wanted to make amends for what your brother-in-law did to me. You wanted to be sure that at least the child he left behind could lead a good life. But things aren't so simple."

"We don't have to talk about that now, even if you are right. Your daughter decided for herself that she didn't want me. I'll admit that she offended me. Her arrogance! I gave you the loan. You know, Finja, I would have never enforced a claim, even though after Klaas's death, I demanded to be repaid. I thought you'd finally help me get justice. We could have brought my brother-in-law before the council so he would have had to pay for what he did to you and my sister."

Finja shook her head. "Not after so long. No one, no council in the world, would be interested in something that happened nineteen years ago. And your sister, buried outside the churchyard in unconsecrated ground as a sinner who took her own life, wouldn't be helped by it anymore either. But now you can make sure that Maren won't lose her child. Now is the time that you can make amends for what your brother-in-law did to me."

Finja stood. She had said enough. Now Captain Boyse had to decide what the next step should be. She reached into the pocket of her skirt and took out the gold pendant and the signet ring with the image of Rán on it, and she put them on the captain's desk. "Your brother-in-law gave these to me then. I kept them, even though I'm horrified every time I look at them. I don't want them anymore. Do with them what you wish."

Finja hadn't expected an immediate answer from him. Rune Boyse was a man who thought before he acted. But she was sure that she'd given him something to think about.

CHAPTER 31

Maren recovered slowly. The fever diminished, and she gradually regained her strength. But it moved Finja to tears when she saw Maren with Angret. There were moments when Maren would stand by the cradle and watch the sleeping child, and tears would run down her face. Then the baby would wake and cry, reaching out her arms for her mother, and Maren would have to turn away. "You take her," she would say, and then Finja would pick up the little one and comfort her and play with her, while Maren just sat there and stared into the distance. She had become too thin, and her hair had lost its shine. The fire in her eyes had gone out.

Maren hadn't mentioned that she might lose Angret since her visit to Thies. Finja knew that Maren was slowly trying to let go of her child, and it was breaking her heart. But she couldn't help her daughter. She had done everything in her power. Every day she waited for Captain Boyse to appear, but he didn't come or even send a message.

Then it was time again for the Biikebrennen. The youths of Rantum piled wood on the highest dune and went from house to house to collect more wood and oil, and the women hung their traditional clothes outside to air.

Finja got her own and Maren's out of the chest and shook them out. "You want your formal wear, don't you?" she asked.

Maren shook her head. "No. I'm not going to the Biikebrennen."

Finja lowered the dress she had been shaking. "You're not?"

"No, I can't. Thies and Grit will be there. I can't stand the sight of them. Do you understand? I'll be holding Angret in my arms, and Grit will look at her and think, or even say, 'Go ahead and hold her tightly. Soon I will be the one holding her.'"

"I understand, Maren. But if you don't go, then she and everyone else will think you aren't going to fight for your child. Some at the fire will be sitting on the council and judging you the next day. If they see how lovingly you treat your child, then they may decide in favor of you. You have to go, Maren, even though it will be difficult."

For a while, Maren stood at the window, looking out over the village that was her home. From a distance, she saw Piet, repairing a shutter on his house. She saw Old Meret, returning from the beach with a bundle of driftwood. She watched the columns of smoke rising from the chimneys, which spoke of comfortable homes.

She stood there for a long time, and she then turned around. "You're right, Mother. I'll go. Everyone must see that I have no reason to be ashamed. Not of myself and certainly not of my child."

It had been snowing all day without a break, but as the first villagers made their way to the Biikebrennen, the snow stopped. The wind stopped too, and the sea whispered softly to itself. It was cold and clear, the stars glimmered, and the moon hung in the sky like a giant golden pancake. Maren had Angret wrapped up warmly and was carrying her over the dunes. She was almost half a year old. She had her mother's eyes, and watched everything that happened around her with lively interest. Her downy hair was hidden under a thick wool cap, and her cheeks glowed, pink and healthy.

She gurgled happily in her mother's arms and even reached out a hand toward her grandmother every now and then. She was joyful, as only a small child can be when it knows nothing of the cares of the world.

Piet came to them and stroked the child tenderly on the cheek with his finger as his wife kissed Angret heartily on the forehead. Old Meret had knit her a pair of tiny warm gloves and had brought the matching stockings one evening later. Angret cooed in Maren's arms, pointing at things and laughing and smiling, and all the villagers were charmed by her.

The flaming wheel was rolled down the dunes to the water, and the bonfire was lit with cries of glee. This year, there was no flock of wild geese, and Old Meret decided not to give a speech. Now the fire blazed merrily, and the young people ran and jumped around it. Others stood around it in groups, drinking hot grog or spiced wine, talking and singing.

Maren stood with Finja, Old Meret, and a few other neighbors, and kept an eye on Thies and Grit. Thies had joined a group of young men at the other side of the fire. Once he looked in Maren's direction, but he quickly looked away when he realized she was watching him. Grit stood with Thies's mother and sister. She was wearing a new cap of seal fur, and Maren knew that she had gotten it as a Christmas gift from Thies. She, too, had once received such a cap from him.

"So, how are you?"

Maren hadn't noticed that Captain Rune Boyse had walked up to her. "Tomorrow our case comes to the council. How do you think I am?" Her gaze swept over his face, and he saw that her eyes were empty and bleak. Then she stroked the child's back to warm her.

"She's getting big," the captain said.

"Yes, she certainly is."

"And she looks healthy and happy. As though she wants for nothing."

"She has all she needs. But tomorrow she may be missing her mother." Maren's voice sounded quiet and raw, and she had to turn away so the captain wouldn't see the tears in her eyes.

"Do you remember? It was here that I asked you to be my wife, two years ago."

"How could I forget?"

"If you had known then what you know now, would you have made a different choice?" Rune Boyse had also lowered his voice, almost to a whisper.

Yes, Maren thought. *Of course. But then I still believed that I loved Thies. And I thought he loved me.* She sighed.

"Would you have made a different choice?" Boyse repeated.

"I still would only marry someone who truly loves me," she replied. "Except then, I didn't know enough about love."

"And now? Do you know more about it?"

Maren thought about her time on board the whaling ship. She had witnessed the captain as a strong-willed man who followed his ambitions with energy and power and had also seen him as a tender lover. If Zelda could be believed, he was able to make a woman happy. And she herself had known him as strong and reliable. And gentle. She thought back to his kiss. The kiss that had burned through her entire body. The kiss that had been so different from the kisses she had shared with Thies.

"Yes. Now I know things that I didn't know before. But what good does it do me? It's too late," she said softly, and she felt an overwhelming sadness rising up inside of her. She felt as though she'd once had happiness laid out before her, but she'd been too blind to see it.

Suddenly Rune Boyse grabbed her by the shoulders and turned her so she had to look directly into his eyes. "You think it's too late? It's not too late. It was never too late. You must only conquer your pride."

Then he kissed Angret on her cap and left. Maren stood there as though frozen. What did he mean?

She lay awake that night thinking for a long time. The thoughts in her head whirled faster than hurricane winds. She was brooding over what the captain had said to her that evening: *It's not too late. It was never too late.* What was he talking about? One part of her was scolding, telling her that this wasn't a good time to be thinking about what he had said. In a few hours, she would probably lose her daughter, but something inside her knew that Rune Boyse's words had something to do with that too. *You must only conquer your pride,* he'd said. What pride? Oh, if she could only speak to him! If she could just tell him that . . .

Suddenly she knew what she had to do. She slid out of bed carefully, so as not to wake Finja and Angret. Then she pulled on her warm boots, slung the heavy oilskin jacket around her shoulders, wrapped a scarf around her neck, and covered her hair with a cap. She got out her father's old fishing lantern, lit the tallow candle inside it, and put a spare candle in her pocket with a little tinder. Then she set off into the night.

It wasn't a pitch-black night—at least the moon was shining to light her way. Maren walked quickly. She had to walk fast because it was far, and in a few hours, it would be dawn. In the distance, she could still hear the noise of the last drunken Biikebrennen revelers who still hadn't made it home to their beds. Otherwise, all was still.

She walked as fast as she could and soon arrived in Westerland, turned right, and almost ran the last stretch of the way. As the first light of dawn touched the sky, she reached Captain Rune Boyse's house. Maren pounded on the door and in her haste almost knocked over the serving maid, slightly disheveled and still hazy with sleep as she opened the door. She hurried past the surprised woman and was about to walk directly into Boyse's bedroom, but then she noticed a glimmer of light shining under the door of the parlor. She stormed in without knocking.

Rune Boyse was sitting in the comfortable armchair in front of the fire, a meerschaum pipe in his mouth and a book in his hand. When he saw Maren, he didn't say a single word, just looked at her. And Maren stood there, suddenly struck dumb, and shifted her weight from one foot to the other. She didn't know what to do or what not to do. Then Rune Boyse stood up and opened his arms wide—and Maren rushed into them.

Later, much later, when the morning was already in full bloom, he spoke. "You haven't said it. You still haven't said it."

Maren closed her eyes and nestled against his broad chest, a little smile on her face. She knew exactly what Rune meant. "You've known it for a long time. You knew it long before I did."

"But that doesn't mean I don't want to hear it. Please, say it. Just this once, and I will be satisfied."

Maren opened her eyes and looked at the man who was holding her hand in his, looking as satisfied as she'd ever seen him. His strong thumb stroked the back of her hand again and again. "I love you, Captain Rune Boyse."

"And I love you, Maren Luersen."

"Did you love me from the start?" she asked. There was so much more to say, so many questions, but this question was the most urgent.

Rune Boyse shook his head. "I barely knew you, barely recognized your face. No, I wanted to marry you because my family had a debt to set to rights with your family. I knew for many years that someday you would be my bride. That's why I never courted any other girl on the island."

"You wanted me, even though you didn't know me? Why?" Maren raised her eyebrows in amazement.

"Not now. I'll tell you later. We have to leave now. Soon the council meeting will begin."

CHAPTER 32

When Maren was called before the council, Finja squeezed her hand tightly, Piet patted her on the shoulder, and Old Meret nodded to her. Then she was led into the hall. At a long table, a dozen men were sitting. They were the municipal administrators from each village on Sylt, and with them sat the bailiff, who was in charge of legal issues on the island, and the beach overseer, who was responsible for keeping the peace on the beaches. Rune Boyse was among them. That year he was the municipal administrator for the village of Keitum, and when Maren looked at him, he nodded to her and smiled.

The bailiff raised a sheet of paper, glanced briefly at Maren, and read aloud. "Today, we are dealing with the case of the unmarried Maren Luersen versus Thies Heinen, regarding the illegitimate child Angret. Thies Heinen, who claims he is the child's father, has requested that Angret Luersen live with him and his wedded wife so that she may become a proper Christian citizen of Sylt, with both a father and a mother."

He looked to the front row of the seats in the hall, where Thies Heinen sat rigidly with his wife, Grit. Grit was holding her husband's hand and wore a self-satisfied expression for all to see. "That's the truth," she answered instead of her husband. "The child should live in a proper family. With us, she'll have a better life than she would with her unvirtuous mother."

Then the bailiff turned to Maren. "Have you understood the petition?"

"Yes, I have."

"Do you have an objection to present?"

"Yes, indeed I do."

"Then tell us."

Maren turned around, smiled at both Thies and Grit, and said, "First of all, I am no unmarried woman, and—"

"What? That's impossible. She's lying!" Grit had jumped up and was pointing a finger at Maren. "She's lying!"

"Order! Sit down, woman, or you will be banished from the court." The bailiff struck his mallet on the table, and Thies urged his wife back into her chair.

"Please continue, Maren Luersen," the bailiff bid her.

"As I said, I am married. That means I have a father for the child and a provider for both of us."

"Who is the father, and why does the council know nothing of these proceedings?"

"My husband's name is . . ." Maren paused and smiled at that point, and she heard Grit squirming impatiently in her chair behind her. "My husband's name is Captain Rune Boyse. And since early this very morning, my name is no longer Maren Luersen, but Maren Boyse."

For a moment, silence reigned in the room after the incredible revelation. Then everyone spoke at once, and Grit's sharp, piercing cries of "She's lying!" kept breaking through the noise.

Finally, the bailiff pounded the table with his mallet again, waited until silence filled the hall once more, and turned to Rune Boyse. "Is it true, what this woman says?" he asked.

"Yes, it's true. The minister married us early this morning. The witnesses are Piet and Old Meret from Rantum. They are sitting outside and may be called to testify."

"Very interesting. And are you, Rune Boyse, prepared to accept Angret as your own and raise her as is befitting a proper Christian?"

Rune stood up, put a hand on his heart, and spoke loudly and clearly. "Yes, sir. I am, as God is my witness. I will love, protect, and provide for Maren and her child as a husband and father should."

Once more, there was a moment of amazed silence, but then the municipal administrator of Rantum began to applaud loudly. Then the administrator of Hörnum joined in, and soon all the others were applauding too.

Rune Boyse stepped forward, took Maren in his arms, and kissed her tenderly before the eyes of all present. The way a loving husband should kiss his wife.

ABOUT THE AUTHOR

Photo © 2016 Jochen Schneider

Bestselling author Ines Thorn was born in Leipzig, Germany, in 1964. Beginning her literary journey as a bookseller's apprentice, she later went on to study German, Slavic studies, and cultural philosophy at the distinguished Goethe University.

In the year 2000, Thorn published her first novel while working in a hospital library. By 2003, she was able to devote her time entirely to writing and has been creating unforgettable historical fiction ever since.

Today she lives in Frankfurt am Main and works as a full-time freelance writer. *The Whaler*, the first installment in her popular series The Island of Sylt, is her first book to be translated into English for the American market.

ABOUT THE TRANSLATOR

Photo © 2011 Alex Maechler

Kate Northrop grew up in Connecticut and later studied music and English literature in the United States and the United Kingdom. Her travels eventually led to the German-speaking region of Switzerland, where she's lived with her Swiss husband and their two bilingual children since 1994.

Today she works as both a professional translator and lyricist, with credits that include songs signed to major labels and publishers. With more than fifteen years of translating experience, Northrop now runs her own literary translation business, Art of Translation. Visit her at www.art-of-translation.com.